The Fountain of Youth

Stories from the Free City, Book 1

By Nathaniel Warner

To Jack and Blue, whose courage inspired me to write their story. To my wife, Mollie, for without her unwavering support, not a single word would have reached paper. And to my son, Lennon, whose positive and energetic spirit strengthened me throughout the process.

From the bottom of my heart, thank you.

Prologue: The Long Goodbye

She sat, still. Watching by the side of his bed. They were both very old now and not long for this world. Even though they had worked together for the past 30 years and loved for almost the same amount of time, she never grew tired of his handsome features and keen intellect. He had lost neither in all this time.

"Taris, wake up," she whispered, seeing that they only had a few moments left before he departed. She swept a stray hair off his face, tucking it behind his long, elegant ears.

Prologue: The Long Goodbye

"RayGina, my love," he responded in a weak tone. His eyes sluggishly searching the room for hers until, after a long moment, they finally connected. "Have they sent word... or replacements?"

"No, they have not. Our fears have been realized. I fear the worst has come to pass. I fear they have been overcome."

"Then, it is lost. It is all lost. We have failed."

"No, my love, there is hope. I will be placing the laboratory into stasis shortly. Should they eventually send transport or replacements, they will find Arlas waiting. With all of our research. We were so close to finding the answers. So close to saving them all."

He nodded, and a small, sad smile appeared on his face. It lingered for a moment then vanished as quickly as it appeared. "I'm sorry. I'm so sorry, my love."

"For what?"

"I should have let you leave with the last transport."

"I could never have left you alone." She insisted. "Besides, you did not know it would be the last. It has been many years since we heard from our home-world or any other outpost. But at least we were able to spend the last of our lives together." She finished, trying to bring him some small comfort.

"Yes, of course, you are right. You are always right," Taris said as his eyes started to lose focus. "Is this the end?"

"Yes." Her voice shaking with the proclamation. "You are beginning the transcendence now. You soon will be on the other side."

"I... I do not wish to leave you. I'm not ready."

"I know. I do not wish for you to leave. I am not ready, either." She said as a single tear ran down her wrinkled cheek. "But do not worry, I will transcend this world too, not far behind you. We will meet again on the other side."

Taris began shaking softly as his physical body started failing. "I love you," he said in slight desperation, not knowing if he would have the time to get it out.

"I love you too," She said back as his eyes began to roll into his head. "I always will."

With a last raspy deep breath and exhale, he went still. RayGina watched him for a moment before leaning over and placing a small kiss on his forehead. She then reached down and pulled the blanket over his head.

RayGina stood and left the bedroom without a word. She gracefully glided through the dorm as if the weight of responsibility had been lifted from her shoulders. Now that the end had come, she was free. Free of guilt, free of failure.

Prologue: The Long Goodbye

She only had a few more tasks to complete before joining Taris on the other side.

She opened the door leading into the holding room. A large, multi-story room that separated the dorms from the laboratory. A space that held the test subjects, chemical vats, power cells, and various other equipment. As soon as the door opened, the animals went wild. Screeching and shaking the cage bars in a violent eruption of sound. She had become accustomed to the racket after all these years. This planet had several native primate species perfect for genetic experimentation—one of the main reasons this site was selected.

RayGina continued on to the primary laboratory, passing the two massive cylindrical test chambers, crossing the open room, and started powering down the equipment and consoles. The hum that was typically ever-present slowly died away. As the final lights dimmed, she headed back into the animal holding room and locked the laboratory door behind her.

She stepped over to another console and initiated the kill command. A robotic arm extended from within the animal's cages, latching on to each remaining primate, and began sending lethal bolts of electricity flowing through their bodies. She continued powering down and securing the equipment as the test subjects thrashed in their last, dying moments. The room went deadly silent, the execution was completed. As she headed back into the dorm, she found the now silent room disturbing, unsettling and, altogether unfamiliar. She closed and locked the holding room door behind her. Just as she had done for the laboratory.

RayGina quietly strode into the kitchen and filled a crystal glass with clear, filtered water. She then grabbed a small bottle from the cabinet labeled poison and opened it. Not wanting to fail in this task, she swallowed the bottle's entire contents and drained the glass of water. Clearing the bitter aftertaste from her mouth.

RayGina took one last protracted look around the dorm, the place she had called home these many long years, before heading back towards the bedroom. She laid herself next to Taris. The thick, ornately carved wooden bed frame barely registering her weight. Within moments she was moving no more. Her transcendence was complete. They were together again. All was silent.

Chapter 1: The Overwatch

Zandar Deek peered out of the transport vessel's window as the captain announced they had reached their destination. Titan's Well was just coming into view. He was anxious as the transport vessel began docking procedures. This was his first time to any Free City. The stories concerning its splendor, as well as its hazards, kept racing through his mind. He wasn't quite sure what to expect as the tiny vessel was swallowed by the unimaginably massive Free City.

Zandar was a Story Teller for the Galactic Trust, a historian with a mind for facts. Although the Trust had no governing control over Titan's Well, if any historical accounts needed to be documented and added to the Hall of

Records, only an official Story Teller could do so. He was also a Tricarion.

Tricarions are singularly unique. They are the last remaining of the original three ancient space-faring species who colonized the stars millions of years before many of the current species even discovered phase space travel. With light blue skin, bright violet eyes, and dark purple hair, they are often referred to as the most beautiful species in the known universe. Besides their breath-taking yet simple beauty, there lay a deep calm personality as their species was also the most long-lived. Their average lifespan stretching to over 1000 standard years.

It wasn't unheard of for a Tricarion to reach 1200 years old and become a celebrated elder amongst their people. Making it to 1500 years meant a life-like statue in the Temple of Life, dedicated to a life well-lived. Over the entire recorded history of Tricar, only 31 life statues existed. While they revered and celebrated life, they also embraced death with welcoming, open arms. Zandar was considered to be coming into his prime amongst his kind, having just celebrated his 451st year.

As with all incoming traffic, Zandar's transport vessel was docked at the lowest ring of Titan's Well. Secured within a pressurized holding bay. Only the larger Star-liners were required to dock using the exterior control arms. The excitement of the travelers waiting to disembark was palpable. "It must be a first time to Titan's Well for many. Or maybe, they just know what awaits them." He thought to himself while standing in line to exit the vessel. Faintly, he could hear the announcements over the loudspeaker.

"Please be sure to have your DigiCard accessible when reaching the security checkpoint. This will maximize efficiency and reduce the time needed for all travelers to pass through the checkpoint. If you have any questions about Titan's Well, please see a Greeter once you have completed your security review."

Stepping out onto the transport terminal, Zandar could see a flurry of activity. Terminal security guards and unloading droids rushing towards the commotion. Not knowing if this was normal or not, Zandar followed their movement curiously. A freighter from Zora Prime had just arrived with some very active live cargo, Dark Zorgs.

Dark Zorgs, with their matte black fur, powerfully muscled appendages, and sharp razor-like claws, are a delicacy for certain adventurous species. Their lack of eyes makes them none the less dangerous, maybe even more so. Most civilized societies try to avoid them at all costs, as they typically needed to be killed, butchered, and eaten within a few hours so that the meat didn't spoil. They are commonly used as gladiator sport in the LightBall arena as a pre-game show and served as the first-course meal for the affluent attendees. The security guards and unloading droids were struggling to bring the cargo to heel. Zandar stood by and watched the scene unfold as he waited patiently in the slow-moving security line.

The Fountain of Youth

He passed through security with no issues, having the needed travel permits. Although the guard was quite curious as to why a Trust Story Teller was on Titan's Well. Apparently, after two centuries of peace, the Trust was still a subject of skepticism aboard a Free City.

After locating a Greeter, Zandar was presented with two options. 'First-time visitors, get introduced to Titan's Well' or 'Ask me anything.' Seeing as he was a 'first time visitor' Zandar selected that option. Instantly a holovid of a beautiful young woman appeared before him and began speaking.

"Titan's Well, one of seven Free Cities scattered across the Milky Way galaxy. It's a sovereign city-state outside the dominating control of the Galactic Trust, the Milky Way's governing body, often just referred to as the "Trust." The Free Cities were born from the Treaty of Binary Star after the 100-year civil war to balance power throughout the galaxy. A method of breaking up the stranglehold the Trust had on all inhabited star systems by moving essential galactic functions under the Free City's jurisdiction.

Although calling it a 'city' isn't exactly correct, it's actually a city-sized space station harboring over 100 million souls from all over the known universe. While it isn't the largest Free City, it is the wealthiest. Being the headquarters for the

Chapter 1: The Overwatch

Bankers Guild, Trade Union, and Gaming Federation has made Titan's Well the center of activity for the entire civilized galaxy.

Titan's Well consists of three enormous spinning rings. The top and bottom ring spin clockwise, while the middle and most massive ring, nearly double the size of the other two combined, spins counter-clockwise. Like dancers, balancing each other as they moved gracefully through space.

The top ring contains the headquarters, offices, and business units for the Bankers Guild, Trade Union, and Gaming Federation, as well as the administration offices for the Free City itself. The middle ring houses residential quarters for all residents and guests, acting as the cities sprawling urban centers. While the lower ring handles all support related tasks such as food storage, incoming and outgoing traffic, waste reclamation, and manufacturing.

All three rings are connected to a central spindle, known to residents as the 'Arm.' The 'Arm' acts as the station's main traffic corridor. Allowing for goods and people to move between the three rings in bulk and at high speed. The best way to describe Titan's Well is to imagine three massive, spoked wheels stacked on top of each other, spaced equally apart, and linked by a single, perpendicular hub. The spokes of the wheel acting as transport conduits enabling movement between the different sections of a ring and allowing easy access to the 'Arm.'

At the very top of the 'Arm' stands the Overwatch. An enormous open domed area with a transparent forcefield roof, qllowing guests an unobstructed view of the neighboring planet, star, and moons. The Overwatch itself houses the Grand Casino, LightBall arena, and the Box. The Box sits at the highest level of the Overwatch and circles it in its entirety. It is the most exquisite collection of restaurants and bars in the entire Milky Way galaxy. More business deals have been negotiated, completed, and celebrated in the Box than anywhere else in the universe."

"That was a bit dry," Zandar thought to himself once the recording stopped. "Maybe they should hire a Story Teller to do the introduction of this place justice." He was once again presented with the two options. This time, he selected 'Ask me anything' and asked for the route and location of the Box in the Overwatch, VIP section 33. After the Greeter had scanned Zandar's DigiCard and synchronized it with the cities digital network, a holovid appeared in-front of him. Showing a three-dimensional map of Titan's Well and the most efficient route to get to where he was going. The route was transferred to his DigiCard for future reference.

All citizens of the Milky Way galaxy are assigned a DigiCard upon birth. Regardless of whether they are a citizen of a Free City or the Trust. DigiCards act as a personal identification and data device that is encoded to each user's unique DNA sequence, making them almost impossible to be forged. After assigned and DNA encoded, they are surgically inserted into the user's forearm, or, for some species, as close to a forearm as they have. Paired with a wireless display screen and holovid projector, they allow the user almost instant access to all sorts of useful information.

Locating the turbo-lift specified by the Greeter, Zandar boarded it, scanned his DigiCard, and the turbo-lift began to move. The trip from the lower ring to the Overwatch was estimated to take 30 standard minutes. Zandar used this time to familiarize himself with Titan's Well. Reviewing the holomap, highlighted attractions, and dismissing the numerous personalized advertisements, he located his guest quarters within the middle ring. An unloading droid at the transport terminal assured him his luggage would be waiting for him in his room. He will be heading to his guest quarters after meeting with the client who requested his services. It was a resort called the Oasis and was listed as the most elegant guest quarters in the Free City. Apparently, the client had spared no expense when it came to room and board. Zandar was intrigued.

Typically, Story Tellers are treated no better than tax auditors, as they usually document recent events for upcoming litigations or obituaries. Every so often, rumors would spread through the Story Tellers guild of a job, documenting a genuinely unique historical account, an actual story worth its place in the Hall of Records. The last such stories all originating from the 100-year civil war. Zandar wondered what type of job this would be.

The trip took closer to 45 standard minutes due to the turbo-lift needing to be redirected because of "Arm" maintenance, although Zandar hardly noticed. He was able to get better acquainted with the Free City. He saved several locations he wished to visit once his business was concluded. He also used this extra time to review the bio information he had gathered from the Trust's personnel files regarding his client. There wasn't much available. He had a name and race, human. He wasn't even sure what a human was, as he had never heard of that species before. He also found this lack of data perplexing, if not outright concerning. The Trust collected and stored almost every piece of data on its citizens.

"Maybe, this client was born outside of a Trust controlled star system? Or maybe Humans are a relatively new species to intergalactic travel?" Zandar commented to himself as there was no one else in the turbo-lift with him. "But still, there should be more data available than this."

Chapter 1: The Overwatch

He shook his head in resignation "This will just take more time to fully document the requested story, needing to complete the Tellers biography as well."

Adding the Teller's biographical data to the Story was a way of authenticating it and allowing future historians to verify its contents. Although it wasn't needed in some exceptional cases, the Story itself acted as the authenticating factor.

When the turbo lift reached its destination, the doors opened, and Zandar stepped out. He was immediately struck by the immense size of The Overwatch. Striding over to the nearest observation deck, he swept his vision around to take it all in. From this position, he could see the Grand Casino level stretching off, far into the distance. Zandar wasn't able to see the two sides connect as the Overwatch was so vast. He could, however, see the LightBall arena entrance, as well as the jumbo holovid that sat atop the LightBall arena. It was large enough to be seen from anywhere within the Overwatch and was currently showing a LightBall game in-progress.

"You can take in the sights after you meet with the client," Zandar chided himself, not wanting to make his client wait any longer than necessary. Punctuality is a top priority for every Story Teller. It sets the right tone for any engagement and lets the client know their Story is of the utmost importance — whether that is true or not.

He pressed the transport request button on his DigiCard. A moment later, a transport vehicle landed directly in front of Zandar. It was remarkably similar to the flying rickshaws from his home-world and was being driven by an operator droid. He scanned his DigiCard, and instantly the operator droid set to work. The rickshaw door closed. The interior light switched from red to blue. They lifted into the air, speeding above all the people and structures below.

"3.24 minutes to your destination, Sir," the operator droid informed, with an air of confidence Zandar didn't know droids could have.

3.24 minutes later, he reached section 33 of the Box, and Zandar now understood why the droid was so confident. The trip was amazingly quick, although quick wasn't really the right way to describe it. It was more accurate or efficient, not a single wasted second or joule of energy.

Stepping down and disembarking from the rickshaw. Zandar could hear the operator droid politely say, "Enjoy your stay on Titan's Well," as he sped off to collect his next passenger.

Entering the Box at section 33 through a majestic golden framed double-door, the gold flecks in the marble flooring glinting, he located the lavish, dark wooden front desk. "May you direct me to table 142?" Zandar asked the well dressed, clean-cut, maître d' who was standing there looking quite ready to assist. "I am looking for Jackson Miller."

"Right this way, right this way," the maître d' proclaimed. "He has been expecting you."

Chapter 1: The Overwatch

The maître d' guided Zander through the VIP section of what could only be called the most luxurious bar in the galaxy. Its platinum flecked marble columns supporting ornately carved animal figurines. Brilliant crystal chandeliers hovered in the air, supported by neither chain nor rope. Floating, casting their soft, colorful light upon each of the guests, as if projecting the colors of their unique souls. Each table has its own holographic waiter, standing politely out of sight, opaque, waiting for the moment to serve.

Not far from the opulent bar that served section 33 was table 142, sitting on its own private balcony, overlooking the planet that Titan's Well orbited. A Human man sat alone waiting for a Trust Story Teller. His name was Jackson Miller. Although Titan's Well had hundreds of species from all over the galaxy as residents, Jackson was one of only two Humans to call the Free City home.

With light brown skin, piercing gray eyes, thick wavy brown hair, and a ruggedly handsome face, Jackson should have looked out of place amongst the cornucopia of exotic alien species, but he didn't. In fact, he looked as if he owned the place. Zandar brushed off this notion since it couldn't be possible. As Zandar approached closer, he got a sense of depth and poise that only many centuries of life could bring. Until now, he had only ever gotten that feeling from fellow Tricarions. Zandar wondered if all Humans were like this or was this Human special.

"Welcome Zandar Deek, please sit," Jack grinned, a welcoming smile gracing his ruggedly handsome face. "I am

Jackson Miller, but you may call me Jack. I have been waiting for you".

"Thank you, Jack. It is a pleasure to meet you." Zandar responded as he pulled out a chair and sat at the table.

"How was your trip to Titan's Well? Good, I hope?" Jack inquired.

"Very well, thank you."

"Did you have far to travel?" Jack asked. "To get to Titan's Well?"

"No. Not far at all. I was in a neighboring star system, having just completed an obituary when I received your invitation. Just a quick jump to get here." Zander responded warmly.

"Good. I've always found that entering and exiting phase space to be a little disconcerting." Jack remarked thoughtfully.

"I know what you mean, but the transport vessel I was on had the best phase dampeners I have ever experienced." Zandar said. "I'm glad they did too. The young lady next to me was looking rather ill. I'd hate to think what would have happened had it been different."

Jack smiled at this comment. There had been many times, he had almost gotten sick when entering phase space, even on short jumps.

Chapter 1: The Overwatch

"Are you familiar with the process of documenting a Story?" Zandar asked, being sure that the small talk had concluded.

"Yes," Jack replied, the slight smile on his face growing into a wide grin. "I am very familiar with your process, although I haven't officially given a story before or met a Trust Story Teller face-to-face. Are you always this down-to-business?"

"Why, yes," noted Zandar with a well-practiced tone that made Jack think he has been asked this before, many times. "You are paying for the time I am acting as your Story Teller. I want you to get the most from my services." He paused momentarily to add a level of importance to this comment. "What made you decide that now was the time to tell your tale?"

"I have been holding onto this Story for far too long. Now feels like the right time for the galaxy to understand," Jack answered, wanting to see how far Zandar was willing to go into the unknown and unanswered. Jack's Story required a Story Teller who was willing to suspend disbelief.

"Understand what?" Zander asked calmly, never breaking eye contact with Jack.

"To understand love and loss and the possibilities and consequences that the universe can present. That is why I specifically asked for you. I have a feeling that only a Tricarion would fully comprehend." Jack said with an air of mystery that Zandar couldn't quite discern. Seeing the slight change in his posture, Jack quickly followed, "You'll see. Somethings can only be known after all is laid bare."

"Ok," continued Zandar, realizing it was a test and not wanting to upset the customer. He was finding himself liking Jack more and more as this conversation continued, although not much had been said up to this point. It was more his presence that he found spellbinding. "Shall we get started?"

"Before we do, would you like to order something to eat or drink, perhaps?" Jack asked smoothly. "Based on the Second Rule of the Story Teller's Code, we will be here for a while."

"You know the Code?" Asked Zandar, slightly surprised that a non-Trust citizen would know such an obscure, and not all that useful, set of rules. Outside of the Story Tellers profession, that is.

"Yes," replied Jack with that same slight smile. "I told you I am very familiar with your process. The Code is the main reason I decided to hire a Trust Story Teller. Should we order?"

Zandar, not realizing how hungry he had become throughout his journey through Titan's Well, agreed to this reasonable delay. Jack pushed a few buttons on his DigiCard, and a holovid menu appeared between them.

Chapter 1: The Overwatch

"Being that you are Tricarion, I would recommend the Tricarion wild boar. It's delicious. They have them delivered fresh, bi-weekly." Jack pointed out praisingly.

Very impressed by this feat of logistics, Zandar agreed. It had been many years since he was able to have fresh Tricarion boar as his professional travels kept him far from home. Remarkably few places in the galaxy would go through the trouble of securing fresh Tricarion boar at that frequency.

After pressing a few more buttons on his DigiCard, Jack ordered two Tricarion boar meals. A few minutes later, the holo-waiter delivered the meals and placed them in front of both patrons. The familiar herbal smell transported Zandar to a far off, fond memory of the red sandy beaches of his home-world. The boar sat over a bed of pureed water root, fire radish, and sautéed figs. All covered with decadent reduced blood wine sauce.

They politely consumed their meal with no conversation between them. Jack remembering it was considered rude to speak during mealtime with a Tricarion. With all the time in the galaxy, there was no need for discussion while eating, which is what they believed. They both slowly, purposefully devoured the meal. When they both had finished, the waiter wordlessly had removed their plates.

"How was the boar? Was it as good as they make it on Tricar? "Jack asked, this being the first time he was able to get a critique by an actual Tricarion.

"Yes, quite exquisite. I would almost say it was better than my grandmother used to make, but not quite. After all, she did have over 1500 years to perfect her recipe, which she coveted fiercely." Zandar responded jovially, a small chuckle escaping his lips.

"I figured as much. As long as it was passable?" Jack hesitated slightly, hoping he wasn't overreaching or possibly offending the Story Teller.

"I would say more than passable," Zandar confirmed.

"Great, I will pass your praise along to the head chef," Jack said, beaming. Within the space of a moment, his face changed to a slightly more serious tone. "I was pleased to hear of your grandmother Milana's passing and her place in the Temple of Life. She was a fierce woman and a strong advocate for the Tricarion people's way of life. She spoke very fondly of you, you know."

"Thank you, and yes, she was extremely supportive. I... I wasn't aware you were acquainted," Zander said, slightly caught off guard. "I mean, she never spoke of knowing any humans."

"I don't expect she did," Jack said mysteriously. "Just know, she was always proud to have a grandson who was the first Tricarion member of the Story Teller's Guild."

"The only Tricarion who has joined the Guild," Zander lamented.

Chapter 1: The Overwatch

"Yes, quite right. But it did make it easy to locate you. And I figured if Milana's opinion of you was so high, it meant something. And that you would be the right one, the only one, to be able to document my Story," Jack said earnestly. "Now, with the necessities out of the way, shall we continue?"

"If we are to continue, I have to officially read the Story Tellers code, and you must agree to each of the Three Rules. Refusal to agree to any Rule will bring our session to an end. However, since you apparently know the Code, I have a feeling you won't object," Zandar professed with a slight smile of his own.

Jack tipped his head once in agreement.

Zandar continued, "Rule One. The Story must be told completely in the third person, even if it is an autobiography. This maintains consistency across documented stories as well as ease of consumption for future reviewers."

"Agreed," Jack said.

"Rule Two. Once started, you may not stop until the Story is fully told. Accordingly, I may not interrupt you in any way. All the questions I have will be presented at the conclusion of your tale. This ensures the integrity of the Story."

"Agreed."

"Rule Three. You must consent to your Story being made available to all citizens of the Trust or any Free City in the Hall of Records. This provides transparency and freedom of information."

"Agreed."

With all three rules confirmed and agreed on, Zandar pulled out his holopad and recorder. He placed them on the table between himself and Jack, then clicked a button on his DigiCard. The holopad illuminated as though it, too, was ready to get to work.

"Please scan your DigiCard on the holopad when you are ready to begin the recording. This will act as your official acknowledgment that you have been read the Three Rules and have agreed."

Jack had been preparing to tell this Story for many years and could feel a sense of excited anticipation. He reached over and scanned his DigiCard on Zandar's holopad. A tiny red light illuminated on the recorder. With that, he knew it was time to begin.

Chapter 2: The Liberty Ship

In a small solar system located in the inner rim of the Orion Arm, about 8,000 parsecs from the center of the Milky Way galaxy, sits a G-type main-sequence yellow sun. That sun has eight planets, five dwarf planets, one asteroid belt, and about 150 moons captured within its gravity, forever revolving around it. There was really nothing special about this particular solar system at all, except for the 3rd planet from the sun. It is called Earth.

Earth, a blue and green marble floating in the darkness of what is otherwise considered lifeless space, harboring over nine million distinct species of life wrapped within its protective atmosphere. Most are simple, single-celled organisms, slightly more complex insects, marine animals, or land-based quadrupeds. However, the planet gave birth to several intelligent species, with homo sapiens rising to the top and coming to dominate them all. They are more familiarly known as Humans.

Humans are incredibly ingenious, creating amazing marvels from weapons to medicine, art to science. They measure everything they can from distances to time and mass to temperature. For humans, time was an ever-present force upon their lives and the thing that they most feared. They busied themselves with trying to leave a legacy, to outlive time. Some built extraordinary monuments to be remembered by, leaving many future generations in wonder. While others caused such tragedy and death in their path to be immortalized, their memory is like poison to the mind.

Humans measure time like this: Sixty seconds to a minute. Sixty minutes to an hour. Twenty-four hours to a day — one rotation of the planet around its axis. And 365 days to a year — one complete orbit of the planet around its star.

Depending on the generation, the average human life span is between 40 and 80 years. That wasn't much time to build a legacy but was plenty of time to forge sorrow and tragedy.

The year was 1943, and the world was at war. The vast majority of the world's nations fighting over territory, beliefs, resources, and, to some, the freedom of the world itself. A Liberty Ship was leaving the recently rebuilt port of

Chapter 2: The Liberty Ship

Pearl Harbor. On its way to bring much-needed replacements and supplies to the island war zones, deep in the Pacific Ocean.

Jackson Miller was a passenger on this Liberty Ship, the Arcadia. The Arcadia was one of the first Liberty Ships off the line in 1941. It had made the dangerous ocean passage many times, ferrying the men and supplies needed to wage war. Showing her age through cracking paint and a rusty edge around her portholes, you never would hear a negative word about her. In fact, her sailors described her as a "sturdy girl" who never let them down, a good luck charm to see them safely through the war. Never suffering so much as a scratch of battle damage, you could understand why they felt this way. The sailors were proud to call her home.

Jack was a member of the United States Marine Corps, enlisting on the day after Pearl Harbor was attacked, December 7th, 1941. The enlistment line was around the block even as the snowdrifts piled up. The call to duty was inescapable for all Americans. The United States of America was ruthlessly attacked, resulting in thousands killed in an unprovoked act of aggression. By doing so, the Japanese unlocked the patriotism and determination of the entire Nation. Jack was just trying to do his part.

Growing up in the small town of Marion, Iowa, about 15 miles from Cedar Rapids, he was the average American. His parents owned the local corner store. Jack would often work there during his summers away from school. His best friend, well his only friend really, was named Blue. At least, that's what everyone called her.

Her real name was Margaret Ann Carter. Her father was really hoping for a boy but ended up with her instead. He even had a name picked out and everything, Bluford, after his father. Thankfully, her mother would not let him put that on her birth certificate. So, for as long as she could remember, he just kept calling her "Blue." It stuck. Everyone who knew her called her Blue as if it was the name she was born with. Blue had pale white skin, the color of fresh snow, deep almond brown eyes, and straight brown hair with faint red highlights. Being that they were the same age, next-door neighbors and their families were very close, they became inseparable.

As they grew from childhood to the teenage years, that inseparable friendship turned towards deep affection, then love. It was only a few days before the attack on Pearl Harbor that Jack had proposed marriage to Blue. And although he didn't have money for a ring, of course, she said yes. She never gave two thoughts towards material possessions, finding more comfort in a warm campfire or good story of the old wild west.

After the news of the attack, Blue also enlisted. The Red Cross was looking for young ladies to serve in the Navy Nurse Corps. This was something she could do. She had experience helping her father in his practice, although he was only a veterinarian. It was enough for Blue to know she wouldn't be squeamish at the sight of blood or the sound of a bone saw. So, she volunteered. It was her way of not being left behind.

Jack was so proud of her. After the Christmas holidays in 1941, they said their goodbyes. For now, at least. As luck would have it, they were both off to San Diego. Jack for basic training and Blue for the nursing school. They kept in touch, writing whenever they had a free moment. During furloughs, they met up and took in the sights that San Diego had to offer.

Jack was there at Blue's graduation. She looked so beautiful in the long white linen stockings, knee-length white dress, a belt synched at her waist, and small pearlescent buttons lining the front of her nurses' gown. The signature round cap adorned with the bright Red Cross only highlighted the importance of the uniform. They celebrated that evening, jumping from bar to bar. Although Blue didn't drink, she enjoyed the social atmosphere and spending time with Jack. Knowing that they would see little of each other over the next few months as they both prepared for war and the trials ahead.

As the year went on, they continued to write daily. In early 1943 Jack and Blue found themselves stationed together again, this time in Pearl Harbor. A staging area for the fight in the Pacific. Jack's unit was told they would be heading east to fight the Japanese in the greatest island-hopping campaign the world has ever seen. And he would be making the ocean crossing aboard the Arcadia. It just so happened that Blue was also catching a ride aboard the Arcadia.

Jack wasn't particularly fond of being at sea, not having spent much time in the ocean in his youth. But he found navy transport vessels to be the worst. The smell of sweat and gasoline was ever-present, making Jack constantly nauseous. It did give Jack comfort knowing Blue was with him, and, when they reached the war, she would be back, far back behind the lines, attending to injured soldiers. However, it didn't alleviate all fear of something terrible happening to her. War was danger, and they were heading directly towards it. He didn't mind facing it himself, but he thought Blue deserved better, deserved to be safe. In his heart, he knew she would never be happy sitting back while others struggled not doing her part. He was at least glad they would spend the next several days together as the ship crossed the vast expanse of the Pacific Ocean.

"Do you know where we are going?" Jack asked Blue jokingly. He had asked her this several times on this journey and knew she didn't know.

"No. You know I don't!" Blue responded mockingly. She knew what he was doing, and it was working as intended. Even with the prospect of an unknown, dangerous location ahead, he was trying to make her smile. That was just one of the things she loved about him. "Why do you keep asking me that?" She prodded.

"I just like hearing the sound of your voice." He said, "Soon I won't be able to hear it at all, and I don't know when I will be able to again." "...Or if I ever will be able to again," he finished to himself. Not wanting to worry her more than she was already.

Even though he didn't say it, she knew what he was thinking. His ruggedly handsome, expressive face and piercing grey eyes a window into his soul that she could easily see-through. All she could do was smile back at him.

The first few days went along without anything notable happening other than the rigor one comes to expect with the life of a serviceman. Jack and Blue stealing moments together as a way to gain strength for the trials each faced ahead.

On the third night, that all changed. An explosion rang out in the distance. The shockwave rocking the Arcadia. One of the ships further up in the convoy column had been struck. The Arcadia sprang into life, each person heading to their assigned action stations. Being fully asleep when the alarms blared to life, Jack took the slightest moment to fully wake up and understand what the commotion was about. He quickly rubbed the sleep from his eyes. Looking at his watch, it was just past 1AM.

"Abel, get up. Get up! We are under attack!" Jack shouted as the noise from the excited passengers and return fire was defining. Jack pulled on his pants, shirt, and belt. Finishing the look by placing his helmet on his head and grabbing his weapon. He was issued a Thompson M1928A1 and M1911A1 sidearm. He had always felt a fierce connection to his weapons, knowing that they would protect him, so he must, in turn, protect them.

Abel likewise quickly shook off sleep and got ready. Abel Green was a member of Jack's squad and his closest friend since joining the Corps. Abel was an average-sized man, with toned muscles, warm ivory skin, and what can only be described as a round baby face that quite accurately matched his overly optimistic personality. Being sure to grab his M1 Garand, he also snatched up several extra loads of *en bloc* clip loaded with the powerful .30-06 cartridge. He draped the additional ammo sashes one over each shoulder.

"Good thinking! Throw me some extra Thompson mags," Jack yelled. He reached up and grab the mags out of the air as Abel threw them. "Ready?"

Abel nodded several times rapidly.

"We need to get to the port gunners," Jack yelled, knowing Abel knew what to do. He was confirming more for his benefit, working up the nerve to get out there. This was his first time in combat after-all. "Okay, let's go."

The two ran down the passageways, up the ladders, onto the deck, took their designated position, and waited. Jack hadn't remembered the ship seeming so big before, a real sitting duck. The sea had gone quiet since the initial explosion and return volley. The deck gun smelled of sulfur, letting Jack know it hadn't been idle. All they could hear now was a ship burning and the drone of propellers humming in the distance. The burning fire creating an eerie orange glow over the ocean's surface. That's when Jack saw it.

A Japanese submarine was eying its next target. Jack could see the reflection of the fires glinting off the periscope's lens.

"Off the port beam!" Jack yelled, splitting the silence. "Off the port beam!"

In an instant, many events started happening in quick succession. First, the deck gunners opened up, raining a hail of bullets towards the submarine. Next, the ship began turning towards it. Jack guessed it was to minimize the ship's target size making it more challenging to hit. Lastly, Jack could see the ocean frothing in a trail headed directly towards the ship. His heart sank. The submarine had launched a torpedo, and it looked like it was on course.

"Incoming!" Several people yelled in tandem, carrying above all other noise. "Incoming!"

The torpedo just missed, sweeping past the bow of the ship and out of Jack's view. For a moment, he felt elation. "The torpedo missed," he yelled excitedly at Abel. Abel did not respond, staring out across the ocean toward where Jack had seen the submarine.

"Incoming!"

This time, it didn't miss, hitting the bow of the ship in a head-on collision. The explosion was deafening. In that instance, Jack thought he was dead. The world was spinning, growing dark and cold. But he wasn't dead. Somehow, he was lying on his back on the chilly, wet deck. He didn't even remember falling. The world rocked back into view as Jack stared into the starry night sky. His ears ringing, mouth and throat aching from breathing in the harsh smoke billowing out of the bow of the ship. He was surprised it was still afloat.

"Abandon ship!" He heard the deck master yell as a different, more frantic alarm whirled to life. "Abandon ship, you worthless bastards! Abandon Ship!"

Jack's only thought was finding Blue. He had to find Blue. Jumping up, he raced into the flaming wreckage, knocking into bulkheads and the frightened people scurrying past. His balance was still off-kilter from the torpedo strike, but he knew, during an action drill, Blue would be in the infirmary. He hoped she was still there. Desperate to find her there. Fear was the only thing keeping him plunging deeper into the raging inferno. Fear is what pushed others to leave it. His fear was different. Yes, he was afraid of dying. Of course, he was. It wasn't until that moment he realized the truth. He was scared of losing Blue more.

"Why couldn't you have just stayed at home?" Jack thought to himself. He instantly regretted his selfish wants. Could he have stayed back while others did their part? No, he couldn't and couldn't ask that of Blue either.

Jack heard multiple explosions in the distance as he barreled down the passageways, his weapon and helmet banging against the ship's steel hull. "They must have hit the

Chapter 2: The Liberty Ship

Japanese Sub," he thought to himself, but the explosion and gunfire continued. A wild rattling hit the haul above him. "What is going on up there?" he wondered in the back of his mind. Knowing he was running out of time, he pressed on, focusing on his immediate goal, finding Blue.

He burst around the corner and froze, staggering to an awkward halt. Blue was here. She was alive! Like always, she was going out of her way to help others. Passing out life jackets to those trying to escape. For Jack, at that moment, everything faded away. The brutal sounds of burning flames, endless gunfire, and even the savage screams of men dying. Jack was awestruck at her generosity and giving spirit, even in a moment as violent as this. A sharp jolt of the ship brought him back to reality. He knew they didn't have long and quickly closed the remaining distance between them.

"Blue! Blue!" Not able to get her attention. "Margaret Ann Carter! We need to leave. NOW!" She looked up just as he grabbed her arm and pulled her towards him. Jack could sense her fear and relief, as well. He gave her a quick kiss, even though he wanted the embrace to last much longer. As they ran out of the infirmary, Blue, thinking quickly, grab two life jackets and a brown combat medic's satchel from a crate labeled Kit No. 1.

It took little time for them to return to the deck as the passageways had been mostly cleared out. This gave Jack hope as he assumed all passengers had made it to the lifeboats and into the ocean, safely away from the floundering Arcadia. He couldn't have been more wrong.

"What? no!" Blue gasped as she cleared the door, crossing the threshold onto the main deck. "How is this possible? Jack, why?"

The ship was mostly empty of the living now. Death was all around them, littering the main deck. Blood streaming off the sides into the dark, uncaring ocean as the ship rocked from one side to the other. Stepping over the countless dead bodies, Jack saw two sailors lowering, what looked to be, the last remaining lifeboat onto the water below.

"What happened? Where are all the lifeboats?" Jack asked with a spark of desperation he couldn't hold back. "Did anyone else get out?" Thinking about his friend Abel.

The sailor closest to Jack leaned towards him as he finished lowering the lifeboat and clearing the Davit system. "Japanese Zeros," he said with detached emptiness. "They strafed us. We weren't ready. They were working to put out the fires."

He suddenly knew what that wild rattling was—a barrage from two 20 mm cannons. The results were devastating. The Japanese Zero was an astonishingly capable aircraft of war.

The ship's deck was getting very close to the waterline now. Not wanting to stand around any longer than needed, Jack and Blue made the small leap into the lifeboat. At the same time, a dark figure came running toward them from the stern of the ship. Jack, hearing the noise, spun quickly and pulled his 1911 from its holster. He disengaged the safety in a single, well-practiced maneuver.

"Don't shoot!" Abel screamed as he jumped into the lifeboat. Blood covered his face from a gash on his forehead, just above his left eye. He was alive. Jack couldn't help but smile.

"Where have you been? And where is your helmet?" Jack asked, with the smile still stretching across his face.

"Looking for you! I followed you below deck but quickly lost sight of you," Abel answered. His naturally smooth voice cracked, breaking into a higher register. For the first time since they had met, Abel's voice matched his youthful appearance. "I got turned around, ended up exiting at the back of the ship. My helmet got knocked off during the explosion. That's when I got this." He finished, pointing to his forehead.

"Well, I am just glad you made it, Abel," Blue said, also smiling. The first time she had done so since the too short kiss with Jack. "Let me look at your head." She rummaged around the medic's bag, found some gauze and a large bandage. "This will do nicely."

"Here let me help you in," Jack said to the nearest sailor as he extended his arm.

"Thanks," the sailor replied with that same detached monotone voice as he grabbed Jack's outstretched hand.

"Now you," Jack urged to the second sailor as he waved him down. He grabbed Jack's hand and jumped in without a word. As he jumped past Jack, he could see his flaming red hair and just assumed the firelight was reflecting somehow. It wasn't until the two sailors were aboard that Jack noticed a woman standing by the nearest bulkhead holding what looked like a book. She was wearing the Women's Army Corps uniform, with a matching backpack, and a revolver strapped to her waist.

"Miss, you need to come here now. We don't have a lot of time." Jack yelled. She didn't move. "Damn, okay."

Jack jumped from the lifeboat back onto the burning deck of the Arcadia. The once "sturdy girl" was listing far forward, moments from slipping beneath the waves with only her dead for eternal company.

Blue turned away from mending Abel's head just in time to see Jack leaping back onto the sinking ship. She gasped in horror. "Jack hurry!" She yelled. "Hurry!"

He rushed a few steps towards the Army lady, grabbed her by the arm, and pulled her in the lifeboat's direction. They made it back just in time. As they both stepped into the boat, the Arcadia gave one final shudder. It slipped silently below the ocean's surface, the force causing the lifeboat to bob up and down violently.

They paddled away from what was only minutes ago, the Arcadia's location, in complete silence. Once they reached several hundred yards distance, Jack could see what all the explosions were about. Most of the ships in the convoy were either on fire and limping away or sinking—the dark dots of the Japanese Zeros disappearing into the night sky. The hum of their engines fading. Jack guessed they needed to return to their carrier hundreds of miles away before running out of fuel. Off in the distance, he could see something on the edge of the waterline, also burning—little men running on the flat deck. Working, Jack suspected, to put out the fires.

"Jack, it looks like we got them too! The Jap Sub. Look!" Said Abel exuberantly. His excitement about retribution did little to ease Jack's worry.

"Keep your voice down," Jack whispered hoarsely as all the yelling had depleted what was left of his voice. "We don't want them spotting us. They don't treat prisoners well if they take any at all."

The lifeboat fell silent upon hearing Jack's warning. They slowly floated away from the ghostly convoy riding an ocean current—the ocean's glassy calm surface concealing the violence and terrors that just occurred. By Jack's estimate, it had only been about 20 minutes since he had been asleep, in his bunk, dreaming. Now he was drifting out to sea, in a lifeboat, with two friends, three strangers, and no idea where they were headed, with little hope of being rescued.

Chapter 3: Boredom and Blind Luck

The calm ocean. Soft rolling waves lapped against the lifeboat's wooden hull. The soothing motion did little to quell the anxiety permeating the boat. The violence from the night before was at the forefront of everyone's mind. It had been hours since they left the battle. Hours since they had seen any sign of either an enemy or friend. The quiet sounds of whimpers, sobs, and whispered prayers were the only things to break the silence.

"Look! The sun is coming up!" Blue exclaimed with as much excitement as she could muster. Hoping the new dawn would revive the spirits of those onboard. "The sun is coming up."

Jack smiled. He knew what she was doing. Blue was always trying to make others feel better, whether in body, mind, or spirit. That is what made her an extremely effective nurse. "It is," he replied, letting her know her proclamation didn't go unheard.

Abel was sleeping in the corner, leaning against the Army lady who, as it turns out, was the one softly sobbing. "It must be one or both of the navy folks whimpering," Jack thought to himself. Realizing it didn't matter, he kicked Abel awake. "Private Abel, it's dawn. Time to get up."

"Yes, Sir, Corporal Miller." Abel instinctively responded as he worked to get into attention, knocking into the Army lady, causing her to suddenly stop sobbing. She apparently noticed for the first time she was surrounded by strangers. At that moment, Jack saw she was a staff sergeant.

Being the highest rank in the lifeboat, Jack asked: "Ma'am, what are your orders?"

She just ignored him, as if she didn't know he was addressing her. Jack tried again. "Ma'am, what are your orders?"

"What?" She mumbled in a barely audible voice.

"Your orders, Ma'am? It appears you are the ranking officer. What do you recommend we do?" Jack asked, feigning deference as he didn't know how by-the-book she was.

"I don't know. I don't know." She stammered, very close to breaking down. The panic in her voice was threatening to overtake her. One of the sailors started to whimper again.

"Ok," Jack said in his calmest voice possible. "Being that I am the second highest rank here, mind if I make some suggestions, Ma'am?"

"Please," She whispered with the smallest voice Jack thought a person could make while still producing a sound. Blue looked on helplessly. Wanting to do something to ease her stress but instinctively knew when to let Jack take the lead. It wasn't compassion they needed now. It was leadership.

"We need to see what supplies we have available to us," Jack decided with a confidence Blue knew he wasn't feeling but was feigning for the others. "We need to know what we have. Our lives depend on it."

The sailors instantly jumped to action, checking the crates marked "Emergency Supplies" stowed neatly below the aft bench, aboard the tiny wooden vessel they now called home. Jack was surprised by their hustle, something he hadn't seen them exhibit up-to that point. Even when fleeing from the sinking Arcadia. He assumed it was because they were asked to do something simple, something they knew they could accomplish.

Once everything was collected, they took inventory. The tiny boat contained the following: three crates of food rations, equaling — 36 individual meals, one large canvas tarp, six oars, a fair amount of cordage and thick roping, 12 full canteens, and one wooden bucket.

"Ok," Jack said, trying to do the math in his head. "We will need to ration. One meal a day each. That gives us six days of food." There were some grumbles, but everyone seemed to agree. "That just leaves the water," Jack hesitated. "With 12 canteens, that leaves two each, and…"

"One-third canteen per day per person" finished the Army lady with a sense of confidence he hadn't seen from her before.

"Yes," Jack acknowledged. "Look, I know it isn't much, but we will make it work. We will need to collect rainwater. A solar still isn't feasible with what we have at hand. I think the wooden bucket should do, although it looked like it has seen better days." Jack wondered who saw that bucket and decided to pack it with the emergency supplies. "They should have thrown it out and gotten a new one," he thought to himself.

Blue grabbed the bucket without needing to be asked and dunked it into the ocean to see if it would retain water. While not entirely watertight, it held better than Jack expected. "Ok, we can make that work."

"Yeah, all we need to do is make it rain now," one of the sailors said, with what Jack assumed was a feeble attempt at humor. Or maybe it wasn't. His mind was foggy from the exhaustion of the previous evening and working much slower than usual.

"We need to find a way to give us cover," The other sailor pointed out. Now seeing him in the daytime, his hair was flaming red after all. "The sun will be brutal soon, and we need to get out of it."

"Good thinking," Jack replied. Happy that they were all working together. "Abel, help them build a shelter. Use the canvas tarp, oars, and some of the cordage."

They began to work diligently and soon had a makeshift shelter covering the front half of the lifeboat, leaving the aft bench exposed to the sun and ocean. They stowed their supplies under the newly covered forward bench, and all moved under coverage as the sun was already starting to beat down on them. "I think introductions are in order," Blue prodded.

"I'll go first," Blue said, not waiting for the moment to escape. "I'm Margaret Carter, but everyone calls me Blue, from Marion, Iowa." Blue looked directly at Jack, and everyone knew he was next.

"Jackson Miller, but you can call me Jack. I am also from Marion, Iowa."

"Did you know each other before the war?" Spluttered the sailor with the red hair and wearing a slightly suspicious smile.

Chapter 3: Boredom and Blind Luck

"They did! They are actually engaged to be married," Abel beamed with a wide smile. At that moment, Jack was wondering why he even bothered to tell Abel anything. Blue wore a smirk that let Jack know she knew he was uncomfortable.

"Wow, what are the odds?" Dully stated the other sailor. A comment more than a question and not requiring a response as the odds were astronomical. They all sat in awkward silence for a moment.

"So, who's next?" Blue asked cheerfully, trying to regain the momentum of the conversation that otherwise had just stopped. "You," Pointing to the sailor with red hair, the one who asked if she and Jack knew each other.

"Kenneth Muck, but you can call me Muck. Everyone else does." He mumbled with downtrodden eyes. "I am from San Diego, California. I'm... Was," he corrected, "a mechanic aboard the Arcadia." He finished with some resignation, realizing his ship was now at the bottom of the ocean.

"It's alright," Blue comforted, lightly placing her hand on his shoulder. "Nice to meet you, but I don't think I can call you Muck." It sounded like an insult to Blue, and she didn't feel right calling him that. "Can I call you, Kenny?"

He brightened at her touch. "No one calls me Kenny, except my mother." He remarked bashfully. "But you can."

"Yes, I think I will. We all will." She said with an absolute finality that let Jack know the matter was decided.

"Tony Castillo, New York City," Tony chimed in, breaking up the pleasant moment with the same detached emptiness he had used to describe the Japanese Zero attack.

"Tony, so nice to meet you. What did you do before the war?" Blue asked, attempting to get more engagement than just a name and location.

"I was a dock worker in Brooklyn. Loading and unloading cargo vessels that regularly crossed the Atlantic Ocean." He said, only in a slightly more friendly tone.

"You must have seen some pretty crazy things working at the docks." Blue pressed, attempting to keep Tony engaged. Jack was always impressed with Blue's ability to connect with people. Even the difficult ones.

"Yeah, you bet I did," was all Tony said back.

Seeing that Tony wasn't willing to say anymore, Blue moved on. "And Miss, you are?" She said as she continued around the small circle of faces.

"Ruth Martin," that Army Lady said in the same small voice she had used before.

"Ruth, that's a lovely name," Blue said with an encouraging tone, seeing for the first time the title of the book she had been gripping tightly all night. The Complete

History of Oceania and the Polynesian People by B. R. Brooks. "Where are you from, Ruth?"

"Flagstaff. Flagstaff, Arizona," She answered with a half grin and a bit more confidence.

"That's a nice revolver," Jack cut in. "Smith & Wesson Model 27 if I'm not mistaken. Not exactly official Army issue."

"No, no, it isn't," Ruth mumbled. "It was a gift from my father when I graduated from college. Just before signing up."

".357 magnum. That's a good gift," Jack admitted, also impressed hearing that she had graduated college. Something Jack could never see himself accomplishing. "What did you study in school?"

"History of Western Cultures," She reported in a practiced tone.

"How is it that you became a Staff Sergeant and not an officer?" Jack asked.

"Well... I'm not exactly what you'd call 'officer material,' but my father fought in the Great War and had some connections. So, I ended up as a Staff Sergeant. But I am nothing more than a secretary for Brigadier General Oats." She said, eyes downcast from having to explain her shortcomings.

"Well, it's so great to meet you all," Blue interjected with a smile that others in the same situation would have had to force, but not her.

"You forgot about me," blurted Abel with mock disappointment in his voice. Having known Blue for almost a year now. Ever since he and Jack joined the same unit, Fox Company, 2nd Battalion, 5th Marines.

"And this, endlessly optimistic Marine, is Abel Green," Jack said, sensing that Abel wanted to be introduced.

At that, Abel stood and took a bow. Kenny and Blue smiled. Ruth let out a small giggle. Jack just shook his head, and Tony showed no signs of acknowledgment whatsoever.

"Now that we are all acquainted, let's start thinking about how we will catch some food," Jack said with that same confident voice. "I think if we pull the strands of rope apart…"

"It won't work," Tony interrupted in a deeply pessimistic tone.

"I'm pretty sure we can make some lines, cutting hooks from the emptied food tins. Several of us have knives," Jack shot back, thinking that Tony's negative tone wasn't helping.

"You just don't get it. We are in the middle of the ocean," Tony thundered with more than a bit of frustration bleeding through. "There is nothing out there! It's mostly a lifeless desert. You will just be wasting your time building any fishing gear."

"He's right, you know," chimed Kenny. Shrugging his shoulders and looking between Tony and Jack with a what-can-you-do look on his face. "We've crossed this ocean several times in the Arcadia and rarely saw anything out this far. Most ocean life lives near the coasts."

Jack, getting ready to argue that doing something was better than just sitting around, "Look..."

Blue placed her hand on his arm, letting him know it wasn't the time to argue. "Thank you for your insight, boys." She said, attempting to defuse the growing tension. Kenny gave her a small smile acknowledging her attempt and showing he too didn't fancy an argument.

"Ok," Jack reluctantly conceded. Knowing it would make Blue happy and realizing arguing wasn't going to solve anything. He continued, "Let's not waste the energy now building fishing lines. Does anyone have other ideas to improve our current situation?"

They all looked at each other, then away, as if they were all deep in thought. After several long minutes, Abel spoke up.

"Well, we only used four of the six ores making the shelter. Maybe we can take turns paddling?" He said, looking at the two sailors for affirmation that his idea was, at its very least, plausible.

"That could work," Kenny said hesitantly. His face screwed up with the effort of thinking it through. "We would need to pair up and spending no more than an hour rowing per group. But it could work. Oh, and we would need to make sure we continued to paddle with the current"

"Obviously," Tony said in an exasperated tone, finding it hard to believe he actually agreed with them. "It won't be easy."

"But it'll be worth it if it means we reach land or get rescued sooner," Abel said in an optimistic tone, hoping that everyone agreed. "Let's pair up."

"If everyone agrees," Jack said, looking at each of them. In turn, they each nodded in agreement. "Ok, Blue and I, Tony and Kenny, Abel and Ruth. Blue and I will start. It's 11:29 AM right now. Tony, I will let you know when it is 12:30 PM for you and Kenny to take over."

He and Blue moved into position, facing the back of the boat, giving them an unobstructed view of the vast, open ocean. The sun glinted off the ocean surface as if it was just a mirage. The massive scale of the scene was simply breathtaking. Jack couldn't think of anyone he would rather be sharing this experience with.

The two quickly fell into a consistent yet steady rhythm of rowing. And although it couldn't be perceived, looking out over the vast ocean, it felt as if progress was made.

Chapter 3: Boredom and Blind Luck

Looking at his watch, Jack just realized it was 1:41 PM. He was amazed that over two hours had passed already with him and Blue rowing, chatting, laughing, and poking fun at Abel. No matter what they were doing, time always seemed to move more quickly when they did it together. "Hey Tony, you're up."

Tony and Kenny swapped places with Jack and Blue, respectively. Jack, sitting under the cooling shade of the makeshift shelter, was struck with a realization. Seeing Tony and Kenny, rowing next to each other, their appearance stood out in stark relief. Tony, short and stocky with bronze skin, silky black hair, and dark, almost black, eyes. Against Kenny's tall, slender frame, ruddy skin, flaming red hair, and dark burgundy freckles outlining his hazel eyes. They couldn't be more different if they tried.

The monotonous rotation actually gave them something to look forward to, keeping their minds focused from straying too far into desperation. Each pair handled the stress and effort of rowing differently. Jack and Blue reminisced about home and family while also talking about what the future would hold. Abel babbled about everything from his feelings about the war to growing up in an orphanage in San Francisco. Ruth, happy that she had some distractions, didn't mind at all. Tony mostly stayed to himself, leaving Kenny only his imagination for company. The early friendliness and cooperative spirit evaporated with the lazy passing of time and the ores' draining effort. When not on duty, each pair tried to catch as much sleep as possible before their next rotation. The three-hour cycle repeated hour after hour, day after day.

Day four brought a fantastic surprise. A pod of oceanic whitetip sharks glided past, just under the lifeboat. Their long fins and purposeful movements gave the impression that they were flying, not swimming. Their graceful movements reminded Jack that even though Humans are engaged in a deadly struggle, the natural world continued on, little effected by man's plight. For some reason, this gave him comfort.

The relative excitement of seeing the sharks quickly died away, the group falling back into their monotonous duty. The ores, their ever-present taskmaster, was all-consuming. By the evening of day four, the sharks were all but forgotten about.

By the morning of the fifth day, the tension was increasing. Tony was becoming more cynical. Constantly spouting off about how they weren't going to make it or how they should all just drown themselves to save them from dying of thirst. Which he claimed to be the worst possible way to go. Often Jack would cut in, scolding him for his attitude. Abel always backing him up. This never failed to kick off an argument between Tony, Jack, and Abel. Kenny and Ruth never got involved. Blue had the unenviable job of breaking it up. Usually just before it came to blows.

They were running out of water and food. There had been no rain to collect. The current, although rapid, was seemingly pulling them to nowhere. Conversation dwindled to almost nothing, even between Jack and Blue. By the night of day six, they were out of food and water.

Day seven was the most brutal, with none of them sleeping much, even when not on ore duty. With dehydration setting in, all of them felt light-headed with muscle cramps that went well beyond the exertions of rowing. Jack and Abel had experienced this before in basic training, but it was clear the others hadn't. By the night of day seven, they had given up on taking turns rowing. Hope was dwindling. As the sun sank below the horizon, Jack just sat with Blue in his arms, not saying a word.

That is when it started. A bright flash of light followed by a violent crack of thunder, louder than Jack had ever heard.

The storm crashed over them with such violence Jack wasn't sure the little lifeboat was going to survive, or them with it. The speed at which the storm engulfed them had also surprised him. It only took about five minutes from the lightning strike that notified them a storm was on the horizon to being fully enveloped. Passing Blue one of the only two life jackets onboard, he stood wooden, thinking about what to do with the second life jacket. His indecision only lasting for a brief moment.

"Ruth, take this. Put it on," Jack yelled over the howling wind. She took it and mouthed what Jack only could assume was, "Thank you."

They all huddled under the shelter even though it didn't last long. The roaring wind was blowing so strong it ripped the canvas roof from the lifeboat, and it quickly disappeared into the dark—one of the ores used in its construction hitting Kenny on the head, knocking him out. The ore quickly followed the canvas tarp into the night sky.

Jack saw Kenny beginning to fall backward. He grabbed his shirt. Preventing him from falling into the churning ocean. "Blue, Kenny's out cold." Jack shouted as he arranged Kenny's now lifeless body into a sitting position against the side of the boat. "You might want to check on him."

Blue bent down and check Kenny's head, then placed the back of her hand against his lips. "Jack, there's no blood, and he is breathing normally. He should be conscious again soon." She informed.

Just as Blue had given her prognosis, Kenny came too.

"What, what happened?" He asked. "How did I get down here?"

"You were hit in the head. Everything's ok, you'll be fine" Blue responded. "Just let me know if you start feeling dizzy."

"Try to fill your canteens," Jack yelled over the roaring noise of the howling wind, now that the incident with Kenny had been resolved. "This might be our only chance."

They all held up the canteens, capturing what they could of the falling rain. While using one hand to hold their canteen, Blue and Ruth used the other to hold the wooden bucket between them, hoping to capture as much drinkable water as possible. But that didn't last long as the bucket quickly proved to be a fruitless endeavor. Leaking far faster than water could be collected in the violent rocking of the tiny lifeboat.

The storm dragged on for hours, each taking turns using the old wooden bucket to empty out the boat. Jack was getting worried about how much water they were taking on. About halfway through the night, they felt it. A violent collision causing them to all lurch towards the front of the little boat. All forward momentum stopped. For a second, Jack had expected another attack and was looking around for the Jap sub. But nothing else happened. The boat seemed to be motionless, in the middle of the ocean, while the stormy seas swirled around them.

The rain was still coming down in thick sheets, although not as hard as before. Jack could hear Kenny praying desperately for relief, for a break in the storm, or maybe even for deliverance. It wasn't until the next lightning flash that Jack saw it.

All he could do was laugh, laugh out loud, and as loud as his dehydrated body and constricted throat would allow him. Elation spreading to every inch of his sore, defeated body. For some reason, this gave Blue strength. She knew it would take more than a storm to make Jack crack. The others, not knowing him as well as she did, just looked at him like he had finally gone crazy. There was nothing more they could do now, not with the storm and darkness. They hunkered down and road out the night.

Chapter 4: A Light in the Darkness

The tired group of survivors huddled low in the lifeboat, partially submerged in the water collected by the boat's hull. Figuring it was better to be wet and protected vs. wet and hounded by the furious wind. By daybreak, the storm had finally passed. With the sunlight beaming over the horizon, they all started to stir. Blue gasped, her hand tightening on Jack's arm. On Jack's other side, Abel stood and gave a wild, jubilant cheer. The lifeboat swayed with the sudden motion.

In the hours that passed, Jack had almost forgotten what he had seen. Passing it off as a lucid dream. More worried about staying warm and making it through the night. Abel's cheer let Jack know it wasn't a dream.

"Whoa," Blue gasped. Seeing the island for the first time. "We made it. We are safe!"

The island's vibrant green plant life standing in stark relief against the endless blue ocean as if the land itself was painted onto the water. Jack could see two mountains from the boat, one small, not far from where they had landed. The other towering, large, as if watching over the island itself. Between them and it was only a wild jungle.

"Well, we are at least out of the boat," Tony said in a dry tone. "But it looks like we need to swim."

They were stuck on what appeared to be an outcropping of coral and sand. As it hadn't taken on any additional water when they crashed, Jack assumed it was just stuck, not damaged. The water was a calm, bright crystal blue, sprawling with all sorts of marine creatures. Jack could see schools of fish and crabs crawling on the reef just from his spot in the lifeboat. A group of sea turtles grazed lazily on the grass growing from the brightly colored coral. The beach didn't look more than 100 yards away. "Well, at least we won't go hungry," Jack thought to himself.

"Looks like we need to swim," Jack confirmed excitedly. He always loved swimming in the lakes back home and was on the varsity swim team in high school. "This shouldn't be too difficult at all."

Chapter 4: A Light in the Darkness

"I c…c… can't swim," Ruth stuttered.

Not knowing if that was from the fear or merely the cold water they had been exposed to all night, Jack asked: "What do you mean? Like you aren't very good? Or can't swim at all?"

"At all," She quietly peeped.

"Ok. Not a problem. Not a problem at all. I can bring you in. You still have the life jacket on, so you won't drown. It will take a little longer, but we will make it." Jack said confidently. Sharing a look with Blue and wondering how it was possible to make it to adulthood, not knowing how to swim.

The others made excellent time to the beach. The gentle waves helped carry them to their destination. Jack, dragged down with weapons and Ruth, took much longer. Ruth's efforts to help only hindering their slow, arduous progress. "Stop Ruth, you are only making it worse." Jack yelled over the suffocating sound of water, pressing against his ears.

Once they finally made it to the beach — the only blemishes to its beauty were the debris that had washed up during the nights' storm — Jack collapsed. The effort had been far more than his tired, hungry body could bear. He laid on the pristine soft white sand, wanting, at that moment, to never move again. Jack closed his eyes, trying to regain a little strength. Not knowing how long he had actually been lying there, he was startled when Blue spoke.

"Open your eyes," She encouraged in a somewhat giddy tone. "Jack, you're going to want to see this."

He slowly opened his eyes. The bright sunlight whitewashed out all details. As he squinted to bring the pieces back into focus, he smiled. Blue was holding up what looked like a melon. A giant, sweet-smelling bright yellow melon. "Take it," she said affectionately. "You need energy more than anyone."

The hollow pit in Jack's stomach growled, yawning open like a bear rousing from hibernation. He sat up and met Blue's steady gaze, avoiding the impossibly ripe melon in her outstretched hand.

Keeping his tone light, he answered, "You go ahead, I'll go find more for both of us."

"Jack," she continued brushing off his attempt at chivalry and trying to stop him from getting up. "Jack, you don't need to. We found loads of them creeping along the jungle floor. Right there." She pointed towards the Jungle. No more than 30 feet away, the tree line was densely packed with palm trees, lush flowering bushes, and a type of short, broadleaf tree Jack had never seen before. Seeing as there was no longer any reason to object, Jack pulled out his knife, drove it deep into the melon, and split it wide open.

He gave one half to Blue and kept the other for himself. They devoured it greedily. Using the rind as a makeshift bowl, ensuring not a single drop of sweet juice was wasted. The others were doing likewise. Looking around, Jack noticed that Abel had already finished three melons, six halves littered the beach just beside him and was getting ready to open his fourth.

"Abel," Blue yelled across the beach, "Slow down. You will make yourself sick," She chuckled.

But he didn't slow down. Abel devoured his fourth melon, throwing each half hastily aside, and started on his fifth. When all of a sudden, he darted into the Jungle. A few minutes later, he came out and wiped his mouth with the sleeve of his uniform. "You got sick, didn't you," Blue asked matter-of-factly. Abel acknowledged with a slight nod of his head.

"I told you so," Blue said as they both laughed. Kenny and Ruth even joining in. It was a needed release from the stress they had all just endured.

After the laughter died down, which took several minutes, Jack got up and surveyed the beach. From here, they had an unobstructed view of the beach in both directions and the open ocean. Their plucky little lifeboat was still stuck on the coral. Jack cautiously strode over to the tree line.

"Jack, whatcha doing?" Abel questioned as he quickly fell in behind him.

"Just taking a short patrol, I need to know what resources we have close at hand and if there are any imminent dangers," Jack answered. "Stay with the group, that's an order." As he saw Abel continuing to follow.

Begrudgingly, Abel headed back to Ruth, Blue, and Kenny. Jack tentatively entered the Jungle and started walking in ever-growing arches outward. Scouting the resources they had in their immediate vicinity. Food and shelter building materials were in abundance, but no freshwater within a 200-yard radius. He headed back to the others, not sure how he wanted to proceed.

Abel was once again diving into another melon as Blue and Ruth laughed at his side. Kenny was standing close to the water's edge so that the incoming waves washed over his feet. Jack could see that he had removed his shoes. "I better leave mine on," Jack said to himself as he sat down near Blue, Abel, and Ruth.

"No more melon's Abel. That's an order," Jack commanded only half-joking.

"Like no more ever, Jack?" Blue asked jokingly.

"No, not ever. How about. No more melon's today," Jack responded.

Abel dropped the half of melon he had left and saluted. "Yes, Sir, Corporal, Miller Sir."

They all sat and rested. Jack figured they had earned an hour's break before starting the difficult work of surviving. However, he didn't want to put off needed tasks for too long. Their very life depended on it, and their water supply was running dangerously low.

Jack had forgotten how therapeutic the sounds of waves crashing on a beach could be. If allowed, he would sit there, listening to that sound for the rest of his life, with Blue by his side. Reality came crashing back with the sight of Tony brooding a short distance away.

Jack got up and walked over to Tony. He was the only person not enjoying their newfound luck. Although Jack was getting rather frustrated with Tony's endless negativity, he asked, "What's on your mind, Tony?" in the most sympathetic tone he could muster.

"Really, Jack?" Tony said dismissively. "You don't wanna know what's on my mind."

"I'm not sure I do, but I need to hear it," Jack said back, trying to maintain his sympathetic tone. "You have good insights… Sometimes I just don't appreciate how you decide to share them. But If we are all going to get home safe, I need everyone's help. Including yours."

This took Tony a little bit by surprise. "Ok, Jack. Ok." Tony started in a matter-of-fact voice "First, we need to find water. Freshwater. The water we can all drink. Our canteens won't last much longer in this heat."

Jack already knew this and planned to take a scouting mission deep into the Jungle to find a freshwater source. It seems like Tony would be joining him. "Yes, absolutely. Please continue," Jack said.

"Second, we need shelter off the beach. So, we are at least a little protected from the weather," Tony Continued.

Again, Jack already knew this but didn't want to interrupt now that Tony was actually trying to help.

"Third, we need to watch out for things like leeches, venomous reptiles, razor vine, etc."

This Jack completely forgot about. Being a Marine, he had spent six weeks training in Panama for jungle warfare, affectionately name Green Hell by anyone who had the pleasure of going through it. Hell, on Earth, it actually was. He remembered the mosquitos and sand fleas most of all. The little bastards never gave anyone a moment's peace. He hated biting insects. Loathed them with every fiber of his being. Turning to look into the Jungle, for the first time, he wondered what horrors awaited them inside. "Right," Jack said, finally acknowledging Tony's last point.

"We probably should also get to high ground so we can get a good sense of this island's size and features," Jack said, not knowing if Tony was finished. But figured he would end this conversation before it could turn into an argument. "Ok, let's go round up the others."

Tony complied without responding, standing and heading over to Blue, Kenny, Abel, and Ruth. "Here's the plan, three of us will head into the Jungle to look for freshwater and a good vantage point to scout the island. The other three will stay back, build a shelter, collect firewood, and gather up some food," Jack said as they all nodded. "Who's going…"

"I'm going with you!" Abel spat out before Jack could even finish his sentence.

"Ok, Abel, you're with me. Need just one more to help carry the canteens," Jack stated, looking from one person to the next. He could tell that none of them were particularly excited about entering the Jungle, finding the beach to be much more inviting. Blue was getting ready to agree when she noticed Jack staring at her with a look that screamed: "No, not you." After an awkward moment of silence, Tony reluctantly agreed.

"It was my idea after all," he said with such resignation.

"Kenny, with you being a mechanic, I can assume you are good with your hands?" Jack asked, even though he knew what the answer would be. He just wanted to give Kenny a chance to be involved. To feel like part of the group.

Kenny, looking up from the pile of sand he was moving around with his foot, smiled. "Yes. Yes!" He exclaimed. "What do you need?"

"You will be in charge of building the shelter. It needs to be large enough for several of us to sleep at the same time. Blue and Ruth will help. Make sure you build it just slightly inside the tree line, just off the beach. We won't get much sleep if we have to contend with sand fleas all night," Jack said. "Once done, start gathering firewood." Kenny saluted vigorously. For some reason, that gesture seemed out-of-place to Jack, given their situation. He brushed the feeling aside.

"Blue," Jack started turning towards her.

"I know. Once the shelter is built, take Ruth and gather food." She said with a smirk and slightly mischievous look. "You want dinner ready when you get home, sweetie?"

"That would be nice," Jack said chuckling. He and Blue both knew that he was the one who actually did most of the cooking, something he learned from his father. Blue just couldn't resist the opportunity to make light of current social stigmas. "Abel, Tony, grab your gear. We need to get going."

"You're the boss," Abel replied, ready as always to follow his squad leader and friend, even into possible danger.

They said their goodbyes, Blue giving Jack a small kiss. Abel leaned in for his. Blue just pushed him away, laughing. "Hurry back," she said, still chuckling slightly. As they stepped into the Jungle, Jack could hear Kenny in the background laying out his plans for the shelter. The Jungle quickly swallowed them, drowning out all sounds. After a few steps, even the consistent sound of lapping waves dissolved.

The light vanished beneath the dense jungle canopy. Air became thick and heavy, making the effort of breathing uncomfortable. Intense heat and moisture weighing down their very bodies as the rancid smell of the decaying vegetation permeated their nostrils. The spongy jungle floor only adding to the difficulty of their task.

To say it was rough going would be an understatement. It was downright brutal. Only having their knives to cut their way through, they spent a fair amount of time weaving back and forth, following the path of least resistance. At one point, Abel shrieked and jumped back. Apparently, he attempted to grab a vine for balance, but that vine was actually an enormous, very alive python. Backing up and giving it a wide berth, they continued on heading towards the small group of rocking outcroppings Jack saw from the beach. It seemed like the best vantage point around and the best chance for rainwater to collect.

All of a sudden, Tony let out a blood-curdling scream. Abel and Jack darted to his side. With all of the commotion, Jack thought he had been attacked by a panther or pit viper. Not even sure if these deadly animals lived on this island. Racing over to Tony, Jack asked in the calmest voice he could muster, "Tony what's wrong?"

Tony pointed to his hand. A large thorn was sticking out. Jack was surprised a thorn was the genesis for all this racket. He wiped his knife clean on the leg of his pants, pressed the tip to the base of the thorn in Tony's palm, and flicked. The thorn popped right out.

"Umm, thanks," Tony said, feeling a little ashamed of what just happened. "It just surprised me, that's all. I thought it was a snake bite…"

"No worries, Tony. Glad I could help." Jack said as Abel snickered softly. "Shall we continue?"

The Jungle was stifling hot, the thick air and moisture making the act of breathing difficult. Causing conversation to be all but impossible. After an hour's walk in, what Jack thought was the right direction and, after having just ascended a steep muddy slope, they stopped. "15 minutes downtime," Jack managed to say through his momentary exhaustion.

"How far now, boss?" Abel asked, also trying to recover from the exhausting climb as well.

"Hard to say. This terrain is brutal. But if I had to guess, I would say about halfway." Jack said, still catching his breath. "Don't start Tony, I'm not in the mood!" Jack said with frustration, seeing Tony's mouth open as if he wanted to argue. He closed it and sat in silence looking as grumpy as Jack had ever seen him.

Tony sat perched against a tree stump, elbows resting on his knees, arms crossed in front of his chest, massaging his left palm with the thumb of his right hand. Jack caught his gaze, seeing the discomfort and his attempt at relief.

Chapter 4: A Light in the Darkness

"How's your hand? Is everything ok?" Jack probed hesitantly, having just erroneously yelled at Tony in frustration that had nothing to do with him.

"Yeah, fine. Just fine." Tony spat, "Thanks for asking." Abel, not wanting to get involved, avoided eye-contact by gazing up into the jungle canopy. Jack decided to let it go. He wasn't going to make progress with Tony and needed his energy for the journey ahead.

They finished the downtime in silence. Every so often, Jack could hear a deep, slow breath or a slap on a piece of exposed skin. He, too, was attempting to keep the persistent, invasive insects at bay.

"All right, times, up. Let's get moving again." Jack said, with little excitement in his voice.

It wasn't long before they stumbled upon what Abel guessed was a game trail. As it was heading in the right direction, they followed it. This allowed them to make a much better time, reaching the base of the rocking outcropping within 30 minutes. Jack swung his Thompson from his shoulder and leaned it up against the rock wall. Then he removed his ammo belt and placed it, with the canteens he was carrying, next to his weapon, and started to climb. Abel quickly began to follow suit.

"No, stay with Tony. We don't know how safe this rock wall is." Jack said with a stern air of leadership. "We only need to risk one of us. You two follow the wall and look for a well or spring." Abel nodded in agreement.

The climb wasn't easy. Loose rocks threaten to dislodge Jack from the wall's steep surface. Sharp edges cutting into his fingertips. Grass and vines clinging between its cracks, making the wall slippery in places. Jack wasn't sure this was going to be worth the effort. After several minutes of hard climbing, Jack heard Abel yell up from below. "Jack! Jack!"

"Yeah," Jack replied, attempting to look down but was not at all sure of the sturdiness of his current grip.

"Water! We found water! It's a spring, filtering out of the base of the rock wall. It leads to a stream. And you won't believe this, but it looks like the stream heads North, back to the beach."

"Nice, we should be able to follow that back to the others," Jack yelled down. "Great find. Now fill up the canteens."

"You got it, boss," Abel said with the most excitement Jack had heard since entering the Jungle.

After a few more minutes of exertion, Jack reached the top of the small rocky hill. The view was incredible. The island was much bigger than he expected. From what he could see, it was several miles wide and more than three times that long. Spinning around to look back the way they came. Far off, he saw the lifeboat still stuck on the coral and the beach they washed upon. It was on the northern side of the island, along with the rock hill he was currently standing on. Following the beach, he panned left. Off in the distance, around the midpoint on the west side, he saw a large clearing with what, could only be, huts. His heart lifted. This could be their way home.

Not wanting to miss anything, he continued panning around the island. Directly on the opposite, southern side of the island was the massive mountain. The remanence of the volcano that formed the island itself, but old, dormant, and weather-worn. It was blocking his view of anything beyond. Jack had no idea if the island kept going, stopped, or even if there was another village beyond. The mountain was that dominating. He decided to continue his survey of the island.

Jack followed the beach towards the eastern side of the island. When he reached just past the mid-point, he stopped suddenly and dropped to the floor—his quick, shallow breaths pushing loose dirt away from his mouth. Sweat pouring from his forehead and dripping off the end of his nose. The Japanese submarine was berthed in a small bay near the eastern shore, next to a sharp outcropping of rocky beach jutting out into the ocean. To be sure he wasn't imagining, he stole another quick glance. It was the sub alright.

He crawled on his belly back to the edge of the small rocky cliff and slowly climbed down. Making sure each step landed purposefully on a sturdy ledge. He needed to reach the bottom safely to warn the others. Thankfully, he made it down without incident, the adrenaline pushing him, and called Abel and Tony over.

"We've got trouble. The Jap sub. It's here. Berthed on the eastern side of the island."

Chapter 5: Scouting Party

"Are you sure?" Abel begged, hoping it wasn't true. "I thought they would have sunk with all that damage. I mean, how is it possible that they're still floating? Are you sure it's them?"

"It looks like them," Jack continued. "I mean, what are the chances it's some other submarine? You can see the damage from here."

"Fair point," Abel conceded. "What's the plan, boss?"

"Well, it doesn't look like they are going anywhere, anytime soon, at least. The entire rear end of the sub looks like a mangled mess." Jack responded pensively. He was thinking about the next move. The next several moves. How was he, the leader, going to get them out of this? Abel's question brought him back to reality.

"Wait, how far away from our beach, are they?" Abel asked, wanting the answer to be far, very far. But it wasn't.

"Not far enough," Jack said as he started pointing his left arm north, towards their camp. "If we are at 12 o'clock," he continued, thinking about where the others were working, having no idea how dangerous this island really was. Then pointed his right arm about 90 degrees out, towards the east, "they are at 2:30." Jack reported in a matter-of-fact tone that made Abel whistle nervously.

"That's a little too close for comfort," Abel confirmed.

"Jap subs typically have a crew complement of 60, although some can go up to 90. We are way outnumbered! We gotta get away from here!" Tony stammered, intense fear creeping into his voice. "Did you see anything else? Any place we could hide. We've gotta get as far away from them as possible!"

Jack could see Tony's flight or fight response happening in real-time. Apparently, the flight was winning. "We have to assume some Japs died in the initial attack and explosion we saw. Remember how devastating the smoke was on the Arcadia?"

Chapter 5: Scouting Party

Tony nodded slowly as he gazed in the direction of the sub. As if he saw through the jungle itself. Seeing the danger close-up. Exposed to it, without any protection.

"Besides, we can't just run. We need to get back to the others and warn them. They have no idea how close to danger they actually are," Jack rebuked forcefully. "There is a natural rocky groin separating them from us. It isn't likely they would want to wade out to go around it. Meaning..."

"Meaning what? You don't think they..." Tony cut in.

"Meaning, they would need to venture into the jungle to even get to our beach. Besides, it's a good bet they don't even know we are here. The only decent vantage point is this small rocky cliff. Based on what you experienced getting here, would you want to spend hours scouting through an unknown jungle?" Jack finished, trying not to let his frustration with Tony show. It was proving difficult after the exhaustion of the climb.

"Yeah, sure, Jack. That makes sense. They are probably staying close to their sub." Tony answered after a long pause.

"We just need to get moving," Jack stated. "Able, Tony, grab the canteens."

Jack picked up his weapon and ammo and began walking, almost jogging down the small stream back towards the beach. Abel and Tony followed quickly on his heels. They passed a cave entrance that looked to go deep into the earth, having been carved out by the stream over many thousands of years. Jack took note as a possible place of refuge, depending on how bad things got.

They reached the beach within a short 40 minutes. Jack paused for a moment to get his bearings. He saw the lifeboat still stuck on the coral and realized they were only about 500 yards away from where they came ashore.

They finished the last 500 yards in a full run and reached a small structure just inside the tree line that wasn't there when they washed ashore. To Jack's amazement, it had three walls, a roof, and even a floor made of split bamboo logs. Although saying it had walls and a roof was a little exaggeration. It was actually just covered with broad, sturdy-looking leaves, layered like shingles.

"Hey, Jack, you're back! Like it?" Kenny asked, seeing Jack eyeing the fledgling shelter. "Banana leaves, that's what we used for the roof. There is a bunch of trees not too far that way." He pointed off into the jungle, towards the banana trees. "Although they didn't have any ripe bananas."

"Yeah, it's great," Jack wheezed, bending over, placing his hands on his knees, and trying to catch his breath. Completely ignoring Kenny's comment on the lack of bananas. "Where's Blue?"

"She's just down the beach aways, with Ruth, trying to collect some crabs," Kenny said, pointing east, in the direction of danger, towards the Jap sub.

Chapter 5: Scouting Party

Jack looked in the direction Kenny was pointing but didn't see blue. "How far, Kenny? How far?" He barked.

"Not, far, just around the bend," Kenny responded weakly, feeling as if he had done something wrong.

"I'll go get them," Abel said, seeing the fearful look in Jack's eyes, and took off at a full run before Jack even had time to respond.

Jack, seeing the downcast look on Kenny's face, apologized. "Sorry Kenny, I didn't mean to..." But he stopped. Not sure what he meant or even what he was feeling. Conversation between Kenny, Jack, and Tony fell silent.

Several minutes later, Abel returned with Blue and Ruth. Both ladened with blue crabs and various bright-colored fruit. "Welcome back, Jack. You don't look so good." Blue joked.

"I bet. Hey, we need to talk. All of us." He insisted, calling them over, feeling like he had regained a little control over his emotions seeing as Blue was safe. "You're going to want to sit down for this."

They all sat down in a tight circle, eating fruit and listening intently as Jack recounted their trip through the jungle and view from the small hill. Only omitting Tony's thorn incident to save him the embarrassment. They all sat in shocked silence. First, elation when he mentioned the little village in the clearing, then horror when they realized the danger they were all in.

"So, what do we do?" Ruth asked as she pressed a small piece of green fruit to her lips and slurped up its juices.

"Well, we need to go check it out…"

"We can't do that!" Tony exclaimed, rubbing the palm of his left hand. His eyes darting between Jack, Abel, and Blue. "It's suicide."

"Tony, we have too. We need to know what we are up against," Jack shot back. "Don't worry, I'm not asking you to come anyways." Tony slumped with relief.

"So, when do we leave?" Abel asked knowingly.

"Not so fast. We need a plan," Jack insisted. "I was thinking it would be best to do this under cover of night. Based on the last few nights, we should have a full moon. That is plenty of light for us to see where we are going and to conduct a proper headcount when we arrive." Jack looked at his watch; it was just after 4 PM.

"Jack, won't that be a little dangerous walking through the jungle at night?" Blue Whispered. Showing a little fear for the first time since they had arrived on the island.

"Yes, it will be. I'm guessing most of the creatures here are nocturnal, so the jungle will be crawling at night. At least it did in Panama. But it's better than being caught in broad daylight if we should come across some Japs." Jack reassured her.

After a moment's reflection, Abel chimed in, "So let's get some grub then some shut-eye."

"I was thinking the same thing," Jack grunted.

"Please eat the rest of the fruit. Ruth and I can always get more," Blue offered.

"Thank you, Blue." Jack said as he threw what looked like an apple to Abel. They quickly consumed what was left of the available fruit. Getting to his feet, Jack looked at each member of their rag-tag group, realizing they were all looking at him to save them. Just then, he wasn't sure he could, at least not all of them. "Kenny, can you wake us up at 9 PM?" He finally said.

Kenny nodded vigorously in agreement. Jack and Abel walked over to the shelter, laid down, and closed their eyes. Jack found sleep came easy. In no time at all, he was dreaming. Dreaming of a red clay tiled roof covering a villa perched on a hill overlooking a small village. It was Christmas time. He could see far off lights decorating a massive conifer tree in the center of town. He had never felt this content before.

"Jack, wake up. It's 9 PM. Wake up," encouraged Kenny. "Abel, Abel, time to get up."

"What a beautiful morning," Abel guffawed playfully as he stretched, lifting both hands over his head. "Oh, that's right. It's still night time."

Jack smiled, although he was sure it was because of his dream and not Abel's lackluster attempt at comedy. They got ready mostly in silence; only the rattles and clicks of their weapons could be heard. Each mentally preparing themselves for the journey ahead. Blue stood by watching. Once they were ready, she handed them both a bundle of fruit and cooked crab meat, wrapped in a banana leaf. "For the road." She offered generously, coming to terms with the task ahead.

"Thank you," Jack said with false cheerfulness, trying to alleviate the concern he saw in her face. "Stay safe, keep your eyes open. And Kenny, no stealing my girl while I am gone."

Kenny awkwardly smiled, "You don't have to worry about that. I won't."

Seeing that Abel was ready, it was time. "Let's move out."

Nighttime wasn't the best time to be trodding through a thick jungle. In reality, there wasn't a good time to ever be doing it, but night time made everything just that much harder. However, Jack noticed they made much better progress without needing to worry about Tony. He and Abel walked in silence for well over an hour. The only sounds were the rustling of the bushes and tree branches as they brushed up against them or the sounds of wildlife going about its regular business. Every now and then, a twig would snap beneath their feet. It was still hot, but the cold night air made the journey more tolerable. Sweat rings had formed under both men's arms and down their backs.

They exited the jungle pretty close to the rocky groin. "Nice job Abel," Jack beamed as he was the one navigating. Lowering his voice to a whisper. "Let's head over to the groin. We can climb up it to get a clear view of the small bay beyond."

Jack walked slowly over to the groin, hunched over as to not be seen. Abel on his heels. They reached the dark, rocky groin and climbed the few feet to the top. They both peeked over.

The sub was still sitting in the bay, the damage more apparent from this close of proximity. A giant hole, about 20 feet across, pierced the back of the sub. The sub was tilting backwards, letting Jack know it had taken on some amount of water. Although he didn't know how much. It was silent, not a sign of life. Dead. Jack panned to the beach to see a single inflatable life raft laying, unused not far from the waterline. Further up the sand, he saw the camp.

Two rows of bamboo mats were spread neatly across the open beach. Jack counted ten mats per row. Closer to the tree line, a small shelter was constructed. Jack could only see a single empty raised cot with a Katana leaned up against it. Around a massive bonfire sat nine men, chatting in Japanese. As neither Jack nor Abel spoke it and was too far away to hear clearly, they didn't know what they were conversing about. It didn't really matter anyway. Jack noticed another man sitting slightly apart, back from the fire. He was wearing officers' clothing, and the men seem to treat him with deference. "This must be the Captain," Jack thought to himself. Off in the distance, he could see three additional men walking down the beach, towards the fire with weapons slung over their shoulders. He assumed they were returning from a patrol. Three other men were gearing up, looking to be switching places with the retiring patrol.

They stayed locked in place, barely moving, and watching the Japanese for about 30 minutes. Believing he saw everything he needed, Jack looked over at Abel, motioned with his head, and started back down the groin. They returned the way they came, staying low to not be seen until they reached the relative safety of the jungle. Jack froze in place, realizing the mistake they had just made. He quickly jumped up, grabbed a giant leaf from a low hanging branch, and headed back onto the beach.

"What are you doing?" Abel hissed. Waving his arms trying to signal Jack back into the concealment of the jungle.

"I need to cover our tracks, so the Japs don't know someone was watching them," Jack responded. He brushed the sand with the giant leaf as he walked backwards, still hunched over, making sure there was no sign they had been there. Satisfied, he threw the leaf down, patted Abel on the shoulder, and wordlessly headed back to their camp.

Chapter 5: Scouting Party

On the way back, they reconciled their counts. Both men came to the same conclusion. 16 Japs but bedding for 21. They were both sure the remaining five Japs were out on patrol, looking for food, water, or hostiles. Their group was outnumbered over three to one. "It could be much worse," Abel said with his characteristic optimism. Jack just wondered how they were going to get out of this situation.

"They all looked like sailors. I wonder how good they will be at soldiering?" Abel asked.

"I'm not sure. Let's hope their combat skills are limited on land. If Kenny and Tony are any comparison, sailors are no match for Marines." Jack said confidently as he began to smile. Abel chuckled. "But I'm honestly not sure the training they receive."

After about 30 minutes of walking, they came upon a fallen tree. "This looks as good as any place to rest, let's take 10," Jack said to Abel. Both men sat, drinking from their canteens, mulling over what they had seen at the Jap camp, and eating the crab meat Blue had so graciously removed from its shell. That is when they heard it—the sharp snapping of a twig. Jack's heart stopped; his breathing caught in his throat. He knew from his time walking through jungles that only a human could make a sound like that.

Both men spun around, jumping to their feet, and dropping their banana leaf bundles, just as five Japanese soldiers emerged from the dark. Two carried what looked to be a small wild pig, tied upside-down, on a thick branch draped between them. Jack's training took over, time seemed to slow down. He raised his Thompson to his shoulder, disengaged the safety, and opened fire. Followed quickly by Abel and the clank, clank, clank of his M1.

The two Japs, not holding the pig, began to swing their bolt action rifles off their shoulders into firing position. At the same time, the third, an officer, reached for his pistol. They were hit before they could even fire back. Their bodies thrashing with the force of each bullet strike. Blood squirting out in spouts. The last two Japs didn't even have time to drop the pig before it was all over. The ping of Abel's M1 letting Jack know he had emptied the entire eight-round clip. The muzzle flash having temporary blinded Jack.

The violence ended just as quickly as it started. Jack mowed down the two with the rifles and one of the pig carriers. At the same time, Abel had finished off the officer, who wasn't even able to clear his holster and wounding the other pig carrier. The echo of bullet fire ringing in Jack's ears.

Walking over to the bodies, Jack looked down. The fifth man, the wounded man, was pinned beneath the pig. A devastating bullet hole shredded his left upper thigh. He was writhing in pain, yelling, probably cursing, in Japanese. Seeing Jack for the first time, he immediately fell silent, staring directly into his eyes, and steeling himself for the moment to come. Jack raised his Thompson, took aim squarely at the man's forehead, and fired a single shot. His head exploded, brain and skull fragments spraying the jungle floor.

This was Jack's first experience with real, face-to-face combat. This was the first time he had used his weapon against another human. The first time he had taken a life. He expected it to feel different. He expected to feel something. But he didn't. He felt nothing for the men's lives he had just snuffed out. He only felt the adrenalin pumping through his body. His heart beating as if it would explode. Blood pulsing in his ear, and his rapid, shallow breathing.

"Abel, Abel," Jack panted, taking a minute to get his attention while he got his breathing under control. "Are you ok?"

Abel shook his head vigorously while reloading his M1. "Yeah, boss, all ok." Jack bent down, picked up the first soldier's rifle and ammo pouch, and threw them to Abel. "What's this for?" Abel questioned, seeing how he already had a weapon.

"It's for Tony and Kenny," Jack explained as he moved to the second soldier, repeating the process. "We're gonna need everyone armed if we are going to survive."

Hoping they were far enough inside the jungle for it to have muffled the gunfire. Jack stood in silence, waiting to see if any Jap reinforcements were coming. He certainly didn't wish to fight all of them at once, but for sure didn't want to lead them back to camp. After several minutes, no one else showed up.

Not wanting to waste the pig, Jack bent down and removed each of the rear legs. It was all they were able to carry back to camp now laden down with extra weapons and ammo.

"Let's go, double-time," He ordered. They jogged back as quickly as the dense jungle would allow. Not a word was shared between them for the remainder of the trip.

Reaching the beach just before 2 AM, they walked along the sand for only a few minutes before finding the shelter. Tony, Ruth, and Kenny were asleep. Blue wasn't. She was sitting by a small fire, prodding it with a long skinny stick. Jack could see a burst of sparks as she moved a log into place. She gasped when she saw them. Running over and giving them both a hug.

"Are you both ok?" She asked, patting Jack down, looking for wounds. The tenseness in her body relaxed once she verified he was safe.

"We are fine. Why are you not asleep like the others?" Jack questioned, although he knew the answer.

"I was too worried to sleep," She admitted. "Besides someone needed to keep watch encase any soldiers showed up."

"Here, we brought you a gift. Breakfast, for tomorrow," Jack announced as he handed the pig legs to Blue.

Chapter 5: Scouting Party

"Where did these come from?" Blue chortled as Jack and Abel laid their weapons against a tree and added the Jap rifles to the mix. "And what are those? Better yet, why do you have them?" She stressed not waiting for an answer to her first question.

"Jap rifles," Abel proclaimed. "We took them from some dead Japs. Well, they weren't dead at first, but we fixed that little problem."

Blue looking incredulous, Jack quickly told her of the Jap camp, sub, and return trip. "I'm glad you all made it safely back. And now we have five fewer soldiers to worry about" She sighed, not agreeing with violence but understanding the need at times like this.

"I'm beat," Jack moaned, "who has the next watch duty?"

"I can take it," Abel volunteered.

"Are you sure?"

"Yeah, I'm way too excited to sleep right now."

"Ok. Stay on watch until 3 AM," Jack commanded, seeing Abel getting ready to say he could do it longer. "And no later. At 3, wake up Tony for his turn. Give him one of the Jap rifles. Then get some shut-eye. That's an order." Abel saluted in confirmation.

With that, Jack and Blue made their way over to the shelter, the day's events draining them to the core. Jack, laid down first with Blue quickly following, curling up next to him with her head on his shoulder. "Love you," "Love you too," was all they managed to say before drifting off to sleep.

Chapter 6: The Village Greeting

Awaking from a deep, dreamless sleep, Jack, not being ready to face the new day, turned onto his side. Listening to the distant sound of the jungle, softly lapping waves, and friendly conversation. Blue was no longer curled up next to him. It was her voice he heard. He slowly opened his eyes.

Blue, Kenny, Ruth, and Abel were sitting next to the fire, eating a green, musky smelling fruit and listening to Abel. He was telling of the time he had stolen a pack of eggs as a child in San Francisco. Jack had heard it often. It was Abel's favorite story to recount. The finale always getting a good laugh. Abel having broken all the eggs in the process of running from the storekeeper. Jack just realized it also had a valuable message. If you are going to do something bold, make sure you can reap the rewards.

Not seeing Tony with the group, he sat up and looked around. Tony was also still asleep. "He must not be used to the middle watch shift," Jack mused to himself. Middle watch shift was always the worst, breaking up your sleep cycle and not allowing your mind or body the full rest it needed. Although Tony didn't look so good. His skin was pale, sweat dripping from his brow, and his breathing was coming in shallow rattles. Jack got up and walked over to the fire.

"Good morning, everyone," Jack announced as he bent down to give Blue a kiss on the top of her head. "Anything happening?"

"Morning?" Abel questioned jokingly, looking at his watch. "Jack, it's half past 12."

Jack, surprised by this news, looked at his watch. He was sure Abel's was just broken. Maybe something happened to it during the fire-fight last night. Sure enough, it was 12:30 PM on the dot. "Why did you let me sleep that long? You know what's out there!"

"Jack," Blue comforted, seeing him starting to get worked up. "That is precisely the reason we let you sleep. We need you at your peak if you are going to get us out of this mess."

Chapter 6: The Village Greeting

Those words had the effect Blue was expecting. Jack instantly became more at ease. "Well, yeah. I guess. But next time..."

"Next time, we will give you a choice to sleep in or not." Blue finished calmly.

That's all Jack needed to hear. "What's wrong with Tony? He doesn't look so good." Jack remarked, assuming Blue already had an answer for that as well.

"What do you mean? He was fine when we relieved him from watch this morning." Blue reported. "I mean, he did look a little out of sort, but we all just assumed he was tired, like the rest of us. Let me go check on him."

Blue glided over to the shelter taking soft, precise steps as if the act of walking would inappropriately wake Tony, aggravating his unknown condition. "Tony, Tony," Blue said compassionately. It never ceased to amaze Jack how quickly Blue could jump into the role of a nurse. Just moments ago, she had been joking around with Abel and Kenny. Now, she was in full healing mode. "Tony, how are you feeling?"

Tony slowly, very slowly, blinked his eyes open and sat up. Being pulled to a sitting position by Blue. Seeing the sweat beading down his brow, she placed the back of her hand against his forehead. "You're burning up, Tony," She remarked, "What happened?"

"I don't know," he croaked weakly. "I was feeling fine just up until the end of my watch. Then I got dizzy and laid down."

"Hmm, maybe you are just dehydrated," Blue speculated, still staring at Tony's sickly figure. "Ruth, get me some water."

Ruth hurried over with a canteen, unscrewed the lid, and handed it to Blue. "Is this one that has been boiled?" Blue stressed not wanting to make Tony worse by giving him contaminated water.

"Yes, yes. I'm sure it is. I got it from the batch next to the fire." Ruth squeaked. "Besides, we have all been drinking the water, it can't be contaminated, or we all would be like Tony."

Blue thought on this for a moment and realized it was most likely the truth. "It's better to be safe. If his immune system is compromised, we don't want to introduce him to something he wouldn't be able to fight." She gently pressed the canteen against Tony's lips and slowly poured its contents into his mouth. He coughed up the first few sips, then his body gracefully accepted the clean, freshwater.

After several more successful sips, Blue lowered Tony back down into a laying position. "Get some sleep. I will check in on you in an hour," she promised. Tony weakly mumbled a few words Jack couldn't hear and quickly fell back asleep.

Chapter 6: The Village Greeting

"This doesn't seem to be just dehydration," Blue confided in Jack, not wanting the others to know she wasn't sure of Tony's condition. "Did he get bit by anything when you were looking for water yesterday?"

"No. Not unless you count a tiny thorn," Jack said, trying not to smile, but couldn't keep the ridiculous memory of Tony and that thorn out of his mind. "I mean, it was nothing. I was able to get it out of his hand." He followed up quickly, seeing the look on Blue's face.

Without a word, she returned to Tony's side, picked up his right hand, and turned it over in hers. Everything looked fine. She grabbed his left hand, turned it over, and gasped. His left palm was red and swollen. A tiny pus-filled hole at its center, circled by a quarter-sized red patch of skin and several yellow blisters. She placed his hand down so that it was resting on his stomach. Blue leaned over to where she had placed her medkit, opened it, and began frantically emptying the contents of the bag onto the shelter floor.

"Jack, most of the supplies are ruined. It must have happened during the storm, our last night at sea." She stammered, "The only thing that isn't destroyed is the morphine syrettes." Mold had already started growing on the exposed cloth bandages. She threw them aside. "What are we going to do?" She pleaded, eyes fixed on Jack, searching for an answer. Although she had taken care of patients before and even lost some, that was at a well-stocked hospital, and they were strangers. There nine days together and shared traumatic experiences had created a bond that was hard to believe. These were not strangers depending on her.

"We need to get to that village," Jack decided on the spot. "If we stay here, he will die. They might have some way to fix what's wrong with him. Not to mention, we need to get as far away from the Japs as possible."

"If we move him now, he might die." Blue pointed out.

"What choice do we have?" Jack said, pleading for there to be a third option as trying to get Tony to the village wasn't going to be easy. "Blue, is there any other choice?"

"Well, let me try to clean and wrap the wound. After a little more rest, Tony might be able to walk," Blue said uncertainly. "I just need to find a piece of clean fabric to make a bandage."

"Here," Ruth offered, reaching into her backpack and pulling out what looked to be a pair of beige Army socks. "This should work."

"Thanks," Blue choked, forgetting Ruth was even standing there, listening to the entire conversation. "This will work." She poured clean water onto Tony's palm, dabbed the injury with one of the socks, then wrapped and tied the wound tightly with the other. Tony winced at this but didn't wake.

Seeing that Blue was finished, Jack began giving orders. "Abel, Kenny, front and center." They ran over and lined up. "It's 1:20 PM, we will be moving out at 3 PM, that will give us four hours of daylight to reach the village. It will be close, but I think we can make it."

"Boss, that's gonna be…" Abel started, but Jack cut in.

"We will make it. We have to. Break camp. It should look like we were never here. We probably shouldn't come back either, knowing the Japs are so close and probably have found their missing patrol by now. They will know they aren't alone." Jack finished. "Go! Don't forget the food."

Abel and Kenny began breaking down camp and collecting their gear. Ruth helped Kenny gather the miscellaneous items scattered around the camp. Abel buried the fire and threw the remaining small logs back into the jungle. At 3 PM, they woke Tony, who was looking marginally better and was actually able to stand. Kenny and Ruth dismantled the shelter with excellent efficiency.

"Ok, time to go. We will make our way west along the tree line. Once we reach the stream, we will follow it towards the rocking outcropping." Jack ordered. "Besides, there is something you all need to see."

"Tony, put your arm over my shoulder. I got you," Abel reassured. "We will make it together. Kenny, be ready to help as needed."

"Yes, absolutely. Here to help." Kenny promised quickly. "Just let me know when you need a break."

The Fountain of Youth

They started down the beach, walking just inside the tree line to not leave tracks for anyone who might be looking for them. Jack and Blue out front, walking side-by-side, leading this ragged group, softly talking between themselves. Behind them followed Abel and Tony, then Kenny and Ruth. It wasn't long before they reached the stream and headed into the dense jungle. When they reached the caves, Jack stopped. "This is our fall back spot. If anyone gets separated, make your way to these caves. It provides shelter, fresh water, and food isn't far afield," Jack said, reassuringly pointing at the entrance then spinning toward the rocky outcropping. "You should be able to see that small hill from anywhere on the island," He continued, now pointing in its direction. "Just head towards it, walk around its base, locate the spring that creates the stream and follow it. You can't miss it," He finished, more for Kenny and Ruth's benefit than anyone else's.

Once everyone had inspected the caves and familiarized themselves with its location, they made a b-line straight for the jungle clearing that housed the village. Tony was still on his feet and mostly walking on his own, but Jack wasn't sure how long that would last. "He's tougher than he looks," thought Jack, smiling to himself, realizing he might have judged Tony too quickly.

The next hour or so passed monotonously, each group member fending off insects, avoiding creeping vines, and watching their hand placements for the thorny tree that infected Tony. Every now and then, Jack would hear birds chirping as if they were commenting on the group's slow progress. Only to be interrupted by a sharp curse as someone tripped over an exposed tree root. It wasn't hard; it was just hard work.

Abel and Kenny switching off helping Tony. Abel was using each rotation as an excuse to tell terrible jokes about manual labor, often mentioning a "sack of potatoes." This made Ruth giggle when she wasn't profoundly focused on the trek and avoiding the jungle dangers. Jack and Blue continued to lead, stealing looks at each other when they could manage and every now and then touching each other affectionately on the arm or shoulder.

They made it to the outskirts of the village shortly after nightfall. Not knowing if it was considered polite to approach, Jack paused. "Blue, what do you think? Should we all just approach?"

"We should approach, slowly, without weapons and only a few of us," Ruth confirmed.

"Ok, Ruth. It's obviously your area of expertise. Who should go with you?" Jack said, deferring command for the first time since the lifeboat. "Maybe, Blue?"

"No, you should come as the Leader. You are in a place to accept any concessions or requirements asked of us as you speak for the group as a whole," She asserted. "We might only get one chance at this."

Jack, not wanting to argue with Ruth when she so obviously knew what she was doing, agreed. He dropped his gear and weapons. Passing his Thompson to Abel, who had just helped Tony to the ground and gave his 1911 to Blue. "Keep that safe until I get back, would ya," Jack teased. With a smirk, Blue saluted with such vigor, Jack knew she was thoroughly enjoying relieving him of his weapon.

Jack and Ruth entered the village, approaching from the beach, not wanting to surprise the villagers. About 50 or so sat in two rings around a large bonfire in the village center, chatting in a very foreign language. Raised wooden huts set further back in circles that mimicked their sitting positions. Cleaned and processed fish hung from lines stretching between the huts; various leaves and herbs drying on racks just outside the fire ring. A large wooden table was set in what Jack could only describe as a buffet. Fish, fruits, nuts, pastes, and roots sat in clay bowls lining the large table. All of a sudden, the villagers fell silent. They had been spotted.

"Say something," Ruth prodded. Jack, not realizing he had also fallen silent. The long shadows cast from the firelight gave the village a mystical and terrifying presence like it was protected by an ancient and powerful force that he had no business interrupting.

"Uh, hello," Jack announced in a voice more like Ruth's than his own. "We washed up on the northern shore and need some help. We have someone who's sick. Can you help us?"

The villagers didn't move. They just stared at the pair. Jack wasn't sure if he should repeat himself or try something completely different. All of a sudden, a young female villager jumped up and ran into a nearby hut, yelling what sounded like "Palila, Palila, Palila!" The villagers didn't look away, transfixed by the strange new pair. A moment later, the same young villager came back out of the hut, helping what seemed to be a very, very old woman. "She must be almost 80," Jack thought to himself.

"That's gotta be the village elder," Ruth pointed out in a low whisper so that the villagers couldn't hear her. "We are making progress. Good Job, Jack."

At that moment, he didn't know if he was doing a good job or a bad one. "Thanks, I think," He hesitated.

"Hello, and welcome to Maha'ina. I am Palila." The old lady announced in passable, yet unpracticed sounding English. Jack was dumbfounded.

"Oh, um, thank you." He stammered, staring at the very short, very round, aged woman. Although she didn't look unhealthy. She looked happy. As if the years had treated her exceptionally well. "Very nice to meet you. I'm Jack, and this is Ruth." Ruth waved, beaming with a wide smile. In the short time he had known her, Jack had never seen her this happy.

"Very nice to meet you both. Are you here to trade?"

"No, not exactly, we need help," Jack admitted, not sure how it would be received. Palila said nothing but continued to smile at them. Jack went on, "We have four other members of our party waiting outside the village, one's sick, very sick. He was pricked by a thorn."

"Please, you are all welcome as long as you mean us no harm," Palila offered, spreading her hands wide in a gesture of acceptance. "It has been a long time since malihini has stepped foot here."

"Malihini?" Jack questioned, not understanding.

"Outsiders," Palila stated, "No 'visitors' is probably closer. It has been many monsoons since I spoke the tongue of the English man."

"Right," Jack said, brushing off the odd phrasing. "Ruth, can you go get Blue and the others?" She slowly turned and headed back towards the village outskirts. A few minutes later, she returned with Blue, Kenny, Abel, and Tony, who looked to have gotten worst in the few minutes since Jack had last seen him.

The villagers beckoned them over to the fire, insisting that they sat and joined them. Jack introduced the members of the group in turn. Each thanking Palila and the village for their hospitality. When Jack got to Tony, Palila stopped him.

"Dragon's breath sickness," she said knowingly. "That's what we call the infection from the dragon thorn. It causes you to heat up as if a dragon was breathing fire on you." She finished seeing the questioning looks on their faces.

Chapter 6: The Village Greeting

"Is there anything that can be done about it?" Blue pleaded, "He's getting worse."

"Maybe," Palila speculated, "If it hasn't been too long since the bite…" She walked over to the rack of dried herbs, grabbed a few, and stuffed them into her mouth. She was chewing the herbs as she walked back over to them. "Let me see the wound, dear."

Blue lifted up Tony's hand, removed the hastily put together bandage, and turned it over, palm up. Palila pulled the chewed-up herbs out of her mouth, rolled them between her palms, and placed the salve directly onto the blistering, pus-filled wound. She pulled a long skinny leaf out of a pouch in her skirt and tied it off. "He needs rest now. We will check on him in the morning. Please, place him in there," She said as she pointed to a hut not far away. Jack and Abel practically had to carry him in and laid him down on a thin, wooden mat.

Walking back towards the fire, Jack could see that Blue, Kenny, and Ruth had been given wooden plates piled with the various exotic foods from the long table. As soon as he sat down, the villagers thrust one into his hands as well. "I like this place!" Abel exclaimed as he stuffed his face with a variety of brightly colored fruit pieces.

"Is this the entire village?" Ruth asked, seeming very interested in the people who lived there.

"Almost, we have ten men who took the outrigger and are off trading with a neighboring island. Tahiti, we call it."

The group looked up in surprise. Tahiti was one of the most famous islands in the Polynesian triangle, along with New Zealand, Hawaii, and Fiji. All the travel and glamour magazines of the time loved featuring Tahiti on their covers. This was due to its turquoise waters and meticulous clean beaches, calling it 'the jewel of the Pacific.'

"We are near Tahiti? Can you take us there?" Jack asked, almost begging. "We need to get back."

"We can," Palila chuckled, seeing his excitement. "But our people won't be back with the outrigger for, now, let me see. They left 10 suns ago" She trailed off softly, talking to herself, working out the timing. "Ah, 13, suns. They should be back in 13 suns."

"Palila, are you saying it is a 23-day round trip from here to Tahiti?" Blue questioned, hoping she got the math right. It was never one of her best subjects. "That seems pretty, far away."

"Depending on the currents and winds, yes, yes. One way is aways with the wind, the other is always against the wind and takes almost twice as long. And they tend to spend a few days trading and gathering supplies. So, yes, normally it takes about 23 suns. Our outrigger is very fast." She finished with pride. "You are welcome to stay here until they return as our guests."

"Thank you, Pa..." Jack started to say but suddenly stop and almost dropped his plate with the shock of recollection. "Palila, we aren't the only ones who recently arrived on this island. There are dangerous, dangerous men here also."

"How do you know they are dangerous?" Palila questioned without a hint of judgment in her voice.

"Our countries are at war. The world is at war," Jack responded hastily. "It isn't safe."

"Just because they are your enemy doesn't make them our enemy," Palila politely insisted. "This is a place of peace, and all are welcome. As long as they don't raise weapons to us or any who stay here."

"They will, that's their way," Jack sadly acknowledged. "They have conquered and enslaved vast numbers of people on this side of the world. Going island to island. Taking what they want. Destroying anything that doesn't benefit them. We need to get help. I'm not sure we are enough to keep you safe."

"That will not be our fate," She remarked without an explanation and in a tone that let Jack know this was the final word on the matter.

A gap of silence grew between Jack and Palila. Not an uncomfortable silence, but a profoundly thoughtful silence. As if she was waiting for him to understand. She wore a warm, motherly smile the entire time.

Attempting to comfort Jack, Blue placed her hand in his. He squeezed it in appreciation. "How is it that you know English, Palila?" Blue asked, breaking the silence.

"Long, long ago, when I was only 11 monsoons old," She started but was abruptly interrupted by Abel.

"Monsoons?" He said with his mouth still full of fruits, the juices dripping down his chin.

"Years," Ruth giggled, looking at Palila for confirmation. She nodded her approval.

"Two giant wooden ships visited our village. We traded fresh fruits and other plants for fabrics and tools; such is our way. Two men decided to stay here to learn about our island and people while their ships continued on their voyage. Several monsoons later, when the ships returned, they left. Having studied what they wanted about us. It is they who taught me English." She finished.

"Wooden ships and speaking English," Ruth thought out-loud. That must have been some time ago. "Did you ever learn the names of these ships?"

"Oh, yes. The men talked about them often. Telling us stories of their travels and the fame of their Captain. A captain named... named James Cook of the Resolute and Adventure they would say proudly."

"Wait, are you saying..." Ruth trailed off as she opened her book and quickly began parsing over the pages. "That can't be. The Resolute was the ship James Cook commanded in his second voyage. That voyage took place between 1772–1775. Almost 170 years ago!"

"Has it been that long?" Palila chuckled, picking up a piece of fruit and placing it gracefully into her mouth. "Too long."

"How, how is that possible?" Blue asked in a gentle yet somewhat skeptical tone.

"We believe that the oceans were created by the water flowing from the Font of Life. In the pre-time before the sun, moon, and earth danced around each other. Every creature sprang from the Font's depths. Life itself is bound to it. If the Font of Life were to ever stop flowing, all life would wither and die. The Font of Life is here on our island. It flows from our very mountain. It is what gives us our long, healthy lives." Palila explained as the group listened intently. "It wasn't until we started trading with other islands that we realize we were different. To us, it seemed that their lives were sped up, moving twice that of ours. Most people don't spend enough time with us to even notice the difference."

"The Fountain of Youth!" Ruth exclaimed. "This must be the origins of the myth! It must be!"

Palila chuckled, "Yes, that is what the men from the Resolute called it as well. If your friend isn't healed by the herbs, you only have one chance. You will need to make the pilgrimage to the Font of Life."

"You'd let us do that?" Jack asked, assuming it would be off-limits. People typically coveted their most revered artifacts, keeping them behind locked doors and away from the prying eyes of others.

"The Font of Life belongs to all people. All life is bound to it. It isn't ours to let you or not let you use it." Palila pointed out in a matter-of-fact tone as if this should have been understood.

"Right, um, thank you, Palila," Jack said, shifting his gaze from her to the rest of the village.

The small group of misfits was welcomed by the entire village as the night progressed. They shared food and laughs. At one point, a group of children started dancing in sync as the villagers clapped and chanted.

"Palila, thank you for the wonderful evening," Ruth said, beaming. "I think I am ready to turn-in. Is there a place I may sleep?"

"Yes, please, join your friend. You may share that hut tonight. You are all welcome to use that hut. Plenty of sleeping mats for all." Palila responded.

"Thank you," Ruth said as she yawned and headed toward the Hut that Tony was resting in.

"I'm getting tired as well," Kenny said as he stood and followed Ruth.

Chapter 6: The Village Greeting

Blue, Abel, and Jack sat by the fire with the Adult villagers well into the night, Palila and the children having retired shortly after Kenny and Ruth. Around midnight, the fire had died down, and the village dispersed. The three remaining survivors headed to the hut and settled in for the night.

Chapter 7: Taking the Pilgrimage

The next morning arrived with little to no fanfare. A crowing rooster dragged Jack out of a deep sleep. The sun was peaking over the horizon, its light gently shining through the gaps in the hut's wooden siding. Jack sat up, slipped on his boots, and stepped out into the village, deciding to let the rest of the group sleep, as they let him the morning before. Not out of retribution, no. Out of fondness for this misplaced troop that had shared so much together.

Daylight had transformed the village. It was no longer the dark, unfamiliar place of the night before. It was warm. It was friendly. Alive with activity. Several people were sitting at the long table, mashing roots into the paste that

Chapter 7: Taking the Pilgrimage

Jack recognized from last night's feast. Others returning from the forest, burlap sacks overflowing with fruits and various flowers. Still, others tended the large garden on the village's easternmost side, backing up to the tree line. A rustic wooden fence enclosed it in its entirety with a small gate facing the village's center and the large fire pit.

A small group of children were playing kickball on the beach. Their laughter brightening the morning air more than the sunlight ever could. Jack watched for a minute, seeing their pure joy at the simplest thing. "What a place to grow up," Jack thought to himself.

He walked over to the nearest villagers. Three young women sat on the ground, legs extended out in front of them, several lashings of vine held tightly within their toes. They were creating rope from the look of it. Jack noticed one of them was the same young woman from the previous evening who had fetched Palila. "Palila?" He offered, hoping this would be enough for the young woman to summon her. It was. She removed the lashing from her toes, jumped up, and ran into the same hut as the night before. Palila soon appeared.

"Good sun rise, Jack. How did you sleep?"

"Very well, actually. Thanks."

"I see you have met my granddaughter, Masina. And these are her friends, Lulu and Fetia."

"Nice to meet you," Jack said before realizing they didn't understand, so he quickly bowed. This just caused all three to giggle enthusiastically. Each had an exotic beauty, with warm, golden skin, dark eyes, and shiny straight black hair. Palila beamed at him with the same motherly smile as the girls continued to giggle.

Palila introduced Jack to several more villagers as they strolled around the village, talking. It wasn't until they reached the garden that he noticed Ruth was already up and helping.

"She has been very excited. Asking many, many questions." Palila chuckled. "Has she never been anywhere before? Or is she normally this curious?"

"I'm not sure," Jack acknowledged, a smile creeping across his face. They stood by for a minute or so, watching Ruth helping a young boy pull out a rather stubborn weed. "We haven't known each other long. Our transport was attacked and sunk. The six of us were the only ones to make it to the lifeboat. I didn't know Ruth, Kenny, or Tony before that night."

"Really, when did that happen?"

"That was…" Jack trailed off, thinking. "Ten days ago." He finished, shocked by the realization. Had it really only been ten days since he and Blue were in the relative safety of the Arcadia?

Chapter 7: Taking the Pilgrimage

"We have a saying here, lana ka manaolana me ka lā hou," She said as if it was a promise. "A new day brings hope."

"Thank you." Jack choked. For the first time in days, he felt that Blue had a real chance of making it home alive.

"Should we wake the others?" Palila asked. "We still need to check on Ton'ei."

"Tony," Jack chuckled, glad that she had changed the subject before he could get too emotional. "Yes, let's."

As the village wasn't very big, it only took a minute to reach the hut. Blue was just waking up as he entered. Abel, Kenny, and Tony were all still asleep.

"Morning, honey. Bring me breakfast in bed?" Blue asked jokingly.

"No, sorry."

"Next time you should," Palila said with her motherly grin, "You should always treat your women well. Food is a gift rarely rejected."

"Yeah ok, thanks for the advice" Jack couldn't help but smile. Blue chuckled knowingly, recognizing a fellow firebrand in Palila. "How's Tony doing, Blue?"

Blue placed her hand on his forehead, then in front of his mouth. "Not good. Still burning up, and his breathing is steady but very weak."

Palila bent down and check Tony's hand. It hadn't gotten worse, but the herbs failed to reduce the infection overnight. "You will need to make the pilgrimage."

Jack and Blue's eyes met. Both were thinking the same thing. "Is it safe to move him?" Blue finally asked, breaking away from Jack's intense gaze.

"Yes, it should be. We will make something to help you carry Ton'ei." Palila said.

"Aren't you coming with us?" Jack inquired cautiously. "I mean, we don't even know where it is."

Palila stared at him for a long moment before answering. "No, you must do this without us accompanying you. Typically, we each make the pilgrimage alone. As a test of character and to prepare our hearts for its gift. But that is our way, not yours. And you don't have that option. You must go as a group. Gather what you need. The trip there and back normally takes from sunrise to sunset. We must hurry."

"Um, Palila," Blue questions hesitantly, like she should already know the answer. "What do we do when we get there?"

"Have him drink some of the water." She said matter-of-factly. "Be sure to pour some over the infected wound as well."

"How will we know it worked?"

Chapter 7: Taking the Pilgrimage

"You will know. Trust me, you will know." Palila repeated, seeing the skeptical look on Blue's face.

"Right, Ok," Blue responded.

As they gathered their supplies, gear, and weapons, the villagers were busy working on a stretcher. It was constructed from two long wooden polls with vine rope weaved between them. It only took them a few minutes to assemble. Jack was thoroughly amazed at their skills.

Kenny and Abel picked up Tony from his resting place in the hut and transferred him to the makeshift stretcher. "Follow the path that leads up the mountain. Follow the stones. The symbols will never lead you astray. Eventually, you will reach its end and the Font of Life. You will see it flowing from a rocky cliff into a small pool that feeds this stream." She pointed to a stream that ran along the village's southern side and emptied into the ocean.

"We can do that. Everyone ready?" Jack asked

"I, I think I'm going to stay back," Ruth announced timidly. "Is that ok?"

"Yes, of course," Blue responded compassionately, seeing Ruth truly happy. "Stay, get to know our new friends."

With that decided, they headed south, out of the village, following a well-traveled path leading directly towards the base of the towering mountain. Several of the villagers had lined up, waving at them cheerfully. Jack and

Abel carried Tony while Blue and Kenny stayed out front. Every 15 minutes or so, they would switch out stretcher-bearers. Kenny replaced Abel, then Abel replaced Jack, then Jack replaced Kenny.

During their trek, Jack noticed the strange rocks lining the path, each with a different engraved symbol. He wondered if this was what Palila meant by "Follow the rocks." Or was she describing the mountain and its rocky walls. He almost wished Ruth was here so she could have a look. She might have even known what the symbols meant.

Walking along a well-defined path significantly improved everyone's mood. They no longer needed to worry about thorns, vines, venomous reptiles, or exposed roots. They were able to converse about the village and its friendly people. It was getting time for the next switch when they came across a slender log bridge spanning a narrow but deep gorge.

"You better let Abel and me get Tony across," Jack said, not wanting to hurt Kenny's feelings but knowing it was for the best. "You can take over once we have crossed."

Blue and Kenny edged slowly across the bridge. Carefully watching each step they took. Blue's eyes never straying into the gorge. Focused on the bridge and on the other side. The bridge was, in actuality, only three logs tied together and laid over the canyon. Barely touching either side.

Chapter 7: Taking the Pilgrimage

Abel stepped out first, inching across, pulling Jack along behind. When Abel reached the midway point, jack stepped out. The thin wooden logs bobbed under their weight. Abel let out a nervous whistle.

"Keep going," Jack said, not wanting to be stuck in this precarious position any longer than needed. That's when Jack saw it. The earth in front of Abel exploded, followed closely by the sharp crack of gunfire.

Looking over his shoulder, he saw about ten Jap soldiers emerging from the jungle and taking up fighting positions. Some took cover behind trees, their heads and rifles poking out. Others in a kneeling position, firing, manually cycling the action, and rapidly reloading after the five rounds had been spent.

"GO!" Jack yelled as he and Abel darted across the gorge. Bullet fire getting so close, he could feel the tiny shockwaves and heat. They made it safely behind a few trees. Putting Tony down, they raised their weapons and returned fire. Blue and Kenny hugged close to a nearby tree for safety. They were separated by the mountain path.

"Blue, stay down, stay undercover! Kenny, we need you to engage. Get your rifle up!" Jack shouted over the roar of gunfire.

Kenny raised the rifle to his shoulder, exited cover, and fired. The force of recoil surprised him. His eyes opened wide, momentarily freezing him in place.

"Keep firing!" Jack yelled.

Jack saw two Japs attempting to cross the small bridge. He took aim with his Thompson, but before he could get a shot off, Abel's M1 rang out. The Japs flailed, falling into the gorge.

"Nice shooting Abel!"

"Thanks, I'm getting good at this," He bragged.

Jack couldn't help but smile. "We need to drop the bridge!" He commanded, "We can't let them get across it. Will never be able to retreat with Tony. Abel, we gotta do it."

"Ok, I will take Kenny and drop the bridge. You provide covering fire." Abel answered.

They both looked at Kenny, who was trembling behind the large tree, frantically attempting to stuff another clip of ammo into his rifle. "Abel, I don't think he will be able to function directly in the line of fire. We need to do it together."

Abel stared at him, resolute. "Ok, you know I got you, Jack."

"Kenny, you need to lay down suppressing fire. Keep them distracted. Wait for my signal," Jack ordered, yelling over the thunderous gunfire.

Chapter 7: Taking the Pilgrimage

Kenny finished adding the fresh clip of ammo to the Jap rifle, smashing the cartridges down into the magazine well, and throwing the empty metal clip aside. He looked at Jack, eyes filled will fear, waiting. After a short moment, Jack nodded once.

Kenny wheeled around, exposing the barrel towards the Japs, who were preparing to send two more soldiers across the bridge. He fired wildly, missing them with every round. But it worked. The Japs retreated slightly. Jack saw the opening he was waiting for.

He jumped up and ran to the bridge, Abel quickly on his heels. They both fired towards the Japs as they ran, pushing them back, undercover. Within the space of a few heartbeats, they reached the bridge. With a mighty effort, they tossed their end into the gorge. The other end quickly followed. "Yes!" burst Abel, "We did it, Ja…" But he didn't finish.

A bullet had passed through the right side of his neck. Abel lurched forward. Apparently, the time it took to dislodge the bridge was enough for the Japs to regroup and resume their attack. Jack had just enough time to catch Abel and pull him away from the edge of the gorge as he began to fall. Dragging him back to the trees in a panic, bullets whizzing dangerously close, Jack was frantic. "Kenny, keep firing!" Jack yelled, trembling, the fear overtaking him. "Blue, help, please!"

Jack whipped his Thompson around, emptying what remained of the magazine, trying to give Blue the most cover fire possible.

She darted across the path and made it safely to the tree Jack was behind with Abel. She froze the moment she saw him. Blood was foaming from his mouth and squirting from his exposed Carotid Artery. She knew, at that moment, there was no hope. Abel only had a few breaths left.

"Blue, do something!" Jack pleaded as he furiously removed the empty magazine and reloaded.

She placed her hand over the wound and press down. Simultaneously, she grabbed a morphine syrette from her medkit and emptied it into Abel's thigh. Abel went limp, the morphine kicking in. His distant gazed past over them. "Ja, Jack. Don't be sad... This is a beautiful place to die... Remember me." Abel said, grabbing Jack's arm, blood bubbles foaming and popping on his lips as he spoke.

"I won't forget you, I won't. I won't..." Jack trailed off, realizing Abel's grip had gone slack. Jack let out an agonizing scream. Blue removed her hand from Abel's neck and stared fixedly at the wet blood dripping from her fingertips.

"Hi o yameru! Hi o yameru!" Jack heard in the distance, not knowing what it was. Thinking that grief had overtaken him. Thinking he had gone mad. The Jap guns fell silent.

120

Chapter 7: Taking the Pilgrimage

"I wish to offer you a choice," a voice rang out.

"No way in hell, I'm gonna kill you! I'm gonna kill you all!" Jack yelled through gritted teeth, vengeance the only thing on his mind. The fury of what they had done to Abel was consuming him. "Who the hell do you think you are, anyway?"

"I am Akira Kobayashi, Captain of the Imperial Japanese submarine, the Sakura," He said. "And since you have robbed me of my last remaining officer, you will have to deal with me now. Luckily for you, I am in a generous mood. I wish to offer you terms."

"Go to hell!" Jack shouted back furiously.

"Please, I know we are enemies, but respect must be shown. I am a patient man, but do not test me. Who do I have the pleasure of engaging with?" Akira asked in a pleasant tone that belied the current situation.

After a moment's contemplation, Jack spat back, "Jackson Miller." Knowing that he didn't have many options at the moment. Talking might buy him some time to figure a way out.

"Nice to meet you, Jackson Miller. Please, come out here. Let's talk face-to-face. You will be perfectly safe. On my honor."

Jack slowly looked away from Abel's lifeless face and stood up.

"Jack, no," Blue hissed fearfully. "Don't."

"It will be fine. Honor means something to them, even if it is a little twisted. I will be safe, for now." Jack commented softly so that only Blue could hear.

He stepped out onto the path, Thompson raised, pointing directly at Akira's heart. Only the gorge and 30 yards separating them. Seeing Akira for the first time in daylight and in close proximity, Jack was struck by his commanding presence.

Akira looked like a man used to being in charge and having people follow his orders without question. His neatly pleated pants, knee-high black boots, and perfectly fitting tan jacket only served to intensify this feeling. Not to mention the katana firmly strapped to his side. "Now, seeing that you're outnumbered more than two to one, it would be in your best interest to surrender." Akira said in a matter-of-fact tone as if Jack had already decided.

"Ain't gonna happen. How about I just end you now and take my chances with the rest of your men. With you gone, I'm betting they will lose some resolve."

"Doing that would be a fatal mistake, Jackson Miller. If you do, my men with seek vengeance, they are duty-bound to do so, and you will have no hope of surviving." Akira said with a finality that Jack found absolutely frightening. "I will give you 48 hours to surrender. At the end of that time, if you are not at our camp unarmed, and I know you know where it is, we will find you and kill you all. You will not get another warning."

Jack looked at Blue. She was shaking her head, no. Kenny was trembling, hidden behind his tree, unwilling to face the current situation. Tony was still unconscious, helpless.

"Take your time to decide. You have 48 hours and not many options. In the meantime, we saw a village down the way. I am sure they can entertain us." Akira said with a sadistic venom in his voice. "Yukō"

With that last command, the Japanese vanished back into the jungle and out of sight. Leaving Jack, Blue, Kenny, and Tony in an empty silence. Grief and fear being all that remained.

"Jack, no. The village," Blue whimpered. "We have to help."

"We can't," Jack started.

"We have too, Ruth," Blue interjected.

"We can't, not right now," Jack said, consoling her. "Without the bridge, it will take us much longer to make our way back. I think he was counting on us destroying it. And with Abel gone," The words caught in his throat, preventing him from continuing.

"We need Tony, back at full strength." Blue finished, realizing the truth of the matter.

"Yes," Jack agreed begrudgingly. He was furious at Tony. If it wasn't for Tony getting hurt, they would have never been on this path. Abel would still be with them. He laid Abel's body down as he wiped a tear from his cheek. Jack grabbed a thick stick and began to dig in the soft earth. "Kenny, get Tony and continue along the path. Blue, please help them. I need to do this. I won't be long."

Jack continued to dig a small grave, finding the manual labor to be almost therapeutic. As if each clump of dirt removed represented a fraction of the anger he felt. Once he had reached a depth of several feet down, he placed Abel in the grave, pulled off his dog tags, and laid his M1 Garand beside him. "I won't forget you, buddy. Not ever." He promised, then pushed the earth over the top, coving him completely. Abel was gone. It was final. There was no going back. Jack picked up his Thompson, placed Abel's dog tags around his neck, and jogged after the others.

Chapter 8: The Font of Life

It wasn't long before Jack caught up with Blue, Kenny, and Tony. His mind was numb, reliving recent events as if on repeat. Doubt consuming him, tormenting his thoughts, crushing his confidence. "Why didn't he notice the soldiers sooner? Did they need to drop the bridge? What would Abel be saying if he was here?"

As soon as Blue saw him coming up the path, she closed the distance between them within the space of a heartbeat. She pulled him in, hugging him so tightly. He momentarily forgot everything. Jack could hear her crying softly. Feeling her warm tears as she pressed her cheek up against his. "I'm so sorry, Jack."

"Me too, Blue... Me too. I'm gonna miss him," They stood, holding each other as the world faded out. "We are going to get out of this for him," Jack said, finding some of his confidence. "And I am going to make those Japs pay, Blue. They will pay for what they did."

Blue was startled by this proclamation. Not having seen Jack consumed with this much rage before. "Jack," Is all she managed to say. Fear was overtaking her. Concern for Jack's safety. Worried for his very sanity. She still held him tightly, trying to anchor him to this world, anchor him to her.

"Let's get Tony fixed up," Jack said, the fury easing from his voice as he stared directly into Blue's deep brown eyes. He wiped the tears from her cheeks with the thumbs of both hands.

"Yes, I just hope it works," Blue replied, having been unsure this entire time but not wanting to voice it, breaking his gaze in shame.

"It has to Blue. They were so sure of it. And Palila." Jack sputtered, directing her gaze back to his, not having considered the fact that Tony might be doomed also. "She is a walking testament. Blue. It has to work. It has to. We have given up too much for it not to." His anger with Tony subsiding.

Blue conceded, seeing that Jack needed something to hope for. His eyes trembling in desperation. "We better get moving," She agreed, wanting to lift Jack up.

Chapter 8: The Font of Life

Jack gazed up the path towards Kenny and Tony. It appeared that they had abandoned the stretcher. Tony was weakly on his feet, swaying back and forth, being helped forward by Kenny. Jack moved along Tony's side, opposite of Kenny, and placed Tony's arm over his shoulder. "I got it now, Kenny. You need a break." It wasn't until just then did Jack realize that Kenny was also in tears. He felt guilty about comforting only Blue, not realizing the impact of Abel's death on the rest of the group.

"Ruth," Jack croaked to himself. Ruth and Abel had become close during their time together and, not only did she not know about his death, but she was also in danger back in the village. "Focus on what you can control," Jack chided himself.

They continued to follow the path per Palila's instructions. Jack continuing to see those strange symboled rocks scattered along the trail, repeating in sets of three. For most of the journey, jungle blanketed both sides of the path as it snaked its way towards the ever-growing mountain. Suddenly, the jungle to their right disappeared, replaced by sheer rocky cliffs jutting sharply upwards.

"We must be getting close," Jack announced. "Palila said the Font starts at the base of the mountain."

It wasn't long before the path opened into a large clearing. The sheer rocky cliffs still stood to their right. But, directly in front of them, was a pond, with crystal clear turquoise water about the size of an Olympic swimming pool. It was lined with smooth flagstones that matched the rock wall. The pool fed the gently flowing stream that ran back towards the direction of the village. Its source water flowing from a gap in the mountain in a graceful waterfall, causing a mist to surround the clearing. This place felt special, like the water itself was vibrating, humming its peaceful intent.

Blue was awestruck. Jack could see her face light up as the soft mist gently touched her skin. "We made it! Bring Tony here, lay him here," Blue pointed at a relatively level patch of earth directly beside the pool.

She pulled out an empty canteen and dunked it in the water. The water felt warm as it slowly rolled over her skin and down into the stream. Blue saw the current swirling in soft little eddies as the water moved from the fountain to the pool, then into the stream.

"Tony, you need to drink this." She placed the canteen to his lips in what was now a well-practiced maneuver and slowly poured.

Tony sipped it up, not spilling a drop. She lifted up his hand, removed the thin leaf, salve, and poured the clear water over the wound. She gasped in horror. As soon as the water hit his infected wound, it began hissing as if it were acid. The injury bubbled in frothy white foam as if Blue had just poured hydrogen peroxide on it. Tony recoiled in pain. His eye's shot open.

"Blue, what? Where? Where are we?" He asked with a hit of fear behind his confusion.

Chapter 8: The Font of Life

"We are at the Font of Life," Jack stated. "The villagers told us it was the only way to save you."

"Villagers? The Font of Life? What's that?"

"It's a long story," Blue started to say.

"We don't have time for that now. How is Tony's hand?" Jack asked although it sounded more like an order.

"Tony, let me see your palm," Blue asked politely, seeing the hurt in Tony's face at Jack's abrasive tone. "Woah. It is completely gone! Tony, how do you feel?"

"Fine. I feel just fine. What's going on here?"

"Great, everyone take a drink. Maybe it will protect us from those thorns in the future." Jack ordered, completely ignoring Tony's question. He dunked his canteen into the water, filled it, and emptied the vessel. He instantly felt energized, like he had just awoken from a deep, restful sleep. All fatigue leaving his sore body. "Wow. Ok. let's get moving. We need to get back to the village, back to Ruth."

"Where's Abel?" Tony asked, not seeing him. "I thought I heard his voice or was I still dreaming? Or did he stay back at the village?"

"He, he didn't make it," Blue said, tears welling in her eyes, emotion threatening to overtake her.

"We will explain everything later, Tony," Jack stated, trying to stop him from asking any more difficult questions.

Questions Jack knew he had to answer. "We need to get back now. Ruth is in danger."

Kenny was eyeing the sheer rock wall, placing his hands at different points along its face. "What's this?" Kenny mumbled as he vigorously wiped crusted dirt from its surface.

"What now," Jack grunted, turning to walk toward Kenny. "Kenny, what's…" His voice trailed off. Kenny had exposed another one of those strange symbols, but this time, it was on the rock wall.

"What are these things?" Jack said mostly to himself.

"You have been seeing them too?" Kenny inquired.

"Yeah, but I thought the villagers placed them along the path as part of the pilgrimage or something. Why would it be on the wall?"

"Maybe it says, congratulations, you made it. Enjoy the water," Kenny suggested with a weak chuckle.

"Maybe," They didn't look exactly like the symbols on the pilgrimage. Those had been carved into the small boulders lining the path. These looked like bricks inserted into the mountain itself. Jack wasn't sure why, but he had a nagging desire to push it. Not able to prevent himself, he placed his hand on it and leaned into it. The rock wall vibrated slightly as the section of rock containing the symbol disappeared. They both took a giant step backward.

Chapter 8: The Font of Life

"What was that?" Blue asked incredulously.

"I'm not sure," Jack replied. "It happened after I pushed on the symbol."

"What made you think pushing on a strange rocky symbol was a good idea?"

"I don't know. I couldn't help it."

"Jack! There's another one here," Kenny said. Jack hadn't even realized that Kenny left his side. "Should I push it?"

But before anyone could answer him, he did. The rock wall again vibrated slightly, and the section of rock disappeared.

"Woah," Kenny snorted awkwardly.

Tony was also on his feet, moving as if he had never been injured, and surveying the rock wall. "Is this one?"

They all hurried over. "Yes, that's one," Kenny confirmed. Tony pressed it in.

This time was not like the others. The rock wall shook violently as a sizable double-door section disappeared into the wall, exposing a short cave. At the other end, Jack could see a faint blinking green light.

As he stepped into the cave, Blue grabbed his arm. "Jack, I'm not sure about this. It might not be safe."

"You might be right, but we need to know what this is. Stay here," His curiosity had gotten the better of him. It was like he was being drawn into the cave, as if he was hooked on the end of a fishing line, the caster reeling him in. "Stay here until we know it is safe. I don't want any of you getting stuck in here if that thing closes."

Jack crossed the short cave with only a few steps. He wiped the dirt that surrounded the blinking green light. "Those symbols again. Wait, these look different." He stated towards the mouth of the cave, where the other stood in rapped silence. He slowly pushed the green light.

Immediately Jack could hear a mechanical sound emanating from the walls, the light switch to red, and smoke issued from the ceiling. Jack thought about running, but it was over almost as quickly as it had begun. The light switched too white. A door in front of Jack opened. He hadn't even noticed it was there.

Looking in, he could see a massive, dark open space. Some indistinct objects were scattered around the room which he couldn't make out. Instinctively, Jack reached around the inner wall for a light-switch. His hands brushing up and down, one side, then the other. He stopped. His hands landing on a significantly large metallic leaver. Throwing caution to the wind, he pulled it.

The room awakened and flooded with light. Jack could now see a large circular room with grated metal flooring and an exposed rocky ceiling—steel scaffolding checkered across its open expanse. Three large control stations lit up to his left, covered in brightly colored display panels and buttons. Following the room around, he saw two giant clear cylindrical tubes. Each had several, what looked like beds or maybe tables inside, with a single metal door set on a rail system. Each cylinder had its own control panel a few feet away, opposite of the metal door. Continuing to pan around, the last notable feature was a sizable open-topped metal table covered with glass beakers and other pieces of equipment. At the far end stood another large door. The entire room was covered in a thick layer of dust.

"It must have been a while since anyone has been here." Jack thought to himself. Seeing the state of things, Jack felt pretty confident it was safe. He called the other over. They hesitated for only a moment. Their curiosity, too, had been peaked. And after what they had just seen from the Font of Life, anything was possible.

They stepped into the room one after the other. As they reached the first control station, a figure appeared, standing in the center of the room. They gasped. Everything about the Being was graceful. From his angular facial features to the way he moved. He had long blonde hair, tightly bound in a ponytail, and reaching down to his waist. His ears were slender, sweeping back in long, high points—his arms were long, longer than any humans, with his hands stretching down to his knees. Reaching about eight feet tall, he was an impressive sight. But the most impressive of all was the fact that he appeared to be made of pure light.

The Being walked gracefully over to the stunned group. As he did, he was speaking to them in a language

Jack didn't understand. This didn't unnerve him as much as he expected. It had become the norm recently. The Being must have seen the looks on their faces, or maybe it was the fact that nobody responded, that he stopped.

He walked over to the central control panel, pressed a few buttons, and a screen flickered to life in the center of the room. It reminded Jack of a movie screen from the cinema back home, but it was floating in place and appeared to be made of nothing but light. Just like the Being.

He began talking again in his strange language. Jack had a sneaking suspicion that it was just to get their attention. It worked. They were all staring at him. He placed his hand over his mouth and opened and closed it while pointing at the light screen with his other hand.

"I think he wants us to say something," Tony pointed out. At that moment, three cards appeared on the screen. One was blue, one was yellow, and the final one was red. He gestured again, motioning them to speak and pointing at the screen.

"Blue, Yellow, Red," Blue said, reading them in order.

He smiled and pressed a few more buttons. This time nine cards came into view. Each card contained a series of small dots.

"We need to count them," Kenny guessed.

Blue again went through the listed items. "2, 3, 5, 7, 11, 13, 17, 19, 23. Oh, prime numbers!" She squeaked excitedly.

The next set of cards came into view. They were pictures of animals. Jack decided he could handle these ones and again read them in order. "Elephant, snake, squid, monkey, jellyfish, horse, whale, parrot, shark."

The screen went blank, a spinning circle appeared as if it was thinking. Jack looked at the being. He raised his finger in a gesture that Jack was surprised to find he recognized. They were being asked to wait. A moment later, the spinning circle disappeared, and six more cards came into view. "I got this one," Tony said. "Tree, grass, flower, cloud, water, snow."

They faded out, and three more appeared. Kenny, not wanting to be left out, said, "Sun, Earth, Moon." Before anyone else had a chance too.

The spinning circle reappeared briefly. Once it disappeared, Jack, Blue, Kenny, and Tony heard the being speak again, but this time they understood. Their jaws dropped in complete shock.

"Hello, I am Arlas, and welcome to the Laboratory."

Chapter 9: The Laboratory

It took several minutes before the shock wore off. Standing in the futuristic yet surprisingly simple Lab, Jack's first thought was back to the stories his mother used to tell him of the lost city of Atlantis. He wondered if this was it, at least, a part of it. Letting his mind wander into the fantastical and back. He was the first one to speak, to break the silence as Arlas just watched on. "What are you, and how are you speaking English?"

"I am Arlas," He answered cordially. "The Artificial Laboratory Assistant" These words appeared on the light screen with the Ar, L, As underlined. "And this is my home."

Blue hesitated, not wanting to insult the being, "What do you mean, artificial?"

"I am a computer program—an advanced algorithm built to decipher the deep and complex genome of many species. I am a science program. This form only acts as an interface between the scientists, computers, and experiments. What you see is a hologram, created from light and forcefields. My body, if you were, and my mind is here." He pointed at the three consoles.

"I'm not sure I understand," Jack admitted.

"The Primori long ago realized that they needed a better interface between themselves and computers. Manual keystrokes work for some tasks but are vastly inferior to any other form of input. Voice commands worked for a time but lacked a higher level of interaction. AI and holograms provided them the interface they long wished for. Not only could they communicate more accurately with computers, but it also allows the computer to interface with the world around it. Participating in the discussion, as it were."

"Is that what the light screen was? A... hologram?" Tony said in a slightly skeptical tone that was more of a statement than a question.

"Yes," Arlas answered. "It is created by those holo projectors, there" He pointed to the small black cylinders lining the ceiling. Jack failed to notice these when he first appraised the Lab. "As am I."

"What is a genome, Arlas?" Blue inquired. For some reason, this stuck in her mind.

"Genome is your DNA. The makeup of any given species genetic code. It is what makes you, you." Arlas patiently explained as if he was giving a school lesson. "It is the very essence of life. Without DNA, no organic life could exist." Blue nodded along in rapped attention.

"Do you mean blood?" Jack probed, knowing he was helplessly in over his head.

"No, it is smaller, much smaller. Most DNA exists within the nucleus of every cell in your body." Arlas continued.

Although he knew what cells were, this was covered in his high school science class. Jack wasn't sure he really understood what Arlas was saying. He was hoping Blue would be able to explain it to him later. So, he pressed on. "And how is it that you can speak English?"

"That was not hard. You did most of the work."

"The pictures?" Blue asked excitedly.

"Yes, I took your vocalizations of the images, paired it against our own, and ran a decryption algorithm to decipher your speech, a simple translation. It was not difficult. Your language is fairly primitive."

Not knowing if he should feel insulted by that, Jack continued. "What is this place?" Shock, disbelief, and

Chapter 9: The Laboratory

wonderment were replaced by his usually confident tone as he realized they weren't in any imminent danger.

"This is a Primori Science Laboratory," Arlas responded matter-of-factly.

"What's a Primori?" Jack questioned. This being the second time Arlas had used that word. Jack wasn't sure if he misheard or if something was wrong with the translation algorithm, whatever that was.

"The Primori were a powerfully advanced ancient race, one of three who first discovered intergalactic space travel using Phase Space. Along with the Tricarions and Dragons."

"Dragons?!" Gasped Kenny. "Did he say Dragons?"

"Yes, Dragons, they have visited many, many worlds. I am not surprised you have heard of them."

"You said they were... were a powerfully advanced ancient race... What happened to them? Where are the Primori now?" Blue inquired.

"I have two hypotheses. They are either extinct or have left this region of space forever. Either way, gone." Arlas admitted. Seeing the confused looks on the stranger's faces, he continued. "After centuries of war with the Dragons, their population had dwindled. A tentative peace was brokered with the help of the Tricarions. It was not long after the peace treaty that the disease emerged and started spreading. It affected the Primori at a genetic level.

Degrading their very DNA. The Primori believed it was a weapon developed by the Dragons. The Dragons denied this and knew it was divine retribution for all the perverse acts of the Primori people." Arlas paused. Jack thought this was a strange thing for a machine to do. Maybe he was waiting for them to understand or paused to allow them time to ask questions. Blue took him up on the implied offer.

"What was the effect of the disease? How did it manifest?" She asked her medical interest peaked.

"Rapid aging," Arlas announced. "It caused their DNA to degrade and incite the aging process, but much, much faster. Once contracted, it would only take three earth months to run its course. If you examined the body of someone who succumbed to the disease, it would look as if they died of extreme old age."

Blue had no response to this. Her medical training couldn't even grasp the problem this disease presented. She stood in silent terror. Arlas continued.

"The disease spread from planet to planet, decimating entire populations. This Lab was created to research a cure. To find a way to protect themselves from the disease. Protection at the genetic level, designed to prevent the decay of their DNA. To delay or control the rapid aging process. The Lab was in operation for over 100 earth years without any sign of a cure. The scientist knew they were close, but the Primori genome is so advanced and sophisticated, even being close meant treatment was still years away. "

"That was when we lost contact with the Primori home-world, Amphalos. The resupply missions stop coming. I believe the last two remaining scientist station here died before their work was finished."

"Why were they at war with the Dragons?" Jack inquired somberly.

"Why are you?" Arlas shot back, seeing the weapons he wore draped over his shoulder and strapped to his waist. The artifacts of war as evident now as they were then. "Why does anyone go to war? Resources, territory, beliefs. This happened to be a difference of opinion. The Primori believed it was their right, no destiny, to rule the stars, including all lesser species. The Dragons believed it was their responsibility to watch over the younger species, providing them knowledge and wisdom as they grew."

"Younger species?" Tony asked suspiciously. "What, how many of you aliens are there?"

"As of my latest data sync, there were 35 known sentient species."

Tony just whistled. Jack was finding all of this a little overwhelming and decided to change the subject.

"What was that smoke when I hit the green button?" Jack asked, wanting to be sure it was safe.

"It was the decontamination process. Making sure you did not bring anything into the Lab that would contaminate the ongoing experiments," Arlas stated.

"Are their ongoing experiments?" Blue questioned.

"No. All experiments were paused when the scientist died."

"How long ago did that happen?" Tony asked bluntly, not wanting to be caught with his hand in their cookie jar.

"10.385 million years," Arlas explained.

Tony coughed, disbelieving. Kenny chuckled nervously. Jack was sure that this time, Arlas had gotten the translation wrong.

"Wait, that can't be right," Jack decided. "Arlas, are you sure about that? That was a long, long time ago."

"Yes, absolutely. My internal clock was synchronized to the earth's time when I was brought online. This planet was chosen because it had primitive life that could be used in experiments but no sentient life to interfere. Apparently, that has changed."

"How, how do you still have power?" Kenny asked, not knowing of a power source capable of lasting any amount of time.

"Geothermal energy. We built this Lab here because of the active volcano. The heat and steam were used to generate power. We stored vast amounts as backups in our power cells." Arlas explained, pausing for a moment and pushing several buttons on the control station. "It seems the tectonic drift of this planet has moved us off that vent. Our backup power cells are down to 3% power remaining."

"What happens when you have no power? Does the Lab shut down?" Jack asked, not sure if he wanted to know the answer. Fearing it would be bad for anyone who lived on the island.

"The Lab goes into a complete lock-down and incinerates. Destroying it in its entirety, with all experimental data and other-wise deadly chemicals." Arlas announced. "It will be completely contained within the mountain. No need to worry." He finished, seeing the looks are their faces. "Besides, without ongoing experiments, 3% should last a few centuries longer."

"What types of experiments were being conducted here?" Blue inquired, scared of what the answer might be.

"Medical mostly. Genetic manipulation, gene resequencing, anti-viral studies, and so on. Specimens would be placed in one of the two test chambers and subjected to any number of tests. Attempting to prevent genetic decay."

"Wait, are you responsible for the Font of Life?" Blue asked incredulously.

"The Font of Life," Arlas repeated, clearly searching his memory banks. "No, I do not believe so. Could you be more specific?"

"Outside of the entrance of this cave is a pool, with magical healing properties. Tony here was near death, and it brought him back. Many legends on earth speak of it. We call it the Fountain of Youth."

"Magic does not exist. It is only science that you have not discovered yet." Arlas remarked confidently. "Can you bring me a sample of this Fountain of Youth to examine?"

Blue snatched up a test tube from the open-faced table, wiped it clean with her shirt, and headed back towards the Font of Life. Jack continued to look around the Lab in amazement. Kenny was also wandering around, thoroughly checking out the test chambers and control panels. Jack assumed that being a mechanic, this place made a little more sense to him.

"What's behind this door?" Kenny inquired awkwardly. Standing at the back of the Lab, between the two test chambers.

"That is the storage and holding room and, further back into the mountain, the living quarters," Arlas explained.

"What's being stored in there?" Jack cut in.

Chapter 9: The Laboratory

"The laboratory machinery, chemical vats, specimen holding pens, backup power cells, and other various items."

Blue had just returned with the test tube full of crystal-clear water. So much so that the extra water was spilling over the edges of the tube as she walked. "Is that where the scientist's bodies are?" Blue inquired interestedly, never having seen an alien before. It seemed that the others were not that excited to be in the presence of dead alien bodies.

Arlas snatched up the tube and placed it into an open chamber in one of the control stations. "Most likely, but I don't know for sure. My holo-emitters are in the Lab only. I cannot leave this room. Analyzing the sample now." Arlas stated, Jack, forgetting that he was the machine. "This will take some time. If one of you is willing, would you please inspect the holding room and living quarters to be sure? I would like to close out their file with an official record."

Seeing as none of the group volunteered, Jack stepped forward. "I'll go," Jack said reluctantly.

"But the door is locked," Kenny responded.

"Not to worry, I can unlock both of the doors," Arlas stated.

With a soft metallic click, Jack knew the door was unlocked. As he slowly opened it, the lights flickered to life. "You won't lock me in, right Arlas?"

"No, my programming prohibits me from locking the holding room or dormitory doors. I am only permitted to unlock them in case of emergencies."

Jack stepped tentatively through the door. He was hit with stale, musky air as if no fresh air had entered that room in a very long time. The room was more extensive than Jack expected. To his left, along the wall, stood several stacked rows of cages. Each row had about ten cages, and there were three rows stacked on top of each other. Nearly half of the 30 pens had old, almost petrified skeletons. Various other desks and consoles filled the room. He could see a railing on the far side of the room as if he was standing on a balcony. He walked over to it.

Looking over the edge, he could see three massive vats, like the ones they had at the brewery back home, but much, much larger. Just beyond them, he could see several large square boxes with all sorts of pipes and wires protruding from them. To his right, there was the second door. "This must lead into the living quarters," Jack thought to himself as he took a deep breath, preparing to enter the room.

Again, as he opened the door, he was struck by the stale air. And, again, as the door opened, the lights came to life. Jack was surprised to see it looked very similar to a house he would have recognized. The room immediately in front of him had a couch, and what even looked like a coffee table. Although the proportions seemed a bit exaggerated. Panning around the room, he saw some bookshelves, office desks, and even a small kitchen. Two doors lead to other rooms. One was open, the other was closed. He started with the closed door as it was closer.

It looked to once have been a bedroom but had since been converted to storage. Boxes and crates were stacked neatly in piles across the floor and bed. He closed the door and moved on to the final room.

This was a functioning bedroom. Jack could see large steel cabinets lining the walls and an ornately carved wooden bed frame directly opposite the open door. He could see two ancient skeletons that looked to be about eight feet tall with elongated arms on the bed. Their hands reached down to its knees, just like Arlas. He could see bits of cloth strewn around the base of the bed. As if the blanket had decayed with the bodies. Satisfied, he returned to the Lab, being sure to close the doors behind himself.

The group was staring at him as he re-entered the Lab and closed the final door. "It's just like you said, Arlas, there are two skeletons back there. They had long arms, like you," Jack said to Arlas.

"Yes, that would be them. I was made in their image after all," Arlas stated. "Thank you. I will add your account to the official record." The room went silent for a minute as each came to terms with what this meant.

"What about the water sample?" Blue inquired, breaking the silence. Everyone's eyes snapped to Arlas.

"Ah, yes, my analysis has completed. It looks like the water has been mildly irradiated by gamma radiation. That makes sense as we have been using the natural water runoff as a coolant for the backup power cells. One of their key elements is the isotope Cobalt—60, which emits low levels of gamma radiation. There are also some of our chemical compounds present, base serum two, by the looks of it. There must be some damage to our storage containers, causing a small amount of contamination to the groundwater. Interesting."

"What do you mean, base serum two?" Blue asked curiously.

"Each scientist was working off one of three base serums created that had shown extreme promise in reversing the disease. They would modify the base serum and run experiments attempting to locate the exact combination that would have the desired results. That is why we have vast quantities of the base serums on hand."

"Are you saying the Font is an accident?" Jack questioned.

"Yes, yes, indeed. A fascinating accident," Arlas puzzled. "Based on these readings, I would guess it has powerful healing properties, at least for small wounds and infections. In its current state, it would not regrow limbs or heal deep, deadly wounds. Maybe with more power or a better delivery method, or both, it could." Blue's gaze snapped to Jack's, and she mouthed, "regrow limbs?"

Something that medical science hadn't even considered to be possible.

"Also, it is very possible, prolonged exposure increases life span. Not by much, but noticeable. I need to review these results and compile them against the work the scientists were last doing. It might hold the key..." Arlas finished trailing off as if he was lost in thought.

"That is how the villagers explain the Font of Life," Blue confirmed. Just then, a red blinking light appeared at the control station.

"I am sensing primitive weapon fire. Here." Arlas stated as a map of the island flickered into life on the light screen. The village had a single red flashing dot.

"Arlas, are you saying something has happened in the village?" Blue said.

"Yes, weapons fire."

"The Japs must have kept their promise. We need to go." Jack commanded. "Wait, Arlas... Does this Lab have communication equipment?

"Naturally."

"Can you send a message to our people?"

"I am afraid not," Arlas stated. "I mean, I could send them a message, but they would have no way of receiving or decoding it. To them, it would sound like solar interference or something. Our communication equipment just is not compatible. However, if you had a communication device, I could boost its power to be heard anywhere on the planet. I would just need to know which direction to focus the signal."

Jack's heart rose, then sank all within the space of a single breath. They didn't have any communication equipment. "Ok, thanks, Arlas. We need to be going. Are you able to close the doors? We can't let the Japs find this place."

"Yes, I can close the doors. If you need back in, just hit the key-code."

"Key-code?" Tony asked, unsure of what he meant.

"Yes, the symbol combination you pressed before entering. It is the order that is visible on the Path. A simple but effective locking mechanism. Mostly to keep out wildlife. The inner and outer door will close once you exit." Arlas finished.

Jack now understood. The symbols on the rocks weren't placed there by the villagers. It was the combination code to access the Lab. It had only been adopted by the villagers and added to the myth of the Font over time.

Chapter 10: Return to the Village

"No use standing around any longer. We need to go. The village is in danger, as well as Ruth. The Japs." Was all Jack could manage to say as he headed for the small cave and exit.

"Hey Arlas, you wouldn't happen to have any ray-guns that would help us with our little problem," Tony asked, half-joking, half deadly serious.

"No, this is a research Laboratory. It contains no weapons."

"Damn, ok," Tony confessed. Kenny handed him the Jap rifle.

"You can have mine. I'm not sure I want it," Kenny insisted, "We left yours back at the village, didn't think we were going to need it." He shrugged.

Tony, Kenny, and Blue followed after Jack and out of the fantastic lab. As promised, the inner door closed as Blue passed it, being the final group member to leave. Then the outer door followed suit.

They raced down the path, heading directly towards the village, not saying a word. Jack's thoughts were swirling in a mixture of hopes, fears, and memories. Even though he had just experienced the Laboratory, he wasn't sure if it was real or not. Or what it even meant. He could touch and smell it, but his mind was struggling to reconcile its new truth. His path back to the village just affording him the time he needed to make sense of it all.

"We're almost there," Blue shouted back at Jack. Her voice sounding oddly distant.

This was the first time Jack realized he was bringing up the rear. Tony and Kenny had already reached it. His mind was racing. "How are we going to get over the gorge," he thought to himself. "How, how, how."

They reached the gorge much faster than Jack predicted. Their recently rejuvenated bodies performing at a much higher rate. He stopped dead, eyes locked on Abel's small grave, just slightly off the path, inside the tree line. Tony saw the shell casings that lined the path and realized this is where it must have happened. He walked over to Jack.

"I'm sorry, Jack," was all he said. Saluting Abel's grave, and turning away. Jack gave it one final look, then turned to follow.

"We need to find a way across." Jack insisted. "It's too far to jump, and we don't have a way of cutting down trees to make another bridge."

"We need to follow it into the jungle. Towards the beach. I think that's our best option." Blue said, having obviously been thinking about the problem as well. "At some point, there will be a way around, even if we need to swim."

"Alright, let's go," Jack ordered.

"They followed the gorge in the direction of the sea. Its elevation decreased as they got closer and closer to the ocean, but the canyon remained impassable. When they reached the beach, they stopped. They were about 20 feet above it, standing on the edge of a small cliff. The stream that created the gorge emptying at its base into an estuary.

"Let's climb down," Jack said, "I will go first, just to make sure it is safe. Once I make it down, follow. No more than one at a time."

"Ok, I'm down. Tony, you're next." Jack said after several tense minutes. Tony completed the decent, then Kenny. "Your turn now, Blue."

Blue tentatively edged over, not being a fan of heights. She had been this way for as long as Jack could remember. When she was young, she was helping her father fix some roof shingles and slipped. Falling two stories and breaking her arm in the process. She never forgot that experience. She made slow but deliberate progress, her hand shaking with each step. At the halfway point, she lost her footing. Sending pebbles flying, bouncing down the wall. She froze, her past drama visible on her sweaty face.

"It's ok, keep moving. I've got you, Blue," Jack assured her. "I've got you."

Blue continued on and, a few minutes later, finished the descent. "Let's not do that again."

"If we can help it, absolutely," Jack responded, never wanting to lie to her.

They ran along the beach, north. They could now see several columns of black smoke billowing into the air against the red and gold sunset. This didn't look like new smoke. The dark-colored trails drifted off far into the distance. Only increasing their fear and the speed of their run.

"Jack, Ruth. The villagers," Blue panted as they rushed across the sand. "It's our fault."

"No, Blue. The Japs would have found the village whether we were here or not." Jack consoled her. "At least we can do something about it."

They entered the village from the beach, mimicking the night before. Only this time was much, much different. They had weapons raised, ready for a fight. Jack entered first as Tony and Kenny snuck around the nearest hut. Blue waited for the signal.

Several huts were on fire, including the one they had stayed in the night before. The cause of the black smoke. A dead Jap laid sprawling on the ground directly in front of their temporary home. The villagers were running around, screaming in terror—some crying over the bodies of their friends or family. No alive Japanese to be found.

The large wooden table had a woman's body lying on top. The clay bowls scattered and broken along the village floor. Food lying in heaps. Visible boot prints embedded in the now spoiled delicacies. Blue gasped in shocked horror when she recognized the body.

It was Ruth. She was laid, spread eagle—arms dangling over the table's edges. A type 30 bayonet thrust into her heart. Her decapitated head impaled on its handle.

Jack stood, anger growing in him. His hands shaking in wrathful fury. Ruth was a timid and gentle soul. She didn't deserve this. No one did. "They will pay. Goddammit! I will make them pay," he spat through clenched teeth, saliva dripped onto his chin.

Palila saw them, standing over Ruth's body. Blue and Kenny in hysterical tears. Tony on his knees, hands covering his trembling face. Jack's jaw clenched in anger. This day had taken too much from them. Her hand shaking, Palila walked over and grabbed Jack.

"Jack, Jack," Palila called out, tears streaming down her face. "Jack, they took Masina and her friends. They took them. Into the jungle... They took them." Jack went slack with the revelation. Fear replacing anger. "Jack, they took them," she kept repeating, "They took them."

"Palila, what? Are they still alive? Please, what happened here?

After about a minute and the great effort of regaining her composure, Palila started, "They arrived shortly after mid-day. Entering from the direction of the Font. They came in with their weapons raised. I greeted them. They were speaking a language foreign to us and not responding, so I tried English. A man stepped forward and introduced himself in kind as Akira Kobayashi, a Captain. He said something in Japanese, and the other men fell silent. I let them know this was a peaceful place and that their weapons weren't needed. He again spoke something to them, and they lowered their weapons, slinging them over their shoulders. We offered them food and water. They sat at our table, we dined together. They asked about the island. They asked about you."

"What did you tell them?"

Chapter 10: Return to the Village

"Nothing, it is not our business to speak of yours."

"Ruth, why did this happen to Ruth?!"

"During the meal, we saw them paying particular attention to Masina and her friends. Smiling and speaking to themselves. Their repulsive intent was all too clear. They are wicked, wicked men, Jack."

"I know, Palila, I know. What happened next?"

"As soon as they were finished, Akira stood and thanked us for the hospitality. He spoke to his men again in Japanese. Three immediately jumped up and grabbed the girls by their hair. Several of our men got to their feet, preparing to help. They shot them. Dead Jack. Dead. On the spot." Palila croaked, her eyes filling with tears again.

Jack gave her a minute to regain composure. Knowing this wasn't easy. He would bet they had endured many hardships before, but nothing like this. When she had sopped up the final tear, Jack asked: "What happened next?"

"Akira then stated his men would need to search the village, to make sure no one else meant them harm. Once they reached the hut Ruth was hiding in, we heard another shot. But this time, one of them was flailing in agony, just outside the door. He died a few moments later. Several more rushed in and pulled Ruth out, throwing her weapon aside. Akira walked over to Ruth, pushed her to her knees, removed his sword from its scabbard, and swung. They then placed her here and said it was a warning to us and a message to you. They then burned several huts after stealing food and vanishing into the jungle. A group of seven heading that way." Jack noticed she pointed southeast, "And two, with the captain, headed that way" She finished sobbing again and pointing northeast.

Jack noticed that three Japs were missing from the count. He and Abel had killed five the first night, Abel took out two at the bridge, and Ruth took this one with her. From the original 21, that left the ten men who attacked the village and three who were most likely back at their camp, guarding it.

"Which group had the girls?" Jack questioned as his voice raised hysterically, "Which group!?"

"The larger group, the seven heading towards Snake Canyon. Jack..." She cried, not able to finish her thought, the effort in retelling the day's events was too much for her.

"Palila, I will get them back. Alive." Jack promised, hoping that Snake Canyon was named for its features rather than its inhabitants. "I will get them back." A single tear flowing down his right cheek. He wiped it off with the back of his hand and strolled over to the dead Jap. In what was becoming a too frequent action, Jack grabbed the Japs rifle and ammo. It was just then he saw Ruth's Smith & Wesson revolver lying in the dirt. He grabbed that up as well. He opened this cylinder to find that one of the rounds had been fired. "Good for you, Ruth," Jack thought to himself.

Chapter 10: Return to the Village

Handing the Jap rifle and ammo to Kenny, he looked at Blue. "Here, take it." He said, holding out Ruth's revolver towards Blue. Its wooden handle outstretched, inviting her to grab it. "You need to be protected. Besides, she would have wanted you to have it."

Blue hesitated. She signed on to save lives, not take it. But Jack insisted. She reached up and gripped its handle tightly. "Thank you." She then placed it into her medic's bag. The weight of it was foreign, awkward.

A small group of children were sitting off by themselves. Jack recognized them as the ones playing kickball earlier that morning. Their lives had changed so much since then. All of their lives had. Blue noticed him staring and, without a word, walked over to the children. Jack wasn't sure what she said or did, but they all embraced. Blue hugging the children as if they were her own.

They spent the night helping the villagers with the bodies of the slain. Palila, having convinced Jack that running off towards Snake Canyon at night was just too dangerous. By the time they had finished, six bodies laid on a hastily constructed funeral pyre, including Ruth's. Just before dawn, the pyre was ignited. The surviving villagers standing by chanting.

"Blue, if we make it back..."

"When we make it back,' She corrected.

"Right, when we make it back, we should contact Ruth's family and let them know what happened. Let them know she died bravely. That she fought to save these kind and generous people. She was a hero." Jack acknowledged.

"I think that is only right," Blue confirmed.

With that difficult task completed, Jack focused his efforts on the rescue. He was still feeling rejuvenated from the Font of Life. "I'm going after them. We need to get the girls back, alive." Jack really wished Abel was here but didn't put a voice to it.

"I'm going with you," Tony affirmed weakly. "I don't want to... But I owe them. These villagers saved my life."

"Ok, thanks. I am going to need all the help I can get."

"I'm, I'm going too," Kenny stammered.

"Ok. Blue, we need to chat with Palila. I have an idea."

As the villagers disbanded from the spent funeral pyre, Jack and Blue caught up with Palila.

"Palila," Jack announced softly. "It isn't safe for you all to stay here. Now that the Japs know about the village."

"It is our home," Palila confirmed weakly, cutting Jack off. "We can't leave."

Chapter 10: Return to the Village

"You have too! The Japs will most likely come back. We need to deal with them before it will be safe to return."

"Where will we go?"

Jack thought about Arlas and the lab, but for some reason, he didn't think the villagers would be able to reconcile what it was or what it meant. The caves presented the better, more natural option.

"A few miles north of here, there is a cave system. It should be large enough for the entire village. It has access to fresh water." Jack reassured as Blue watched on. "Blue knows where it is and can take you there."

"Yes, I can. Palila, we need to get the children to safety."

Palila stood silent, contemplating the proposal. "Yes. Yes. I think you are right. We need to gather up supplies. Let me round up my people."

"Before you do, we need your help with something else."

"Jack, you know we are peaceful and cannot raise a weapon against others."

"I know, I'm not asking for that," Jack admitted, although more warriors would have been a welcome offering. "We had to drop the small bridge, over the canyon, on the pilgrimage path." He stopped expecting to be scolded. Palila just stood there waiting, her motherly smile faintly showing. He continued, "We don't have tools and might need to get back to the Font in a hurry. Depending on how things go…"

"You want us to build a new bridge?"

"Yes," he admitted, glad that she had understood without needing to be asked. He felt guilty about damaging any part of their beautiful island and somewhat responsible for the damage that had already occurred. "Are you able to?"

"Yes, it is the least we can do," Palila confessed, finally feeling like her people are helping. She called over two young men, spoke to them in their exotic language. They picked up an old, well-worn ax and headed up the path towards the gorge.

"Do they know where you will be when they are done?" Jack asked, making sure.

"No, but they will find it," Palila said confidently. "When you live in the jungle as long as we have, it speaks to you. It will tell them where to go."

Palila gathered all the villagers at its center, around the unlit fire pit. She was speaking to them, explaining the plan. They were nodding along as she spoke, some shaking their heads. It was apparent they didn't want to leave their homes. Once she was finished, they busied themselves with the preparation to move. Gathering up supplies for what Jack guessed was several days.

Chapter 10: Return to the Village

Seeing that the villagers were ready and waiting to be lead, Jack turned to Blue. "Remember how to get there?"

"Yes,"

"Ok, don't stop. Don't walk on the beach. Go as fast as you can." Jack announced, clearly worried. "We will catch up once we have the girls."

He pulled her into his arms. Their embrace was watched by the entire village, but Jack didn't care. He knew what was at stake. It wasn't only the villagers; it was his whole future with Blue. He was proud to see she wasn't crying. She was tough and had a mission to complete. Jack knew it would get done.

He watched as they entered the jungle to the north of the village. Towards the small hill that he had stood atop just three days ago. A mountain that had changed his perspective. He looked at Tony and Kenny for a long moment. "Alright, let's go."

Chapter 11: Predator or Prey

Standing at the edge of the village, its welcoming friendliness vanishing with its people. The huts fires burnt down to ashes glowing a soft amber. "Wanton destruction. That's all we are capable of, even in a place like this. If that is the case, I will bring furious devastation to those Japs." Jack promised to himself. Coming to terms with what had been growing inside him since the Arcadia had been hit. Since Blue had been placed in danger. Since Abel and Ruth's needless deaths.

Tony and Kenny had already started on the way, Southeast toward Snake Canyon. Not wanting to take a final look at the village, to be reminded of what they were heading into. Jack could see the fear in their eyes. They hadn't signed on for this. Hadn't been trained for this. Jack realized this made them very brave.

As they walked through the jungle, Jack was explaining potential future engagements. Battle plans for his rag-tag army of three. "The only chance we have is to catch them in a crossfire or by surprise. We will need to be close to make sure we don't hit any of the girls." Jack often said, hoping repetition and planning would keep their minds focused and away from desperation.

"What if the girls aren't with them?" Tony commented each time, "I mean, are we sure Palila saw it right?"

"We only have her word to go off of. Besides, she was right about the Font. And it helping you." Said Jack matter-of-factly. "We have to trust her. When we catch up to the Japs and kill them, if they aren't there, we will head to their camp at the beach. Either way, we will find them. We will get the girls back."

They continued southeast for almost two hours. Crossing a wide, shallow stream that looked to be emanating from the direction of the Font. Often discussing their plan and coming up with contingencies. Jack wanted them prepared. During their last engagement, they were caught with their pants down, and Abel paid the price. That wasn't going to happen again.

The Fountain of Youth

Looking ahead, Jack could see a bright patch of sunlit ground. They momentarily paused in a small clearing. He guessed they had reached the midway point between the village beach on the west and the beach lining the island's eastern side. "Let's take ten." He ordered, pulling out his canteen and some dried fruits the villagers provided. He sat down, leaning up against a tree, one of many that lined the outside of the clearing.

Tony was also sitting in a spot, purposefully several feet away from Jack. His negative attitude having returned. Always doubting their plan but offering no suggestions in return. Kenny leaned his rifle up against a thick tree root and began walking around the clearing. Eyeing the beautiful multi-colored flowers growing there. Bending down and smelling them. The jungle canopy no longer strangling out the sunlight. Jack assumed he was just pacing nervously. Each person handles stress differently. Since the first time they met, Jack could sense Kenny's awkwardness, like he didn't belong in this world or this time. Or even in his own body. Jack wasn't sure what that was about but found him to be a much better traveling companion than Tony.

All of a sudden, a sharp crack rang out in the clearing. The jungle floor shook with the force of it. Jack jumped to his feet just as Kenny disappeared into the earth. His scream of terror seeming to last far longer than the two seconds it actually did. It reverberated in Jack's mind. He then heard an echoing splash, as if a large object was dropped into a bottomless bucket.

Chapter 11: Predator or Prey

He hurried over to where he thought Kenny was last standing. Taking soft, steady steps, listening for more cracks. But none came. He laid down on the dirt floor. "Tony, grab my ankles. I need to get a look at him."

Tony did as ordered with no argument. Jack slowly peaked over the opening. The sunlight illuminating the large bowl-shaped cavern below. Kenny was treading water about 30 feet below him, "Jack, help!" He sputtered, spitting muddy, opaque water from his mouth.

"Hang on, Kenny, hang on," Jack shouted into the hole, his voice echoing off the smooth rocky sides. "We need to find some way to reach you."

"Jack, the vines, in the jungle. THE VINES!" He shouted back up through the iris opening, panic overwhelming him. The cold water mixed with fear causing him to shiver violently.

"Can you touch the bottom?"

"No, hurry." He yelled hysterically.

"You need to find a place you can reach. I am not sure how long it will take us to get enough vine. It needs to be long, able to reach you, and hold your weight. You might not be able to tread water that long. "Jack pointed out. "Try next to the walls."

Kenny swam cumbersomely around the circular cave, noticing for the first time, its size matched the clearing above. He found a small ledge that held his weight and was large enough for him to climb onto. He jumped up and sat on it. His feet dangling into the cold, muddy water. "Of course," he said to himself, "those tree roots couldn't grow into this solid piece of earth. That explains the clearing." Having gathered his wits about him now that the immediate danger had subsided.

"Ok, I'm sitting along the wall. Mostly out of the water," Kenny yelled back up, for the first time noticing the echoing timbre of his voice as the sounds collided and multiplied. He waited for them to stop. "Please hurry."

Jack, knowing that Kenny was safe, at least for the moment, knew it was time to act. "Kenny, we are going to find some vines, built a rope, to get you out. Just sit tight." He said through the opening as he began to slowly crawl backward. "Tony, we need vine, 50 feet or so. Enough to throw it down there and for us to be standing safely back as we pull him up."

"Yes, obviously," Tony replied

Shaking off the feeling that he wanted to punch Tony, he continued. "We also need some of those big broad, sturdy leaves to drape over the hole. The friction as we pull might cause it to snap.

This, Jack had learned the hard way, in basic training. His unit was repelling down a steep incline, each member being lowered by the next in a mock rescue action. Jack had lowered Abel down and was getting into position when the rope snapped, its ends frayed. He fell, 20 feet landing on several squad members as they attempted to arrest his fall. He landed mostly unharmed, only a few bruises to show for it. But one of his squad members fractured his thigh. It took him out of the war. Jack couldn't help but feel responsible.

"Let's gather the vine first," Jack ordered as he could hear Kenny's echoing whimpers below. They both took off, separating into the jungle and looking for the thick vine.

Jack found a long section hanging from a high, very high branch. He guessed it to be almost 30 feet by itself. "This will get us halfway there," Jack mentioned to himself as he pulled on the vine, a basic test of its strength. It moved slightly then sprang back upwards, like a giant rubber band. He applied more force to the pull with the same results. For his final test, he jumped up, hanging onto the vine with his full-body weight. It bobbed up and down with the same elastic motion.

"Yes!" He said excitedly. "This will work."

Jack called Tony over. "I need you to give me a boost."

"What, no, ain't gonna happen," Tony denounced automatically, without having a chance to think it through. "Fine, ok" He quickly admitted seeing as there wasn't another option.

Jack stepped up into his open hands, Tony's fingers weaved together, providing Jack with an adequate platform. Tony huffed with the effort of lifting Jack. He grabbed onto a thin broken branch protruding from the trunk and pulled himself up. Jack continued to climb from limb to limb until he reached the branch the vine was clinging to. He pulled his knife from its sheath, placed it in his mouth, and gripped the blade between his teeth, like a pirate from those old silent films. Slowly, he inched his way out towards the base of the vine.

The branch was swaying under his weight. Jack worried it wouldn't hold. He focused his mind on the task at hand. Feeling like he had steadied himself, he started to cut. It took several minutes of sawing for him to sever the vine clinging to the tree. The branch shook violently with its release, causing Jack to drop his knife with the desperate need to hold on.

"Tony, look out!" Jack yelled, not wanting the knife to impale him. Tony jumped back just in time, the blade burying itself deep into the earth.

"Thanks," Tony conceded, just glad he wasn't the victim of this hapless accident.

Making his way back down the tree and safely onto the ground, Jack dislodged his knife from the earth. It was buried up to its hilt. He brushed the blade against his pant leg to remove the dirt and debris. He then grabbed up the vine and pulled it towards the clearing. "Ok, only 20 more feet. Tony, go check over there," Jack pointed slightly further into the jungle. "I'm gonna take care of this section, then I'll catch up."

Chapter 11: Predator or Prey

Jack pulled the vine within 20 feet of the opening and began rolling it up. He was looking around for Tony when a nightmarish scream echoed out of the opening. "Kenny, Kenny! What is it?" Jack yelled back as he laid down and inched toward the dark hole. "Kenny!"

Jack's fear was rising. Kenny wasn't visible. "KENNY?" He continued to yell, the echoes reverberating forcefully. Ripples could be seen in the muddy water below. Jack wondered if Kenny had fallen in and drowned. His mind leaping to the worst possible outcomes. He was getting ready to yell down again when he heard the whimpers. "Kenny?" Jack said, removing the fear from his voice, replacing it with concern.

"Jack," Kenny whispered back. "Jack, there... there's something down here. Something in the water. It brushed up against my feet. Jack, hurry!"

"Can you see what it is?"

"No," Kenny started, then let out another harsh scream. This time Jack saw it as it passed directly below the iris. A long grey, snake-like body with a thin flat tail. Its eyes were deep-set over a wide gaping mouth full of needle-like fangs. Tiny fins sat just behind its head.

"Kenny, it looks like an eel." Jack calmly announced, not sure whether or not it was dangerous. He figured it would be best to not encourage Kenny's fear. A gasp was all he heard. It seems Kenny had some understanding of the situation Jack did not. "I need to finish getting the vines.

Kenny, I need to go. Just for another few minutes. You gonna be ok?" Jack asked but knew it didn't matter. Kenny didn't have a choice. Besides, Jack knew he wouldn't be alright in Kenny's situation, but took comfort knowing he could do something about it. He was able to help.

"Yeah, Jack. Please hurry." Kenny sputtered fearfully.

"Yes. I will." Jack promised as he edged away from the opening. Once he was several feet back, he jumped up and sprinted after Tony. He caught up with him deeper into the jungle than he expected. Tony was cutting down a 15-foot section of vine, using what look to Jack like a sharp rock. The vine dropped quickly once the final fibers were severed.

"Nice job Tony!" Jack started, "Now…"

"Thanks for the help." Tony criticized sardonically. "Where have you been?"

"We have a problem," Jack said, trying not to get upset with Tony. "Kenny isn't alone down there. I could see an eel."

"Are they dangerous?" Tony asked, all flippantness receding from his voice.

Jack just shook his head. "I'm not sure. But we better hurry. We just need one more piece."

Working together, they soon found another suitable vine. Tony helped Jack into the tree without saying a negative word. Jack detached the vine and watched it drop to the ground. He followed it down.

They each carried a section of vine back toward the dark hole. Jack lashed each section together, end-to-end, using a double fisherman's knot, making one long continuous cable. He added a piece of broken tree branch about three feet long to one end. Tony retrieved several large banana leaves and returned.

"What's the stick for?" He asked, not sure of Jack's intentions.

"It's for Kenny to sit on. With his hands wet, he won't be able to hold the vine tight enough to hang on," Jack admitted.

"Well, Jack. That's pretty good thinking," Tony pronounced.

Jack was taken aback. In the short time he had known Tony, he had never heard a positive comment. "Um, thanks."

Jack lowered himself down into a laying position and edge back out to the opening. "Kenny, we are ready. We will be throwing down the vine. It has a stick for you to sit on when you reach it. But Kenny, you will need to swim out into the middle of the chamber." Jack stopped hearing the soft whimpers coming from below. "As soon as you get seated, just tug twice hard, and we will pull you up." He finished.

"I can't," Kenny said back after a moment's silence.

"You have to. There is no other way."

"Ok, ok, ok." Kenny trembled.

"I will stay here and keep watch until you get closer to the rope. Then I need to join Tony to pull you up," Jack noted, trying to explain the upcoming process to Kenny so nothing would cause panic. "We will be about 10 feet away from the opening. We aren't sure how much weight this ledge will hold and need to make sure we all don't end up stuck down there."

"Ok, ok, ok." Kenny trembled again. And with that, Jack began lowering the makeshift rope into the chamber below. Being sure to make as little an impact on the water's surface as possible. Not wanting to draw the creature's attention.

"Ready? I don't see the creature. You got this, Kenny. Just swim out and grab it." Jack reassured, trying to prepare Kenny with overwhelming confidence. "On the count of three."

Kenny just whimpered.

"One... Two... Three!" Jack yelled with enthusiasm, hoping it would steel Kenny against the task. Kenny jumped into the water from his tiny ledge and began frantically swimming towards the vine. Only a few more seconds than he would be there. Jack started to back up but stopped, frozen the moment he saw it. The eel, breaking the surface, was swimming directly behind Kenny and approaching fast.

"Kenny, hurry!" Jack yelled in a panic. Recognizing the behaviors of a predator. But it was too late. The eel latched onto Kenny's ankle and dragged him under. He let out a terrifying scream that ended abruptly in wet gurgles. The chamber fell deadly silent as to announce its new purpose, a tomb.

Without thinking, Jack grabbed a small rock and threw it into the chamber, towards the opposite wall. It slammed forcefully into the water, its splash reverberating. He was hoping to grab the creature's attention. Enticing it to let go of Kenny.

"What's happening?" Tony shouted from where he stood, still holding onto the vine, prepared to pull. "Jack! What happened?"

As Jack turned to answer, he could hear a violent splashing from within the chamber; he looked back down. Kenny had emerged from the murky water and was making his way back to the vine. The eel was cautiously swimming to investigate the rock Jack had thrown.

"Get me out of here!" Kenny yelled as he tugged hard repeatedly on the vine.

Throwing caution to the wind, Jack jumped up and sprinted the ten feet to Tony. Kenny's muffled sobs emanating from the opening. They pulled with reckless abandon. The vine stretched like a giant rubber band as Kenny's weight was absorbed. They pulled and pulled, walking back towards the tree line.

Finally, after what felt like hours of pulling, Kenny's head emerged out of the opening and then his torso. He collapsed onto the rocky floor from sheer exhaustion, all the adrenaline depleted from his body. Jack ran out, lowered himself down, and inched towards Kenny. He grabbed his arm and pulled him to a safe distance. Jack noticed a few small red dots on his right leg. A souvenir from the creature's apparent interest.

Tony dropped the vine and walked over. All three men were panting from the effort. "I don't know about you all, but I think we have earned a break," Tony announced as if the decision was made.

"Tony, I think you are right," Jack stated, too tired to argue. "I am too tired to be effective in any sort of fight right now." Jack looked into the sky. "It's just past mid-day. Let's sleep until dark. Then we have to continue on. They are counting on us."

They walked back into cover, just inside the tree line, and found a nicely conceal area under some thick tree roots. "I will take the middle watch. Who wants the first watch?" Jack asked in resignation.

"I will," Kenny said weakly. "It's only right."

Chapter 11: Predator or Prey

"Ok," Is all Jack managed to say, surprised by the fact Kenny had volunteered. Jack looked at his watch. "Kenny, wake me no later than 3 PM."

With that, Jack laid down and fell asleep.

Chapter 12: Ambush at Snake Canyon

"Jack, Jack," Kenny whispered, poking him with a long, slender stick. Jack sat bolt up-right and unholstered his 1911, ready for an attack. "Woah, Jack. It's me. Kenny. It's your watch."

Jack slowly returned his weapon to its holster and got up, rubbing the sleep from his eyes. "Thanks, Kenny. Anything happened while I was out?"

"Nothing much." Kenny stated, "I mean, a few small animals ran across the clearing. I'm not even sure what they were." He finished.

Chapter 12: Ambush at Snake Canyon

"No Japs?"

"None, it has been quiet on that front."

"Ok, get some shut-eye."

Jack took his place, watching out over the clearing, listening to Kenny get comfortable with the sounds of Tony's snoring ever-present. The only thing on his mind at that moment was Blue. Wondering what she was up to. He was comforted by the fact that she was with the villagers. "It didn't help Ruth..." said a small voice deep inside his mind. He shook this off—the villagers were peaceful, and he couldn't blame them for not fighting back. But if anyone could keep her safe in the wild parts of this island, they could.

He sat in silence for a long time. Watching a line of carpenter ants carrying bits of leaves off into their nests. For an instance, Jack wondered what it would be like to live in that tiny world. With small worries. And even smaller dangers. A self-contained world only a few yards long.

Jack took this opportunity to do inventory and take stock of what he had on hand. Three magazines for his 1911, 21 rounds total, seven of which were currently inserted into his pistol. He checked his Thompson mags, four 30 round mags full, not including the partially spent mag attached to his Thompson. "Plenty to get the job done," Jack thought to himself. Although, honestly, he wasn't entirely sure. He was attempting to bolster himself up.

About halfway through his watch, it started sprinkling. A light, refreshing tropical mist. It had an extraordinary impact on Jack's mental state. He felt renewed as if the mist was washing away some of the horrible recent events. Cleansing him of doubt. Leaving only a confident rage, dedicated to avenging his lost comrades and saving the girls.

It was 5:30 PM when Jack woke up Tony, the rain coming down much harder now. The sky had turned from its bright sunny blue to a melancholy gray in a very short period of time. Jack found a relatively dry patch of earth, covered by an arching tree root and laid down. This time, he didn't sleep, though he certainly tried. He just laid there, thinking of Blue and the challenges that lay before him. Sleep evading him, Jack decided it was time to get up.

"Time to get moving," He said to himself as he slowly stood and headed towards Tony, who was still watching out over the clearing. Even with the clouds covering the Sun. He knew it would soon be dark.

"Tony, wake up, Kenny. We should get moving." Jack insisted.

Tony walked over and shook Kenny. He was also apparently awake but was showing no signs of wanting to continue. "How do we know they are still out there. Wouldn't they have just returned to their beach?" Tony asked. "That's what I would do."

"Well, yeah. That is possible. But I have a sneaking suspicion the Japs are still over there." Jack answered. "Look, there is only one reason they would split up. They have a second camp. They most likely set it up after we ambushed them that first night in the Jungle. It's what I would do. I mean, we sort of did, by abandoning our camp and heading to the village." Jack finished seeing the disbelieving looks on their faces.

"Then why did some of them head back that way?" Tony said questionably and pointing in the direction of the Jap sub and camp.

"Akira told us to surrender and meet them at their camp. The camp at the beach," Jack stated. "Right, you were out of it when that happened," forgetting that Tony was delirious during this conversation, he continued." He said we had 48 hours to surrender, unarmed. Meaning they had to stay there until at least the time was up. I bet they left a small contingent of their forces in case we actually did. And I would also bet Akira is with them. He would want to be there if we did actually surrender. Look, he is obviously very smart if we surrendered, then great. He could meet back up with the rest of his troops and be fine. If we didn't and decided to attack, he has reserve forces waiting."

"Isn't splitting his forces a bad move? I mean, it helps even out the odds," Tony asked.

"Sure, but he has the numbers to take that risk." Jack pointed out. "Even if we can take out all of the Japs in Snake

Canyon, we are still outnumbered two to one." Tony and Kenny both thought about this.

"Yeah, ok, I can see what you mean," Tony conceded. "But what if we took out everyone at the beach, Akira, along with his men."

"He made it very clear that if we took him out, his remaining men would fight on," Jack said. "So, either way, they have enough men."

"Jack," Kenny cut in, "Wouldn't he expect us to go after the girls?"

"I'm not sure about that. Since Akira sent his larger force with them, he must know it is possible. But probably thinks we don't even know that he split his forces."

"What do you mean?" Kenny asked curiously.

"Well, we only know that he split his forces because the villagers told us. I don't think he was counting on that." Jack responded.

"Now, what makes you think that Jack?" Tony contended. "I mean, wouldn't he have expected them to tell us everything after what they did?"

"That's just it. I think the Japs only shot those villagers and burned those huts to cause panic and cover their retreat." Jack concluded. "I don't think he was counting on the resilience of the villagers. He misjudged them."

Chapter 12: Ambush at Snake Canyon

The realization of what they were dealing with hit all three men differently. Tony stood in a brooding silence. Kenny whimpered softly, saying a prayer under his breath. Jack's face became hard with resolve, knowing what had to be done.

"Grab your gear. We need to get moving," Jack ordered, having reassured the others.

It took a little while for Kenny to find his rifle. With all the excitement around his fall, he had forgotten where he left it. They spread out and searched the tree line. Jack found it leaning against a large root. "Don't lose this again." Jack barked, furious with Kenny for being so lackadaisical with the one thing that could save his life out here.

They started on again, walking around the outside of the clearing, heading directly towards Snake Canyon. Or at least that is what Jack hoped. The deluge continued muffling the now-familiar jungle sounds. Jack actually found this comforting. The group's approach would be much harder for the Japs to hear.

It was now pitch dark. Only a soft silver patch could be seen in the sky—the waning Moon covered by the relentless storm clouds. Faintly, Jack could see an empty void ahead and knew what it was. They had reached Snake Canyon.

Jack turned to Tony and Kenny and put his hand up in a gesture to stop. "Jack, what…" Tony started.

"Shhh!" Jack hissed, placing a single finger over his lips. Demanding silence. Jack motioned for them to back away and regroup behind an enormous group of boulders. "Stay here and stay quiet. I am going to go scout it out. See what we are up against." Kenny nodded while Tony sat staring, his upper lip quivering with the retort he couldn't give.

Jack headed back towards the void. As he got close, he hunkered down, crawling through the drenched muddy earth. He reached the canyon's edge. The drop wasn't sheer like he was expecting. It was a gradual decline, like the shape of a giant V. He looked to his right. The southern end of the canyon wasn't far, and no Japs could be seen. He looked left. The northern end of the canyon was nowhere in sight. But something else was. About 100 yards away, Jack could see a tiny flickering orange glow. He backed away from the edge and crawled in its direction.

Jack knew he was close when the orange light could be seen bouncing off the opposite side of the canyon. The chatter of Japanese could be heard, even over the relentless rain. Jack stopped, knowing he was at the right place and carefully peeked over the edge again.

Five Jap soldiers sat underneath a tarp, held up by two poles, and tethered into the canyon wall. The small fire burned beneath its protective cover. Bedrolls stretched out behind them, also protected from the weather. Several feet south of the shelter stood two Japs, soaking wet and guarding Masina, Lulu, and Fetia. They were sitting on the ground, sunk into the mud, and shivering. Just behind them was a wall of rock and earth. From the looks of it, remnants of a landslide, providing the Japs cover on one side.

"That's not a great spot to camp." Jack thought to himself, wondering why they had chosen this position. "A little exposed and vulnerable. Although that landslide does give them a little cover and prevent the girls from getting away easily. We will just need to take advantage of the high ground."

He slowly, painfully, made his way back to Tony and Kenny. Jack found himself also shivering, surprised by how cold the rain was. "Palila was right. The seven Japs have the girls in the canyon. It looks like they are planning to stay the night."

"What makes you think that?" Kenny whispered.

"They had bedrolls set out, next to a fire, and covered," Jack answered.

"So, do we go now?" Tony asked reluctantly.

"No, I think we should wait for first light. We have the element of surprise, and I want to be sure we know what we are firing at. I will come up with an attack plan. You two, try to sleep." Jack finished, his mind already drifting into the upcoming battle.

Jack patrolled their tiny speck of land around the boulders, more to gather his thoughts than lookout. He knew with the rain the Japs wouldn't venture far from their camp. The night seemed to drag on, whether it was the anxiety for the upcoming battle or the continually unrelenting rain. Daylight just seemed like it wouldn't come. Jack was anxious to get this over with. To return safely to Blue. With Tony, Kenny, and the girls in tow. With seven fewer Japs on this island.

After pacing for some time and building a scattered battle plan in his mind, Jack decided it would be best to get a little more organized. He had the time after all and needed to use every advantage he had. He made a miniature model for the canyon with sticks and stones laid out on a banana leaf to keep it out of the mud. He went through the various scenarios he had running through his mind. Mercifully, the sky began to brighten.

"Wake up." Jack hissed as he kicked Tony and Kenny awake. "It's time." Jack led them over to the miniature and started briefing them on his plan.

"I will be here." He pointed to the rock opposite the rockslide replica. "This will allow me to pick off the two guards and prevent anyone from escaping south. Once they are gone, I can then engage the other group. One of you will need to be here." He pointed to the rock directly opposite the shelter. "Your job will be to provide the main fire against the five Japs in the shelter. The other will be here." He pointed to the rock further north along the canyon wall. Your job will be a flanking position. Trying to keep them from focusing on a single target."

Tony and Kenny just looked at each other. "Look, as soon as the two guards are down, I will rain .45 ACP slugs down on the main group. If we hit them hard and fast, this shouldn't last more than a few minutes. Who wants center position?" Jack hesitated. Knowing one of them would be in more danger than the others. He would have volunteered if he felt confident in their ability to dispatch the guards without hitting the girls but knew they didn't have that kind of skill behind a rifle.

"I'll do it," Tony said resolutely. "I told you, I owe them for saving my life."

"Alright, Kenny, you have the northernmost position. We will take our spots along the canyon's edge. Wait for my signal before firing."

"What's the signal?" Kenny asked weakly.

"The first dead Jap," Jack said with a confident smile. "I will line up the shot, being sure not to miss. As soon as you hear the first shot from my Thompson, engage."

They walked back to the canyon in silence, each thinking of the task. The jobs they had been entrusted to complete. Jack knew they both knew what was at stake, so he didn't bother mentioning it. The torrent of rain showing no signs of stopping. When they reached the canyon, Jack again hunkered down and made his way into position. Tony and Kenny waited for his confirmation that the Japs were still there. He flashed them the ok sign, and they each slowly moved into position.

Waiting made Jack very uncomfortable. And the wait seemed to stretch on forever. All it would take is a single twig snap to lose the element of surprise. Jack could see two guards still standing over the girls. He was hoping it was the same two as last night. They would be exhausted and slow to react. But he had a feeling it wasn't. Of the other five, three were still lying in bed, two were tending the fire. "This is perfect." Jack thought to himself. Seeing Tony and Kenny in position, he lined up his Thompson.

Looking down the peep sights and lining up his front post on the nearest Japs head. The Jap was pacing back and forth, sometimes becoming obscured by the landslide remnants. Feeling confident of his victim's rhythm. Jack steadily pulled the trigger.

The Jap dropped dead before ever knowing he was in mortal danger. The effect was immediate. The remaining Japs jumped into action, grabbing their weapons and searching for the location of the gunshot. The three sleeping Japs taking the longest to engage. Just then, Tony opened fire. A Jap sunk to his knees as Tony's volley made contact.

Jack lined up his next shot, targeting the second guard. He was obscured behind the fallen earth. Jack needed Kenny to engage, to draw him out. After what felt like an eternity, Jack could hear a second rifle roar to life on the canyon's edge. His next target came into view, not knowing the fate that awaited him. Another purposeful, steady squeeze of his trigger had the desired results. The guard dropped.

Chapter 12: Ambush at Snake Canyon

The four remaining guards now firing wildly in every direction, unsure of the locations of their targets. Tony kept up a steady barrage. After every five shots, he went momentarily silent as he reloaded. Jack made sure to keep up the covering fire. His Thompson clicked, empty. Jack pulled another magazine out of the pouch on his belt and inserted it. He unloaded the entire mag into the small group of dizzied Jap soldiers. Two more dropped.

Only two left, he thought to himself. Just then, he saw a Jap bend down. Jack just assumed he had been hit. It wasn't until he stood back up that he understood. A small dark cylindrical object was protruding from his right hand. A grenade. "Get down," Jack yelled toward Tony, seeing the Japs intended target. He just finished reloading his Thompson and raised it towards the Japs just as he smashed the striker against his helmet and threw it. Jack was too late. He watched the grenade traveling through the air like it was happening in slow motion.

"Tony get down!" Jack yelled as he fired at the two remaining Japs. But Tony did not take cover. Tony continued to fire at the remaining Japs, unaware of the danger hurtling towards him. Out of the corner of his eye, Jack saw one of the Japs drop. Then it happened. Tony's eyes opened in shock, having just seen the grenade. It exploded only a foot away from his face—the force throwing him backward, away from the canyon's edge.

Jack leaped into ruinous action and slid down the muddy, slippery canyon wall. His judgment clouded with vengeance. Sliding and firing towards the last remaining

Jap. His Thompson's barrel steaming from the heat and rain. When he reached the bottom of the canyon, his Thompson clicked empty again. Jack tossed it into the mud, all logical thought extinguished from his mind and unholstered his 1911. He would have used his bare hands if his 1911 was unavailable.

The Jap was frantically trying to attach his type 30 bayonet to his weapon. Jack knew this meant his ammo was spent. He closed the distance between them, his 1911 raise towards his target. The Jap stopped fiddling with his weapon and stood resolute in obstinance. The two stared at each other for a brief moment.

"Watashi wa meiyo o motte shinu," the Jap said just before Jack fired several shots into the man's chest. His 1911 locking open with the final shot. It was over.

Jack holstered his weapon and rushed over to the three girls. They were crying softly, huddled against the dank canyon wall. "Hey, Hey. Masina. It's ok." Jack said, compassionately, knowing they didn't understand his words but might possibly understand his intent. At the sound of her name, she looked up. The sight of Jack only made her cry more. He assumed this was out of relief.

Jack helped the girls up, and they headed towards the canyon's southern end. The quickest route out and back up. On the way out, Jack made sure to collect his Thompson and clean off the mud. He needed to check on Tony and Kenny. Although he had a gut feeling that Tony didn't survive. Who could? A blast that close. Point blank. He knew it wasn't possible.

His gut was correct. Tony was lying dead, half sunk into the muddy ground. Kenny was over him, still, unmoving, and weeping intensely. The girls joined him when they saw Tony's disfigured face. Tony's eyes were frozen open, a macabre remembrance of the shock of his last moments. Jack reached down and closed them in respect of the service Tony had performed. "Kenny, take the girls back to the group of boulders we stayed at last night," Jack instructed. "There's something I need to do."

Kenny just stared at Jack, eyes red with the constant, yet familiar tears. Lulu must have seen his despair as she reached for him, pulling him into a consoling embrace. Jack made a walking motion with his fingers and pointed to Kenny. The girls understood and began to pull Kenny towards the boulders. He went without argument as the group staggered out of view.

Chapter 13: Beyond Words

Jack once again had the unenviable task of burying a comrade. Although he wouldn't consider Tony a friend, it was still a significant loss. In twelve days, he had lost 50% of his companions. To make matters worse, the villager's trading crew wouldn't be back for another ten days. Ten days was an eternity on this island. By the end of those ten days, either the Japs would be dead, or he and Blue would be.

The rain continued to pour down in thick sheets, soaking the ground, making it hard for Jack to keep an open grave for long. The thick mud kept oozing in, frustrating any progress he made. He did his best with the tools at hand and dragged Tony's lifeless corpse into the hastily dug hole. He pushed the mud back on top and placed several large stones directly above his body. Jack didn't want the rain to wash him away.

Before leaving, He grabbed two sticks, one slightly larger than the other, shaped them into a T, and tied it tight with a thin section of vine hanging from a nearby chestnut tree. He then drove it into the ground as a makeshift headstone.

With the grave completed, Jack slid back into the canyon and pillaged the Jap camp. Looking for food and supplies. He was only able to find a few extra clips of ammo. "At least they are almost out," Jack thought to himself. He placed the seven Jap rifles in a pyramid with the small fire burning beneath it. He added more dried wood to the pile. Soon the Jap rifles would be out of commission. He watched as they were consumed by the flame, wanted to be sure they were gone. He needed to be sure. Blue's safety depended on it.

After the damage was irreparable, he headed to collect Kenny and the girls. The rain was still pouring down in thick sheets. Jack was wet, and he was cold. But most importantly, he was lost. Not physically, no. He knew how to find his way back. But emotionally lost as if he was empty inside. "Don't let this island beat you," He said to himself. "Don't let it."

The elation of finding this place after several long days in the open ocean had been replaced by fear and wonder. This island held many secrets but even more dangers. Jack slowly trudged through the muddy, slippery, wet jungle until he reached the boulders. Kenny was there, Lulu still holding his hand. He was still crying. The girls seemed to be more at peace. Their nightmare had come to an end.

"Kenny, how long did you know Tony for?" Jack asked gently, thinking that Kenny needed something to take his mind off of what just happened. Something to move him towards closure.

Kenny looked up as if his head was jerked into position. Noticing Jack for the first time, "Almost two years. We, we served aboard the Arcadia since the day it rolled out of the dry dock." Kenny lamented. "Although we didn't know each other well. I was always below deck, working on the engines, and I always ate alone in the mess hall. I'm not even sure what he did on board."

Kenny fell silent, and Jack understood. He felt the same way about Ruth. "How was it possible to spend time with other people and really not know anything about them?" Jack thought to himself.

"Kenny, we need to get back. Are you good to make that trip?" Jack asked. "It is a long way to the caves from here. I'm honestly not even sure we will make it before nightfall."

Kenny just nodded as his unfocused gaze drifted across the jungle floor. The three girls were pointing towards their village and speaking in their foreign language. Jack shook his head no, trying to get them to understand.

Chapter 13: Beyond Words

"Masina, Palila." He said, pointing in the direction of the small rocky hill and the caves beyond. "Palila."

This seemed to have the effect he was hoping for. The three girls looked at each other, then nodded in agreement. Still speaking, though, Jack had no idea what they were saying.

Jack decided it was best to travel directly for the caves, through the jungle, and avoid the village at all cost. At least until he knew all the Japs were gone. He figured the concealment provided by the dense jungle was the best bet even if it would slow their progress. They started off at once.

Lulu remained by Kenny's side for the first hour of the walk. Talking to him, most likely providing encouragement or maybe even thanks for the daring and dangerous rescue. Jack was sure that Kenny didn't even notice her at his side. He was in a trance. Walking, stumbling through the jungle. Eyes fixed on the ground.

This continued on until mid-day. The rain was still beating down as if to make up for the past several sunny days. Jack wondered when it was going to stop. It had been raining non-stop for just about 20 hours. That is when a thought hit him. Abel had been gone for 48 hours, and their time limit to surrender was up. As if it matters anymore. The Japs were sure to find the carnage they left in Snake Canyon and know that surrender wasn't an option.

The group made slow, tedious progress, crossing the dense jungle. The tiny streams swelling with the constant deluge. They took these opportunities to rest and drink, filling their canteens at each stop. Jack had to fill Kenny's for him as he was still in a zombie-like state.

They made several stops like this over the course of the day, once after Kenny had tripped over a particularly nasty tree root. He didn't even try to get up. He just laid there—the girls by his side, attempting to help him into a sitting position. Jack decided the group needed to rest. It would be getting dark soon. This was as good as any place to stop for the evening.

With the stress of the last two days, Jack had forgotten the last time he had a proper meal. It must have been the night they arrived in the village. Since then, he had been subsisting off dried fruits. He was famished. Jack stood up and motioned towards his lips, mouthing the word "food," Masina understood.

Together they foraged through the jungle, looking for fruits and nuts. Jack was so hungry he would even eat a rat if they found one. Masina did one better. She disappeared for a short moment and returned with a dead python, about six feet long. Masina was beaming. She draped it over her shoulders, and they continued to gather food. They returned with a cornucopia of jungle treasures.

Lulu and Fetia began building a fire under cover of a giant strangler fig tree growing over a pair of twin boulders. Its gnarled roots providing open dry patches in the otherwise drenched jungle floor. Jack wasn't sure there was enough dry wood to get a fire started but was soon proven wrong.

Chapter 13: Beyond Words

Generations of jungle knowledge had clearly been passed on to these three young girls.

Just then, a realization hit Jack. He wasn't sure how old these girls were. To his eyes, they looked to be in the young 20s, the same age as Blue and himself. But after what he had heard and seen, they could be in their 40s or even older. He made a mental note to ask Palila when they spoke next.

Masina placed the python on a dry rock next to the fire pit and pointed at it, then Jack. He wasn't sure what she was asking. Again, she pointed at the snake, then Jack, then his Ka-bar knife. "You want me to skin it?" Jack asked, unsure. Masina smiled.

He stepped over the small fire, picked up the dead python, and pulled out his knife. Jack had never eaten a snake before, let alone skinned one. However, he was familiar with the process. As a kid, he would often hunt squirrels and rabbits with his old .22lr. He and Blue would build a small fire in the woods just outside Marion, where Jack would clean, skin, and process the fresh meat. Sometimes they would stay out all night, sleeping under the stars, content, with a full belly. Jack went to work.

First, he removed the python's head. Then, he slipped his knife underneath the snake's soft belly skin and sliced it along its length. Once the blade reached the tip of its tail, he placed it aside and flipped the animal around. Grabbing the end that once supported its broad, sturdy head. He pulled on the now detached layer of skin. With considerable force, the skin peeled away, exposing the muscle below. He scooped out the internal organs and threw them on a banana leaf. Masina quickly reached and grabbed what looked to be the heart. Apparently, she wanted to eat it.

They skewered the processed carcass and tiny heart onto a sharped stick and leaned it over the open fire. Fetia then took the remaining internal organs into the jungle and returned sometime later. Jack assumed she had taken them far enough away so as not to encourage predators. Although Jack wasn't sure what predators lived here as he hadn't seen any sign of them in his many treks through the jungle.

The snake cooked over the open flame, its fingers licking the white flesh, for well over an hour. Jack wanted to be sure all parasites had been killed before devouring the beast. Once Masina assured them it was ready, they began cutting pieces off. Masina handed Jack the first piece and motioned for him to eat. Being so hungry, he didn't hesitate. The meat was hot in his mouth. His breath could be seen as he blew air in and out, attempting to cool it. Jack was surprised. It tasted like chicken, although considerably chewier.

The group ate diligently, being sure to savor each mouthful. Food has a magic all of its own. Its magic worked quickly, lifting their spirits with each bite. Even Kenny was starting to regain some life. Returning to his awkward yet friendly self. For the first time since the battle, it seems he had noticed that they actually succeeded in rescuing the girls. This seemed to raise his spirits even more.

Chapter 13: Beyond Words

As Kenny regained his focus on the world around him, he also began to rub the eel bite on his leg. The girls must have seen this a Fetia darted off into the jungle, returning a short while later with a strange-looking fern.

She broke it, perpendicular to its spine. Exposing a thick, clear, viscous gel. She motioned to Kenny to raise his pant leg. Lulu rolled down his sock, revealing the tiny, needle prick teeth marks from the eel.

Fetia generously slathered the wound with the thick gooey sap, and immediately Kenny sighed in relief. Lulu wrapped the bite with a few leaves and a thin vine.

"Jack, mind if we take a minute to pray for Tony?" Kenny asked solemnly. "Not just Tony, but Abel and Ruth as well."

Jack never found much comfort in prayer but decided it was for the best, now that Kenny was responsive again. "Sure, let's do that, Kenny."

Kenny bowed his head, his hands together in supplication, and began. The girls seem to understand that this was a solemn moment and didn't interrupt. Their cheerful giggles fading away at the sounds of Kenny's voice.

"Blessed and holy are those who share in the first resurrection. The second death has no power over them, but they will be priests of God and of Christ and will reign with him for a thousand years. Revelations 20:6," Kenny finished as the group remained silent. The only thing that could be heard was the consistent patter of rain.

Jack wasn't sure what this meant but saw it gave comfort to Kenny. That's all that mattered. They went back to eating and even laughing. Feeling the joy of being alive. The majesty of this place was hard to escape. Between moments of sheer terror and magical wonderment, this island was omnipresent—a part of them on this wild adventure. Jack decided right then, he would live each moment to its fullest.

"I'll take first watch, Kenny you get some sleep."

"Jack, you haven't slept in a while. I know you didn't sleep at all last night. You go first, please." Kenny begged, seeing the effort Jack was making just to stay upright.

Jack was feeling completely exhausted, the rejuvenation effect from the Font having completely evaporated. Forgetting he hadn't slept in over 24 hours; he was grateful to Kenny. "Ok, can you give me five hours of shut-eye?" Jack looked at his watch as Kenny agreed. It was just past 9 PM. "Wake me at 2 AM."

With that, Jack laid on the soft dry earth, protected by the strangler fig and warmed by the fire. He drifted off into a deep sleep.

Kenny woke Jack at 2 AM as requested. It appeared Lulu and Fetia had remained awake with him all night.

Chapter 13: Beyond Words

Masina was asleep not far away. "Thanks, Kenny. Anything happened while I was out?"

"Nothing," Kenny remarked, though the python had been almost wholly consumed.

"Get some sleep. I will wake you at dawn. In about five hours."

Jack took up his position towards the outside of the strangler figs roots and looked out into the dark jungle. The rain was still beating down. The normal jungle noises all but drowned out. "Most creatures are probably hunkered down, out of this rain," Jack thought to himself.

As Kenny laid down, taking Jacks sleeping place by the small fire, Lulu woke Masina. She took up position beside Jack, watching out over the dark, silent, and seemingly empty jungle.

Jack wondered if the girls were scared of being alone after what had happened. "No, probably not." He said to himself. It was as if they didn't want Jack or Kenny to be alone. Alone with their grief. Jack appreciated the gesture, but it wasn't needed in his case. He couldn't explain it, but it wasn't grief; he was feeling. It was a determined resolution. He was going to survive, and Blue with him. He would rid this paradise of the Japanese infection and return it to peace. His fury bubbled right below the surface, giving him strength.

The Fountain of Youth

The night passed like so many others before it. A calm quiet that hid the terrors of tomorrow. Jack occupied himself by twirling a tiny vine around his fingers while watching the jungle for movement. He wondered what Blue was up to. He wondered what the remaining Japs were up to. "Only six left," He thought to himself. "That's much better than 21," Abel's voice creeping into his mind. He couldn't help but smile. Even from beyond, Abel was still keeping things in perspective.

With an hour left before dawn, Jack decided he should have some breakfast ready for the weary group. He stood up slowly—his body stiff from sitting in virtually the same position all night. Masina looked at him and began to stand. Jack gently pressed on her shoulder, letting her know it was ok to stay. He motioned to his mouth the pointed to the jungle. She understood. Jack was going to forage.

It wasn't long before he found a banana tree, some figs, and those delicious yellow melons. He gathered them up, wrapped them in a large banana leaf, and headed back to camp.

Dawn's glow came predictably on schedule. The grey, raining sky showing no signs of abating. It looked like it was going to be another long, wet day of trekking through the muddy jungle. As the darkness receded, Jack woke the others. Not a complaint was heard. Each, as it seems, had a restful night sleep.

They all ate, energizing themselves for the journey ahead. In the daylight, albeit gray, Jack was able to see the small rocky hill. It wasn't as far as he expected. They had made better progress the previous day than Jack realized. They probably only had an hour or two left before reaching it. Then it was just a short way from there to the caves.

Seeing that they all enjoyed the lazy, light-hearted start to the day, Jack let them take it in. They sat and ate. Laughing and joking. The language barrier wholly eroded with food and shared experience. It seemed they could understand each other's positive intent well enough without knowing the meaning of individual words.

"Did everyone have a good breakfast? Ok, Let's get moving." Jack announced as he used his fingers to show a walking movement.

"How much longer, Jack?" Kenny asked, getting to his feet.

"Not long. We should be at the cave, back with the villagers before mid-day."

The positive atmosphere continued as they strode through the jungle. The girls giggling at something Jack couldn't understand but none the less enjoyed. When all of a sudden, Jack heard a strange rustling in the bushes to his left. He spun around, whipped his Thompson into position, and waited for the Japs to emerge. He couldn't believe he had been caught off guard again. Kenny and the girls fell deadly silent.

Just then, a suckling pig emerged from the underbrush. Squealing and running directly towards the startled group. Once it saw them, it veered off wildly, back into the jungle. They must have startled it. But Jack wasn't taking any chances.

He quickly moved behind the cover of a mossy tree, ordering Kenny to do likewise. "Get your weapon up," He hissed at Kenny. The girls ducked behind another nearby tree. Jack was still pointing his Thompson in the direction of the pig. But nothing else happened. After several long, silent minutes, Jack was sure it must have been they who startled the pig. The rain muffling their sounds until they were almost on top of it. He lowered his weapon. Kenny followed suit.

"Everyone good?" Jack chuckled, releasing the pent-up nervous energy. Laughter erupted from the group. "Let's keep going." He got to his feet, not even realizing he had moved into a prone position and began to walk. The base of the small rocky hill was in view. He ran up and touched its rough walls. The memory of the climb seemed far off and distant. They followed it along its base. It was much larger around than Jack imagined. But eventually, the spring came into view, and with it, the stream.

They began the last leg of their journey, the short hop from the small hill to the cave entrance, along the stream, now swollen from the unceasing downpour. Almost twice the size it was from a few days ago. Jack hoped that the caves hadn't flooded.

Chapter 13: Beyond Words

When they reached the cave's mouth, Jack saw four small figures, kicking around a small ball. Blue sitting against the cave wall, watching and laughing with Palila by her side. Evidently, the cave hadn't flooded, the villagers constructing a knee-high levee in front of its mouth out of earth and stone.

Jack just stood there for a minute, watching Blue. Her laughter lifted him up more than any restful night sleep or a belly full of food ever could. Masina let out a gleeful scream, and the villagers turned towards the mouth of the cave. Everyone let out a collective gasp in relief as they rushed towards the weary band, hugging them. Patting them on the backs. Babbling in their exotic language. Palila beamed at him with her motherly smile. Blue waited for the wave of villagers to subside.

They embraced. Sharing a long, passionate kiss. Jack could faintly hear the cheers and jeers from the villagers. Just then, the rain stopped, and the sun came out like awakening from a bad dream. He and Blue looked out of the cave mouth towards the sparkling stream.

"I'm glad you're back."

"Me too."

"Welcome back, Jack," Palila said, finally catching up with them standing at the mouth of the cave. She was looking up and down the stream. "Wait, where's Ton'ei?"

The Fountain of Youth

Jack knew he would have to explain the events of the past two days. He just wasn't sure he was ready for it.

Chapter 14: The Plan

"Tony didn't make it. He died fighting to free the girls. He is a hero." Jack said resolutely as Blue and Palila looked on with horror. He may not have like Tony; in fact, sometimes he found him downright unbearable. But he was a hero, and without him, the girls most likely would still be in the hands of the Japs. He shuttered at the thought.

"Without Tony, the girls would have died for sure or worst remained captives," Jack explained solemnly. "I don't think I would have been able to save Kenny from the eel alone, either."

"Eel? What eel?" Blue asked incredulously.

The Fountain of Youth

Jack just shook his head, rubbing his face with his hands. Pausing for a moment, he decided it was best if they knew everything and began recounting the events of the past two days. Starting from the moment they left the village and completing with the view from this very cave opening.

Blue and Palila sat in rapped attention. Hanging off every word. Every now and then stopping him, asking to clarify a minute detail or repeat a specific series of events. Every now and then, Kenny would interject a detail that Jack didn't have. An event that happened when he wasn't around, or a comment made by Tony out of ear-shot. Jack's voice was hoarse by the end of it.

"So, you got them all?" Blue questioned hesitantly.

"No, unfortunately not. We got seven." Jack answered in disappointment. "By my guess, we have six left." He finished.

Palila turned to Masina and got her recount of events. Or at least that is what he assumed happened. When Masina had finished talking, Palila turned back to Jack, beaming. "You honor us. Your bravery is beyond measure. Not many strangers would do what you did for our people." Palila said, her eyes watering. "From this day, until the day you die, we consider you one of us. Po'e o ke ola. And you, as well as your offspring, may call Maha'ina home."

Jack found himself unable to respond, emotion welling up within him. Blue responded on their behalf, "What does po'e o ke ola mean?" She asked earnestly.

"People of Life," Palila answered. "That is what we call ourselves. We live in reverence of the Font of Life. Ka Poe, for short."

"Ka Poe?" Blue stated questioningly.

"The People," Palila answered.

"We consider ourselves honored to be considered one of the Ka Poe," Jack said, now able to put words to his feelings. He didn't save those girls for accolades or rewards. He rescued them because he believed they had the right to a free and safe life. It felt more of a responsibility than a desire. He realized then he didn't really have a choice. They deserved freedom and safety. And so, did Blue. He was determined that they all would remain safe.

They spent the next little while recounting the lighter events of the previous day. Jack telling a shocking tale of the devilish suckling pig who attacked without warning. Its vicious intent and frothing rabid mouth a gap as it charged recklessly.

Blue laughed out loud at his over-the-top story-telling. Something he was known for back home, being overdramatic. She was happy to have him back, safe, and by her side. Jack could feel her pressing against him whenever they were near each other.

In a moment of recollection, Jack turned to Palila. "Palila, why is it called Snake Canyon?" Jack asked, having been curious since he had seen no sight of a serpent in the canyon.

"We believe it was the maturation place of Ndengei, the creator, who was disguised in the vestige of a snake. Once he emerged from the Font of Life, he laid, resting and growing for many, many years." Palila answered. "The weight of his body pressing into the earth is what formed Snake Canyon. It is where all newly dead souls must pass through to be judged on their way to the afterlife, joining the ancestors. "She finished.

"Ah, ok," was all Jack could say. The look on Palila's face let him know she knew he didn't really understand. But as always, she didn't push the matter, knowing he would come to his own understanding in time. "And how many monsoons are Masina and her friends?"

"This will be their 37th monsoon. They are approaching their bonding year."

"Bonding?" Blue asked.

"Yes, when they reach 40 monsoons or so, they will choose a man and bond for life. Starting a family," Palila announced.

Jack and Blue looked at each other knowingly. They too, had started the process of bonding with Jack's proposal. And hoped to one day start a family once the war was over. Jack knew Blue wanted to have many, many kids someday. Not now, but eventually.

Chapter 14: The Plan

"Blue, I am so sorry. We have only been talking about what happened to us." Jack said, his eyes downtrodden in shame of his own selfishness. "What happened to you and the Ka Poe?"

She smiled at his use of the people's language. "Where to begin?" She said questioningly with a sly smile.

"How about the moment you enter the jungle, from the village?" Jack answered, wanting to know everything.

"Well, we left the village and entered the jungle." She joked, chuckling a little at the look of indignation on Jack's face. "Then we headed towards the small rocky mountain. The villagers quickly returned to normal. The children kicking their snake skinned ball between them. The people talking merrily amongst themselves. Jack, I have to say they are amazingly resilient. After the horrors of the day before, it is hard to believe."

"I noticed the same. The girls bounced back from their ordeal with the Japs much faster than Kenny or even me," Jack confirmed. "What happened when you reached the caves?"

"Oh, that is the craziest part!" She said excitedly. "They split into three groups. Some went back into the caves and began preparing them."

"Preparing them for what?" Jack asking.

"For us! They flattened out some of the earth, laid down the sleeping mats, and built these small fire pits. Then they went to work building the levees. They must have known it was going to rain." She said, still astonished at what happened. "The second group headed down to the beach and returned a short while later with all these fish. And that rather large shark." She said, pointing to a line of drying fish strung between the walls of the cave. "The third group took up positions around the cave, out in the jungle. Watching encase the Japs decided to come our way."

"Did they?" Jack asked fearfully. "Did they come this way?"

"Oh no, we haven't seen hide nor hair of them. We just assumed you got all the Japs." Blue answered.

They talked long into the night. Jack recounting the process of skinning a snake and the chewy chicken-like taste, while Blue described the kickball games the children had played in the stream, using its currents as strategy and the streams banks as goals. Jack was so glad to be back with her. The horrors of the last few days melted away. The people provided them with food and entertainment. Recounting the tales of the creation and the origins of the Ka Poe.

When it came to the point where the Ka Poe landed on Maha'ina. Jack stopped them. The laughter taking a minute to die off. "Palila, what does Maha'ina mean?" Jack asked, expecting it to be tied to their mythology of the Font. But he couldn't have been more wrong.

Chapter 14: The Plan

"When the Ka Poe landed here, they had been at sea for many, many days without the sight of land. When they finally came ashore, they said Maha'ina. All right." She paused. "All right, this is as good as place as any." They all laughed. Jack, even getting a stitch in his side.

After the stories and laughter died down, it was time for bed. Jack hadn't had a full night sleep since the night they stumbled into the village needing help for a gravely injured Tony. He was grateful they offered to keep watch and would wake him if anything was coming near.

Blue lead him over to the pair of thin wooden mats lying next to a small, warm fire. Its orange glow flickering on the cave walls, creating the illusion of movement. She laid him down, leaning his Thompson against the cave wall, and reached down for a kiss.

"Tomorrow," She said sweetly. "You need a bath." She finished. They both chuckled.

"Ok, tomorrow," Jack promised. He fell asleep as soon as his head hit the ground. Just catching a glimpse of Blue laying down next to him as he drifted off. Soon he was dreaming. Dreaming of an open grassy field. A blanket spread out with a picnic basket set in its center. Holding it down against a gentle breeze. Its corners flapped with the light wind. Placemats for seven were set. He could hear Blue in the distance, talking and laughing.

When he looked in her direction, he saw five young kids playing tag with Blue. Three older boys and two young girls. It was the family he and Blue had always talked about. They sat and ate together as a family. Just before dessert, Jack woke up. Ending the dream and leaving him feeling more content than he ever had.

Bright sunlight was pouring through the cave opening. The sounds of the people busying themselves came into sharp focus. Again, Blue was already up, helping the people prepare breakfast or maybe lunch. He checked his watch,10:17 AM. "Probably lunch," he confirmed to himself.

Jack sat, looking around the cave. His shoes had been removed, and a clean pair of socks had been placed on his feet. He found his boots, now dry, next to the fire. He pulled them on and laced them up, finishing by covering the top of his boots and lower pant leg with his canvas gaiters.

Now that he was back in uniform, he strode over to Blue and sat on a small mat next to her. She handed him a wooden plate laden with flaky white fish meat, fresh fruits, and a starchy tuber of some sort. "Where did the clean socks come from?" Jack asked curiously, happy to have the clean fabric pressing against his toes.

"Ruth's bag," Blue confirmed. "She had another pair. "I hope you don't mind."

"No, thank you," Jack said, looking at Blue compassionately.

Chapter 14: The Plan

"Blue, I've been thinking, we need to go after the remaining Japs." He declared with as much tenderness as he could muster. He knew Blue had just gotten him back, but they needed to finish this. And right now, surprise was the only advantage they had. They needed to press it.

"Yes, I have been thinking about that as well," Blue admitted. "Since you said you thought there are six left," She confessed.

"Look, I am pretty sure they are back at their camp on the beach." Jack started. "Based on Palila's description of the location, they headed after leaving the village."

Palila looked up at the mention of her name. Blue sat mute for a minute. "I'm going with you."

"No, Blue. It will be dangerous."

"Jack, the people are safe here. You need the help if…" She started saying but was cut off by Jack.

"No, look. The only thing keeping me from going crazy out there is knowing that you are safe."

"I will be just as safe with you." Blue proclaimed. "Besides, you can't do this alone."

Kenny was staring at them both, listening intently to the conversation. "He, he won't be alone."

They both turned and looked at him. "Are you volunteering to come?" Jack doubted but felt that Kenny's comment required an explanation.

"Yes. I am." Kenny blurted more forcefully than needed. Jack knew he was just trying to force a level of confidence he didn't have.

"Ok, Thanks, Kenny. You are always welcome." Jack noted. A quiet moment grew between the group. Jack lost in deep thought of the upcoming raid. Trying to find words that would explain his strategy.

"Jack, I'm going with you too." Blue dictated resolutely.

"Yes, yes, you are." Jack conceded, knowing she was right all along. "I want you with me, always. You know that. Besides, we might need a nurse."

"So, what's the plan?" Kenny asked, confident that Jack had already worked it out like he did at Snake Canyon.

"I'm not sure. I think it would be best to attack in broad daylight. I think the Japs will be expecting us to do it at night. Keeping up a vigilant watch. Making it almost a certainty that some will be asleep during the day." Jack asserted.

"Ok, so we need to leave before first light tomorrow to make it in time, right? It is already too late today?" Blue asked, pretty sure just based on the distances involved.

Chapter 14: The Plan

"Yes, exactly. We have all day to come up with and refine our plan. I have an idea."

"Let's hear it," Blue announced.

"You two will be behind the rocky groin. Protected. Blue, you will hold the ammo for Kenny. Kenny, you will be firing as rapidly as possible. Getting clips from Blue. Your job is to draw their attention."

"What will you be doing, Jack?" Kenny asked.

"I will be flanking them. I will sneak up behind their camp through the jungle. You will start firing when I get into position. On my signal, you will start, then I will. We will catch them in a crossfire. They won't know what hit them!" Jack finished, feeling the excitement of a foolproof plan.

"Kinda like snake canyon. The Japs had a hard time deciding which one of us to focus on," Kenny said to Jack's surprise. He was pretty sure Kenny had his eyes close the entire battle. Apparently not.

"Yes, exactly. I have two mags left for my Thompson, another two for my 1911. 74 rounds should be plenty to deal with six Japs. What about you? How many Jap clips do you have?" Jack asked Kenny.

"Let me see," He said as he rummaged around the pouch attached to his belt. "five, plus the three rounds loaded in the gun."

"Ok, 28 rounds. Not the best, but plenty to get the job done."

"You forgot about the five I have left in Ruth's revolver." Blue pointed out as she opened and closed its cartridge cylinder, "I've got five, .357 magnum rounds."

"Right, let's save those to the very end. You never know when you will need those bullets. I want you focused on having ammo ready for Kenny." Jack contended, wanting not to make her a target by firing at the Japs.

"What will the signal be?" Kenny asked, "You taking out a Jap again?"

"No, I was hoping to stay hidden until you had their full attention," Jack answered sheepishly, knowing Kenny wasn't going to like this idea.

"Jack, may I make a suggestion?" Palila cut in. "We can teach you to whistle like the goshawk. We have been using it since we arrived at the caves. That is how the lookouts communicate."

"Um, sure. Can you teach me by tomorrow?" Jack asked, unsure since he was never very good at making duck calls when hunting with this father as a kid.

"Jack, we could teach a young child to make this call before the sunsets. You should be no problem."

But Jack was a problem. He really struggled with it. He practiced all day, Blue and Kenny by his side. Taking turns assisting. Blue master the whistles within the first hour. Kenny learned soon after. Palila's motherly frustration was being pushed by Jack's inability to learn a simple bird twitter. Once even throwing her arms in the air, speaking in the people's language, and walking away flabbergasted. When she returned about 30 minutes later, in a much calmer mood, they continued. By bedtime, Jack had finally mastered three distinct calls.

"That man may be brave, but he is very thick." Jack could hear Palila telling Blue once they finished. Blue just giggled at this proclamation. He had always been dreadful at school. But when it came to real-world things, he considered himself very quick on the uptake. "Today must have been too much like grade school," he thought.

Sleep again came easy. Again, Jack dreamed of the grassy field. A dream about his future. The family he and Blue would have one day. One of the people awakened Jack very early. The cave opening had just the slightest gray tinge to it. Dawn wasn't far off.

Jack got ready and gathered his gear. When he was done, he woke the others. While Blue and Kenny got ready, Jack made them all breakfast. It was a large meal of dried fish and fruits. Jack couldn't help but think it might be their last. He quickly banished this thought and chided himself. "Stay focused," he said inaudibly.

"What?" Blue asked.

"Nothing," Jack stuttered quickly." Almost ready to go?"

"Yes."

"I'm ready, too," Kenny said hesitantly. "Should we get going?"

They exited the cave. A small group of the Ka Poe was awake, bidding them a cheerful farewell. Jack instinctively turned towards the small rocky hill. Blue and Kenny followed without question. The walk was easy as the stream had returned to its normal size.

They made excellent time, this being far from their first trek through the jungle. Jack, Blue, and Kenny had become adept at avoiding its dangers and hang-ups. The only thing slowing them down now was the sheer distance.

"Should we rest or keep going?" Jack asked after a solid hour of walking. He didn't need the rest after two nights of uninterrupted, restful sleep but figured it was best to ask. The group decided to push on and to rest infrequently. Opting instead for steady progress. Wanting to finish the job. Wanting to be safe, even if it meant engaging in danger sooner rather than later.

They reached the beach, exiting the jungle at almost the exact spot he and Abel had several nights before. The dark rocky groin only a short stride away.

"Ok, Kenny, Blue. Walk over and climb up. Be sure to stay out of view until you hear the signal. I will whistle twice. Once I hear you engage, I will open up." Jack ordered.

They just nodded and moved into position, staying low, just as Jack had told them. He disappeared into the jungle. Needing to take a wide berth, deciding it was prudent to ensure he wasn't discovered. It took longer than expected to get into position.

Jack could see the submarine through the trees and off in the open bay. The red life raft was still parked on the beach. Jack inched closer to where he believed the camp to be. The spent bonfire was now visible. Jack sat and listen, waiting to hear the familiar sounds of soldiers at camp. He heard nothing, not a sound. He inched closer.

There was no movement, no sound. Just then, Jack realized he had made an awful mistake.

Chapter 15: Unforgivable Mistakes

Jack exited the jungle and stepped out onto the pristine white beach, which only a few nights before housed the remaining Japanese soldiers. The cool ocean breezed was inviting, betraying the desperation of the current situation.

"Kenny! Blue!" Jack yelled towards the rocky groin. "It looks like they are gone, nothing is..." But he didn't finish.

Crack! Jack heard the bullet whizzed past. "Kenny, stop! It's me." Jack shouted, trying not to get shot. Waving his arms towards Kenny. "There's no Japs."

Chapter 15: Unforgivable Mistakes

Kenny looked over the groin. To his dismay, only Jack stood in the location that used to be the Jap camp. "Where are they?" Kenny yelled back questioningly, almost desperate. Hoping that Jack wasn't upset about the misplaced bullet.

"Gone. I'm pretty sure we've waited too long. Based on the fire, I think they have been gone a while." Jack shouted confidently, having spent many, many nights camping. "I don't think there is much here we can use either," He finished as Kenny and Blue scaled the groin and descended the other side, towards Jack.

By the time Blue and Kenny had reached the spent bonfire, Jack had already canvased the entire area. "Yep, there's nothing left here. That means they didn't leave in a hurry. This was planned. Probably soon after, we didn't show up to surrender." Jack confessed. His eyes drifted towards the red inflatable life raft, then the sub anchored in the bay. "What about the Sub? Arlas said he would be able to boost a signal if we had communication equipment..." Jack trailed off, weighing the potential dangers with the benefits.

"Jack, what if the Japs are onboard?" Blue asked hesitantly. "I mean, wouldn't it be a good place to stay? It's safe, remote, and dry."

"Yeah, it would be, but it would also make them a sitting duck, with no way of escaping. Besides, I am pretty sure they aren't out there," Jack answered.

"What makes you think that?" Kenny questioned.

"The raft," Jack started explaining. "If they were on the sub, the raft would be over there, not here. This tells me they are on the island somewhere."

"Do you think they are watching us now?" Kenny asked hesitantly.

"No, I don't think so," Jack answered confidently.

"Jack," Blue started. "Are you sure? We're pretty exposed right now."

"Yes, that's exactly why I'm sure the Japs aren't around. If they were, they would have attacked by now. Remember the log bridge? They didn't even hesitate."

Blue and Kenny just looked at each other. Jack could see them also weighing the possible outcomes, and it seemed they both determined they were safe for the moment, and it was worth it to attempt to search the sub. Their eyes returned to Jacks, now with a resolute firmness that let him know it was decided.

"Kenny, I need you to come with me. I have no idea what a Jap radio looks like." Jack admitted. "Don't worry, I will go first and make sure it is clear of any Japs."

When Jack turned towards Blue, he could see a fearful look in her eyes. He knew she wasn't fond of tight, small, and dark spaces. "Blue, I need you to stay here, hidden. We need someone on lookout encase the Japs come back." He decided though he was sure she wouldn't argue. "I don't want to be caught out there by surprise."

Her face immediately changed from tense anticipation to relief. The lines near the corners of her eyes relaxing. "Right, I can do that. I will give two goshawk hoots if I sense anyone approaching."

"Perfect, you should hide inside the tree line or behind the rocky groin. The beach is too exposed, as you pointed out earlier. Take my Thompson." Jack said as he offered it to her.

"Won't you need it?" Blue asked incredulously. "I mean, what if there are Japs on that sub…"

"It will just get in the way. I am betting it's pretty tight in there," Kenny nodded in agreement. "Ok, let's go, Kenny," Jack said as he walked over to the red raft and began dragging it into the ocean. Blue made her way back over the groin. Not a bad choice as she will have an unobstructed view of the tree line, beach, and sub.

Jack walked the raft out into the ocean up to his knee. The water filled his boots, but it wasn't uncomfortable. It was warm and inviting. In a different circumstance, this would be a beautiful day at the beach. He and Kenny both awkwardly stepped into the raft, sat on their knees, and grabbed a paddle. Jack found the little raft unstable, making it difficult for him to stay upright.

"Jack, I have to admit," Kenny stated, "I'm a little excited about this. I have always wanted to work on a submarine."

"Let's take this nice and slow, Kenny. When we get there, I will enter first. When I know it is safe, I'll call you down. But Kenny, please stay alert. You never know what might be waiting for us. If you hear gunfire, I want you to get in the raft and get back to the beach." Jack explained.

"Jack, I can't leave you..." Kenny started but was quickly cut off by Jack.

"You might have to! If they get me, you need to get back to Blue and hide. Find the people and wait until their traders come back. You both need to get safely off this island." Jack said firmly. "I'm counting on you to keep Blue safe if I can't."

Seeing Kenny's downcast gaze at his firm scolding, Jack attempted to bring the mood back to a more neutral place. "Why didn't you request to serve on a sub, Kenny? You were already in the navy. I am sure they had some open opportunities."

"I could never work up the nerve," Kenny responded.

"Well, what made you join the Navy in the first place?" Jack asked.

"My dad said it was the only one that would take me," Kenny said matter-of-factly as if all parents held little confidence in their children. Jack wasn't sure how to respond. Blue would have known exactly what to say in a situation like this.

"Kenny, you're a fine sailor." He finally said.

They finished the short trip in silence. The ocean was calm, allowing them to make steady progress. Bright sunlight was glinting off its glassy surface. Jack could see an abundance of marine life swimming below them. Going about its own business unaffected by the struggles above the surface.

When they reached the sub, Jack grabbed onto a hull piece to steady them as Kenny exited the tiny inflatable life raft. Jack followed after, throwing Kenny the small guide rope. He pulled the raft onto the sub's deck. He stood for a minute, listening for any sounds that would hint at the presence of other humans. After a long, uncertain minute, he heard nothing other than the ocean lapping against the hull.

Standing on its deck, Jack could clearly see the extent of the damage it has suffered. It started from the aft deck gun, which had been completely destroyed, and continued all the way to the aft radio mast. It's twisted, charred metal open to the decks below, now flooded. Jack could see remnants of the crew quarters, with personal effects bobbing ghostly in the water. "Kenny, please tell me that the comms equipment wasn't down there…"

"No, no. From what I remember, that would be in the command room, in the middle of the ship." He finished.

"Ok, I'm going down. Stay here. Stay alert!" Jack ordered as he climbed up the conning tower. The hatch was closed. Jack hoped this meant they had closed it on their way out. He reached down and spun the hatch lever. It required a forceful pull, and, with a screeching metal on metal sound, it opened.

Instantly, the stench of diesel fuel, hydraulic fluid, human excrement, and rot hit him. Almost knocking him over as if an invisible fist had smashed into his face. Jack quickly covered his mouth and nose with his right hand as he waited for any sign that he wasn't alone. Hearing nothing, he stepped onto the ladder and began his descent. The clanks of his boots on each ladder rung split the silence below. Jack was sure to keep his 1911 in hand and ready as he entered this unholy mausoleum.

He reached the first deck and squinted into the dark. Sunlight drifting down through the open hatch was a bright contrast to the dark corners of this room. Jack could faintly make out multiple wooden tables bolted to the walls and floor. Papers and some sort of mechanical equipment lay spread over one of the tables. A multi-layered navigation chart littered another. A damaged sexton lay sprawling in a corner. A bookcase filled with binders covered in Japanese characters stood against one of the walls. "This must be the navigation deck," Jack mused.

He again waited in silence. Listening. After not hearing anything again, he continued down the main ladder. Deeper into the darkness. Again, the only thing that could be heard was the clank of each step. Jack, taking shallow, nervous breaths, reached what looked to be the control room. He stood still, allowing his eyes to adjust to the near darkness. The sun's rays struggled to penetrate the subs depths.

After several minutes, he was able to make out the main features of the room. It had many varying operating consoles that controlled the different aspects of the sub. Each control station was tightly packed with multiple levers, pressure gauges, and valve wheels. Large knots of wires draped along the walls, only increasing the feeling of claustrophobia. At either end of the room were doors heading forward and aft. A lone chair sat empty in the center of the control room.

The aft door was sitting slightly ajar, open to the room beyond. Jack walked over to close the door, knowing that only devastation lay beyond. Before doing so, he glanced around the room. Bright sunlight was beaming through the exterior damage. Only the far corners remained hidden. As he panned around the room, he froze, breath catching in his throat, as if time skipped a minute.

Multiple piles of dead bodies lay stacked to either side of the aft door. Just out of reach of the water line and protected from the sun's damaging effects. Jack now knew the source of the rotting smell. He pulled the aft door closed and sealed it as tight as he could. Holding back the need to vomit.

As the back of the ship was severely damaged, partially submerged, and full of the dead, Jack decided he only needed to search the front half. He made his way towards the front of the sub. Its eerie silence made the hairs on the back of his neck stand on end. As he passed hatch after hatch lining the main corridor, he looked in and appraised each room. Satisfied that no dangers lied within, he closed and locked the hatches. "Don't want someone sneaking up behind you, Jack." He said to himself.

He passed through a machinery room. Its equipment was dead, no longer able to fulfill its designed purpose. The sun's rays beamed through small bullet holes that penetrated the submarine to its very core. Its iron pipes and riveted walls dripped, causing the room to feel cold and dank. Jack could hear the scurrying of cockroaches and rats somewhere within the room. He shuddered at the sounds of their tiny feet scraping against the metal flooring. The smell of diesel fuel was being replaced by the musky scent of grease and something Jack couldn't place.

A closed-door stood at the forward-most end of the machinery room. Jack headed directly towards it. When reaching it, he found it wasn't locked, so he pulled it open. He was immediately hit with the sharp smell of sulfur. He had discovered the torpedo room. From the smell of things, some of the explosive cores had been exposed. A partially dissected torpedo sat on a machine table. He closed the door, thinking it was for the best to avoid that dangerous room.

Seeing that the sub was satisfactorily empty, Jack called out for Kenny. "Kenny, it's all good, come on…" But he didn't finish. All of a sudden, a blurry figure lunged towards Jack. Its movements erratic, scared, not inherently dangerous, not even human. That's when he noticed the flapping wings. A royal albatross was barreling towards him. Its wings so large they hit the walls, floor, and ceiling as they flapped frantically.

Jack ducked, rolling past the wild animal who snapped its beak ferociously in his direction. It was scared, and it was trapped. A dangerous situation to place any animal in. Jack wished he could help it but thought it was best to leave it for now. He backed up slowly, keeping his eyes on the bird as he reached the door heading back towards the control room. He exited the machinery room and closed the door behind himself. Locking the scared animal inside. "I will let you out before I leave," Jack announced through the closed door.

"Jack, is everything all right?" Kenny yelled down through the open hatch.

"Yeah, just a bird. Come on down. It's safe."

Jack could hear the metallic clanks as Kenny descended the main ladder. He waited for Kenny in the control room. The cacophony of putrid smells causing Jack's head to spin. He wondered how sailors could live in conditions like these. "Kenny, I'm gonna head topside. I need fresh air. Are you gonna be ok down there?"

"Yeah, sure. Don't worry about me. I'll be up as soon as I have the comms equipment." Kenny mumbled as he began walking around the room. Looking for their prize that would see them safely off this island. He was also closely examining the various Japanese control stations, as if on some macabre tour.

"Let's not waste time down here," Jack reminded Kenny.

"Right, sorry," Kenny said as he refocused his efforts.

It didn't take long for Jack to reach the surface. The fresh salty ocean air rejuvenating his lungs with each breath. The sunlight was so bright compared to the dark below. It again took his vision a few moments to adjust. By this time, Jack's head had stopped spinning.

"Jack," Kenny yelled up the ladder. "I don't see any radio equipment. Do you think they took it with them?"

"I'm not sure. Unless they know about the lab, I'm not sure how much good it would do them." Jack answered, pondering this strange twist. "What about the seaplane. Isn't one normally stowed in the forward hanger?"

"Yeah!" Kenny yelled back more out of excitement than for the need to be heard. "I can get to it. Give me a few minutes."

Jack looked down the hatch and could see Kenny ascending a level. Dismounting between the command room and the navigation room. He had utterly missed this level during his descent.

"Be careful, Kenny. I missed that level when searching. I don't know what will be there."

Chapter 15: Unforgivable Mistakes

"The planes here!" Kenny exclaimed. "And no Japs, either."

"Great, is the radio still intact?"

"I'm not sure yet. Let me look."

Jack could hear a soft banging from below as Kenny opened the plane's canopy. Not having heard anything in a few moments, Jack yelled down. "Need help?"

"No, I almost got it," Kenny grunted. "Ok, got it... Oh, it looks like the wiring is missing."

"What do you mean, missing?" Jack asked, but it sounded more like an accusation.

"I don't know. It's almost as if the seaplane was never finished. Based on the state of things," Kenny answered. "Wait, I am pretty sure I can find the correct wiring in the control room. Just give me a few more minutes."

Seeing that they weren't presently in any danger, Jack agreed. "Ok, hurry up, though. I don't like being exposed out here any longer than needed."

"Sure." Was all Kenny said back as Jack saw him descending once again into the control room.

Jack could hear Kenny moving equipment and consoles around below. Looking for the right type of wiring, he guessed. After what felt like several minutes, Jack yelled down, "Need help Kenny?"

"Jack!" Kenny yelled up, but this time all excitement had vanished from his voice. It was replaced by terror. A fear that froze Jack in place. "Jack, get off the sub now. GO!" Kenny shrieked.

"Kenny, what is it?" Jack asked, faltering. He had seen Kenny scared before, even terrified. But this was different. It had a level of desperation that made Jack tremble.

"Jack a bomb, behind the console. Its timed. Not much left. GO!"

"No! Not without you, Kenny. Hurry."

"Can't, 13 seconds left. GO!"

Sensing the imminent danger, Jack knew he couldn't save Kenny. His only option was to run. But not before thanking Kenny and saying goodbye. Kenny just whimpered back, only faint prayers escaping his lips.

Jack ran towards the edge of the conning tower. It was only three steps, but they seemed to stretch into infinity. The conning tower seemed to elongate as his fear rose. When he reached its edge, he jumped. Hurling himself into the open air and towards the calm ocean.

The blast happened just as Jack left the conning tower. Its shockwave tossing him through the air. He toppled end-over-end. Jack didn't even feel himself hit the water.

Chapter 15: Unforgivable Mistakes

The last thing he heard was Blue's distant scream as the world faded out.

Chapter 16: When All Else Fails

Jack woke with a start. He was on the beach, Blue by his side. They were both completely soaked, sand clinging to their wet clothes and exposed skin. He coughed out the salty water that had invaded his lungs. Throat burning from its salinity. The world was blurry, making it hard for Jack to comprehend. His ears ringing, drowning out Blue. He could see her mouth moving but couldn't hear what she was saying.

Seeing Jack's confused but much alive face, Blue kissed him frantically all over his forehead and face. She helped him into a sitting position. His ears still ringing, although it was fading. He could now understand Blue.

Chapter 16: When All Else Fails

"Jack are you ok? Jack, Jack." Blue said softly, seeing him coming around, eyes drifting into focus. "Jack."

"Yeah. Yeah. I'm ok." Jack croaked. "Blue, Kenny." He finished looking into her deep brown eyes. "Kenny was down there. When it exploded. He warned me…"

Her eyes began watering, but she didn't let out a sound. They sat in silence, each showing a moment of respect for their fallen comrade. "Jack, what happened? Why did it explode."

His mind raced, looking for something he missed while he was onboard the Sub. Clues that would make sense of what just happened. As if a key was turning a lock, it all clicked. "The torpedoes." He finally confessed. "Blue, when I got to the torpedo room, I could smell the sulfur. I just assumed they had been damaged during the battle. But now I am sure they used some of the cores to make a bomb. Kenny said it was on a timer."

"Do you think they were expecting us to board the sub?"

"Maybe, but I think the timing was just a terrible coincidence. No way they could have planned it that accurately." He lamented. "I think they just meant for us to never be able to use it to our advantage. Based on the battle damage, it wasn't going anywhere. So, their only option was to destroy it." He finished.

"How long was I out?" Jack asked

"Not long. You were only out for the time it took for me to swim out and pull you back to the shore. You started coming to the moment we hit the beach."

Jack could see the Jap sub still ablaze in the small bay. Its frame and shape mostly intact. Carnage from the explosion now littering the once pristine bay and beach. A line of diesel fuel flaming on the ocean surface as it drifted out to sea. "Blue, I'm sorry. Kenny. It was my fault. It was all my fault." He said, starting to tremble.

"No, don't say that. It wasn't. No."

"It was my idea to search the Sub. I was the one who said it was safe. I left him alone down there." Jack finished weeping, leaning into Blue and grabbing her tight. "It's my fault. All of it. I couldn't keep them safe, Blue," He groaned, continuing to bawl uncontrollably.

Jack was trembling in Blue's arms. "Jack, it's not your fault. It isn't," She said emphatically as if she could bring him back just with the force of her will. Slowly, with great effort, Jack was able to regain control. Blue's strength, giving him strength.

"We need to get out of here," He finally said as he broke away from the embrace. "We need to get back to the villagers and the caves. I'm not sure how safe we are here."

They both stood. Jack much slower than Blue. His body was stiff from the explosion. His ears still slightly ringing. For the first time, he felt a warm liquid dripping

238

down the side of his face. He reached up and touched it. His right ear was apparently bleeding.

"Don't touch it. I will bandage it when we get back to the caves. But for now, leave it alone." She chided. Jack never made a particularly good patient, and he felt sorry for Blue having to deal with his injury. "Do you think we will make it back before dark?"

"No, probably not. We can stay at the strangler fig," Jack said, quickly finishing his thought after seeing the look on Blue's face. "You'll see."

Once again, they headed into the dense jungle. Away from the horrors of the small bay and possibly towards more danger. Jack's mind was racing. "Blue, I'm not sure how we are going to find the remaining Japs."

"Maybe we need to let them come to us?" She responded absentmindedly as she avoided a dragon's thorn tree.

"I don't think so," Jack said back. "The only thing we have is the element of surprise. We need to use it. But we need to find them first."

"Maybe the villagers will help? Now that we are one of them?" Blue asked, unsure of how much leeway being a member of the people would buy them.

"That's what I was thinking. They didn't seem to have a problem being on watch at the caves. But we need to make sure they stay safe. Blue, we have too," Jack said with conviction. "This is our war, and it has already had too much of an impact on these wonderful people."

Jack and Blue trudged through the jungle. Now that the rain had stopped, the hot, sticky humidity had returned. Jack decided he preferred the rain to the heat. It was utterly draining. Sapping them of every ounce of strength and endurance. They stopped more times than Jack could count. Resting, drinking, eating those dried fish and fruits.

With an hour left of daylight, they reached the strangler fig stretched out over the two large boulders. The place where only two nights ago, Jack had shared a meal and laughs with Kenny. The place where Kenny had prayed for Tony.

"Blue, would you mind saying a prayer for Kenny," Jack asked. This must-have seemed out of nowhere, but this place had brought the memory back into stark relief. "Please, Blue. Would you. I know he would appreciate it?"

Blue had been religious her whole life. Her family was members of the Latter Day Saints. Mormons. Although Jack had never found solace in religion, he supported Blue and her need to be close to God. And she, in turn, accepted him for what he was.

"What religion was he?"

"I'm not sure. This is the spot where he prayed for Tony. I figured it's only right."

Chapter 16: When All Else Fails

"Ok," She lowered her head in solemn respect. "And it came to pass that I, Nephi, said unto my father: I will go and do the things which the Lord hath commanded, for I know that the Lord giveth no commandments unto the children of men, save he shall prepare a way for them that they may accomplish the thing which he commandeth them. 1 Nephi 3:7."

"Thanks, Blue," Jack said after a moment of silence. A small pile of dried wood still sat neatly under the gap in the strangler figs roots. Jack wished they could have a fire. It always made the nights more bearable. But tonight, it didn't feel safe. It would be a beacon announcing their position to anyone looking to find them.

The two of them sat and talked about everything that had happened over the last two weeks. Smiling with fond memories of Abel, Ruth, Kenny, and even Tony. After they finished their meager dinner, Jack slowly stood. "I'll take first watch. Blue, you get some sleep."

Just like a few nights before, nothing much happened. Although, without the constant rain, the jungle was alive. Jack saw several small mammals sauntering past, not even noticing him sitting there. The birds vocalizing exuberantly now that they were able to spread their wings. The insects returned. Jack fending them off his exposed skin. He really wished they could stay on the beach.

Halfway through the night, he woke blue. It was her turn at watch. He gave her is Thompson, locked and loaded. "Wake me if anything happens. I mean anything, Blue."

"Ok, I will. Get some sleep. You need it. You look like crap." She chuckled.

He laid down in much the same place he did several nights earlier and slept. This time, it wasn't a deep, restful sleep. He found himself jolted awake, covered in a cold sweat several times. For each instance, Blue comforted him and laid him back down. The final time this happened was just before dawn, as the sky began to turn its odd shade of gray. Jack decided it was best to just get up.

They ate a small breakfast, then headed towards the caves. By mid-morning, they reached them. Palila was sitting by the stream bank, watching the children play. When her eyes met Jack's, she knew Kenny didn't make it.

"I'm so sorry, Jack." She said compassionately. Her motherly instinct showing. "Did you honor him?"

"Yes, we did, Palila," Jack promised. "Blue spoke a wonderful prayer in his honor." Palila beamed at Blue.

"Kenny's spirit will be at rest," Palila affirmed. "I will inform Lulu. She had grown very fond of him."

The villagers welcomed them back just as before, the children hugging Blue, the men patting Jack on his back. Masina and her friends sat back, slumped against the cave wall. Palila, having just finished telling them about Kenny.

"Palila, I think we need the Ka Poe's help." Jack said, "No, not fighting. But finding the Japs. They weren't at their beach camp. I think they have taken to the jungle and dug in somewhere. We need to find them before I can finish this. I will go with them."

"Yes, Jack. We can do that. But please, you need to rest. Stay here. Let us do this." Palila said as she called over several men. Some young, while others old. She spoke to them in their foreign language. Once finished, they immediately gathered some food packs and headed out. Jack watched them leave in several different directions. Heading to scout the island.

"Will they be safe?" Jack asked Palila. "Please, they need to stay safe."

"They will be. They will be like a ghost in the jungle. The Japanese will never know they are there." She explained. "This is our island. We are born from it and are part of it. We are the jungle."

"Right. Anything we can do?" Jack asked, not wanting to just sit back. Waiting was never one of his stronger skills.

"No, just rest. You will need your strength once we locate the Japanese."

"I agree with Palila." Blue said, "Jack, you have been going non-stop since we arrived on this island, eight days ago. Take a day to rest. We need you at your best."

Had it really only been eight days? That means it had been 16 days since the Arcadia sank. To Jack, it felt like a lifetime. Everything before the Arcadia was a distant memory like it was from someone else's life. The only thing anchoring him to the here and now was Blue.

"Ok. Please let me know when the Ka Poe return." Jack conceded. He had always found it difficult to trust others. Ever since he was a kid. During the Great Depression, his father had hired a pair of drifters to work at the store. They said they just needed work, money to get them to their next destination. But that was far from the truth. The pair robbed the place after only a week—just enough time to scout the location. Jack never forgot this experience or the lesson it taught.

"Jack," Palila hesitated. At the sound of his name, he made eye contact. Palila looked like she had something difficult to say.

"What is it, Palila?" Jack prodded.

"Blue was right. You look worn down. You need to rest. To regain your strength." Palila stated. "Not far from here is a pond, filled with fresh, clear water. Our children go there often to play and forget the responsibilities of village life. I think you and Blue should go. It isn't far."

Jack thought this over. How could he go enjoy himself knowing that the Japanese are out there, somewhere? "Palila, I'm not sure that is a good idea. What if the Japs come?" Jack responded.

"Don't worry, Jack, some of our people will stand watch. They'll whistle if danger is coming too nearby. You will have plenty of time to react." She pointed out. "Please, Jack. You have done much for us. Let us do one more thing for you."

Jack conceded. Together with Blue, they followed several of the people out of the cave and into the jungle. And Palila was correct; it wasn't far. If jack had to guess, it was only about two miles as the crow flies from the cave mouth.

The pair stepped out into a small clearing where a beautiful shimmering pond stood. The water was crystal clear. So clear in fact, Jack could see small boulders strewn across its floor about 20 feet down. The pool itself was probably 30 feet wide by 30 feet long in almost a perfect circle. Around its banks grew tall soft grass, plenty of space to layout, under the sun or stars. A single large rock, larger than a man and the perfect height to use as a diving platform, stood at the northern most end of the pool.

The people vanished back into the jungle, taking up their assigned posts. Jack looked at Blue, who was already gazing into his deep grey eyes. Jack could see a slightly guilty look on her face that he understood. Understood all too well. How could they be here enjoying themselves when others were still in danger. She must have seen the same look on his face.

"Jack," She said softly. "It's ok. Abel would want us to enjoy every moment. He wouldn't want us to pity him or waste a beautiful day like this."

"I know," Jack said as a smile began spreading on his lips. He thought how Abel would have thrown himself into this pool without a second thought. "Your right."

Together they stripped down into their underwear and jumped in. The water was cold and refreshing. The little fish that lived in the pool didn't seem to mind the company. In fact, they seemed curious about the newcomers. Approaching close and softly nibbling on their toes.

The two enjoyed the afternoon swimming and diving. The large rock was indeed the perfect diving platform. When not swimming, they laid in the tall grass talking, its soft stems providing ample padding. By the end of the afternoon, they had almost forgotten all their worries. This island was truly unique. Its power to revitalize one's body and soul Jack had never experience before. As if the Font's energy seeped into the very earth.

"Blue," Jack asked, "What is this place?"

"Well," Blue started, "I believe Palila called it a 'Pond'. Whatever that is." She finished with a wide grin and a small laugh.

"No, I mean. I know what this place is." Jack responded, also laughing. "I meant this island. What is this place?

"I don't know," Blue answered in all seriousness. "All I know is it feels special. With everything we have been through, all that we have lost. It almost feels as if the island understands and is helping us overcome it. Helping us bear it. I know it sounds crazy."

"It's not crazy. I know what you mean," Jack answered as he looked into her eyes. At that moment, he realized just how much he needed her in his life. How much he loved her—the sun's light causing the red highlights in her hair to really pop. "I love you, by the way. If I haven't told you that recently."

"I love you too," she replied with a smile and placed her head on his shoulder.

As dusk began to fall, the villagers returned and informed Jack it was time to return to the caves by pointing in its direction. The pair got dressed and, again, followed the villagers.

By the time night had fallen, they had reached the caves and realized the scouts had not returned. Jack and Blue prepared for another night in the caves. The small fires still burning. Even more fish hung from lines tethered between the cave walls. They laid on the same thin, wooden mats as the night before.

When the next morning arrived, Jack and Blue awoke early and enjoyed a breakfast of smashed roots and fish. Soon after they finished, several of the scouts had returned.

They reported their findings to Palila, who translated for Jack and Blue. "They are camped just outside the Village. It looks like they are waiting for us to return."

"Ok," Jack started, then stopped. Drifting off into deep thought. After a moment's silence, he asked: "Did you tell them about the Font?"

"No, they had no need of it," Palila confirmed.

"Ok, great." Jack proclaimed. "That's one less thing we need to worry about."

"What do you mean, Jack?" Palila asked.

"It's just good that they don't have yet another reason to want this island. Once we have dealt with these Japs, it should be over for the Ka Poe." Jack stated, not wanting to give away the existence of the lab. He was pretty sure it wouldn't be good for either of their governments to know of its existence.

"I will sneak towards their camp and open fire when the timing seems right. That's plan A, but I need a plan B if that doesn't go the way I predict. I don't want to leave too much to chance. I don't have much ammo left and need a way to deal with them for sure." Jack said, looking towards Palila and Blue for answers. "Any ideas?"

"Jack, what if we lay a trap like you do when we hunt rabbits?" Blue said hesitantly.

"I was thinking the same thing. But I think we need a little more force behind it." He pointed out. "What about those pits that have wooden spikes at the bottom, like in those old jungle adventure movies we saw as kids."

Chapter 16: When All Else Fails

"That would require a lot of digging," Blue remarked. "Palila, is that possible?"

"Is what possible?"

"We need to create a pit, several feet deep by several feet wide. Deep enough for a man to fall in and not be able to get out. With sharpened wooden poles driven into the ground and pointing upwards." Jack said. "The goal being that the Japs will chase me, then fall into the hole. Being impaled by the spikes." He finished watching Palila intently, not knowing how these peaceful people would feel about it.

"Yes, I think we can do that. We often use this method for hunting wild pigs. We call it a lua'a" Palila confirmed. "Although we can't participate in the actual fighting."

"That's fine. I understand." Jack agreed, happy to have any help he could. "When can the pits be ready?"

"How many do you need? And where do you need them?" Palila asked.

Jack drew a small version of the island on the cave floor, using a thin twig. He added the rocky hill, the Village, the enormous mountain, and snake canyon. He drew two Xs north of the Village and just south of the small rocky hill. "I will engage the Japs at their camp. Here." He pointed just outside of the Village. "If I can finish them off, great. If I run out of ammo before I can, I will run down these game trails and towards the pits." Jack said as he drew the route on the cave floor. "I will need a way to clear the pits. They should be too big to jump over."

"Vines, Jack," Palila exclaimed. "We can hang a vine for you to grab onto and swing to safety."

"Perfect!" Jack proclaimed. "So how long will it take to get these built?"

Palila conferred with several of the people. It seemed as if they were working out the details. "We can have them done before the sun rises."

Jack's jaw dropped in surprise. "Really! That soon?" He said after collecting himself.

"Yes," Palila said, beaming with pride. Just then, most of the people gathered up tools and supplies and headed out of the cave opening.

"Palila, that's a lot of people. I don't want the Japs to be aware of them." Jack cautioned.

"They won't, Jack. Remember, we are like ghosts." She said with her warm, motherly smile. "This is our jungle."

"Right, I will inspect the traps tomorrow morning, then make my way towards their camp. Either way, this ends tomorrow." Jack announced confidently.

Jack spent the day walking between the pit locations, helping the people when he could. Most often, it just felt like he was in the way. The progress was astonishing. Both pits had reached the depth of five feet just as the sun was setting. He headed back to the caves. For what he hoped was his last night there. If everything worked out like he planned, they would all be back sleeping in the Village tomorrow night.

Before bed, Jack decided to clean his Thompson and 1911. It had been a brutal, muddy few days, and wanted to be sure they were ready for the fight. After stripping them both down, he laid the parts on top of a large banana leaf and wiped them clean of the grime that had collected. Palila provided him with the oil from a coconut as a lubricant. He then reassembled his weapons; confident they were now up to the task. It was now time to sleep.

Jack was awakened by Masina about an hour before dawn. He got his gear ready, and like most mornings before, he had breakfast. Although today he wasn't hungry. It was more out of habit. The nervous anticipation was pushing all other needs aside.

It was time. Before leaving, Jack woke Blue. They shared a few private words and a loving embrace. It wasn't a long hug. Not a goodbye. It was more of 'see you soon.' A promise Jack intended on keeping. "Don't worry, Blue," Jack said, just before leaving. "I don't plan on breaking my eggs." She smiled, remembering the lesson from Abel's favorite story.

The trip to the pits took little time. Jack had become well versed in jungle travel. When he reached them, he gasped. The jungle floor showed no signs that it had ever been disturbed. The pits were covered with the flora and fauna that perfectly matched the surrounding area. The camouflage was complete.

The people walked around its edge, showing Jack exactly where the pit began. Several small rocks were placed at 12, 3, 6, and 9 o'clock. Designating its boundaries. Jack lifted up the edge of the covering. He could see a deep pit. Much deeper than the height of a man. Sharpened wooden poles could be seen pointing skyward. A vine hung from a tree branch on its southern side. The side Jack would be approaching from if plan A didn't work.

Jack walked the short distance to the other pit and examined it in a similar fashion. And again, he marked its boundaries with rocks. He didn't want to take the chance he would accidentally fall in, along with his intended victims.

Confident that all preparations had been made, Jack thanked the people and motioned for them to return to the caves. Jack was ready to end this ridiculous adventure. And he would finish it alone.

Chapter 17: Antagonizing the Enemy

Jack stood next to the pit for a minute or two. Gathering his nerves. Preparing himself for the upcoming violence. Surveying the scene that might end up being his last hope. When he was ready, he stepped back from the pit's edge and headed towards the village.

He walked in silence, alone. Making no sound. Attracting little attention from the jungle's inhabitants. His weapon at the ready. This time he wouldn't be surprised. Not by anything. He was on a collision course towards destiny, towards possible death. One that couldn't be changed, one that he wasn't looking to change. "What will happen, will happen," Jack thought to himself.

Jack had been preparing for this moment, maybe for his entire life. His training as a Marine had made him sharp, like an arrow, searching for his target. His love and friendship with Blue, turning him warm, compassionate towards the island's people—the need to protect them strong. His fierce burning responsibility driving him when others would have failed, given up.

For the first time, he could really feel the jungle all around him. Like it was an extension of his own heightened senses. The sweet smells of the brightly colored flowers, the musky odor of the decaying plant material, and the pressure of the humidity against his body. He had experienced this all before, but today it felt more apart of him. Urging him forward. Pressing him on, as if it understood his own desires.

Time passed differently than before. Before, he was always worried about the other's safety. Whether it was Blue, Ruth, Abel, Kenny, Tony, or even the people. His mind had continuously been fixed upon them. But not today. He was solely focused on the task at hand. His own body felt disconnected from his mind. Like he was controlling it via a wireless remote.

Seeing that he was approaching the village, he slowed down. Being sure not to make a single noise. Even his breathing seemed too slow. Jack circled the village under cover of the jungle. When he reached the point nearest the village garden, directly east, he heard them.

Chapter 17: Antagonizing the Enemy

The small contingent of Japanese soldiers sat in hastily dug foxholes. Jack counted all six. "Yes, they are all here." Jack thought to himself. The Japs were overlooking the village. Assuming that danger would be coming from its direction. Jack smiled and sunk back into the jungle, decided his best bet would be to attack them from behind. Slowly, purposefully, he moved into position.

From this position, Jack had an almost unobstructed view of the small camp. The Japs already had bayonets fixed. "They must be really low on ammo," Jack said to himself as he took cover behind a thick tree. Four of the six Japs were looking fixed on the village, most likely expecting them to return. Akira was hunkered down in his foxhole, reading what appeared to be Moby Dick. The final jap was standing, not far away, over a small fire. Cooking. A makeshift table had been constructed, holding up a few pieces of Japanese equipment. Jack guessed that the missing sub radio was one of them.

He lined up his Thompson, preparing to engage in what he hoped was the final battle in the game of chess with the Japs. A game that was being played with their very lives. Just then, a large goshawk let out a piercing scream. The Japs looked in its direction, perched high on a branch, of the tree Jack was hiding behind. He ducked back behind the tree, hoping to evade their questioning gaze. Based on the racket, he wasn't exactly successful.

The sounds of soldiers preparing for an attack could be heard. The thuds of rifles on earth as they turned in his direction. Quick, fearful shallow breathing emanated from their direction. He was found out. All element of surprise was gone. His mind raced, looking for a solution. Searching for a way to salvage plan A.

He decided his only hope was furious violence. So far, the Japs hadn't proven themselves adept at soldiering. Most likely because they were submariners. Jack thought this was his only way. He waited for the anticipation to grow, for the moment to stretch uncomfortably.

When he heard them chattering amongst themselves, he raised his weapon and swung around the tree trunk.

Jack unloaded his Thompson. Emptying an entire magazine. The shock of the rapid, unexpected violence had the desired effect. The Japs struggled to return fire, hastily taking aim and squeezing off a few rounds that missed Jack by a wide margin. He, however, had lethal accuracy.

During the initial volley, Jack hit one of the Japs. Its head exploding. Spraying blood onto the face of the Jap directly to its left. Jack used this momentary distraction to terrible effect. The blood-covered Jap sunk into his foxhole. Jack could tell by the burst of red mist that he had hit his second intended target.

Expelling the spent magazine, Jack reloaded as quickly as his adrenaline-fueled body would allow. The short pause in his attack was enough for the remaining four Japs to regroup. Akira was yelling at them in Japanese, coordinating their efforts. The tree jack was leaning against exploding as their rounds made contact. Splintering wood made Jack recoil, protecting his eyes from the projectiles.

The gunfire ceased; Jack assumed that some were reloading. He turned again and engaged. Pointing his Thompson wildly in their direction. Each round missing an intended target. Jack's mental count of the shots screaming at him. He was almost empty. With the last round, he hit another Jap. His lifeless body was thrown against the side of his foxhole. His body bent in half. The torso was exposed lying on the open earth, while the lower half was dangling in the hole. Three Japs left. And his Thompson clicked empty for the final time.

Jack swung his Thompson back over his shoulder, securing its sling over his head. Its hot barrel pressing against his back uncomfortably. He reached down and unholstered his 1911. Akira saw the desperation in Jack's face and quickly blurted orders to his men. The second Jack opened fire; they took cover. Seven rounds emptied very quickly. Too fast, Jack thought.

The sounds of gunfire ended abruptly. His 1911 locked open. The Japs peaked out of their foxholes just as Jack returned his 1911 to its holster, feigning that he was entirely out of ammo. Locking eyes with Akira for the briefest moment. Instantly Jack knew what was going to happen next.

He took off into the jungle towards the pit. Plan B was now in effect. Jack could hear Akira yelling orders in

Japanese and the sounds of soldiers exiting cover. The remaining two soldiers, along with Akira, were on his trail.

Jack slowed just enough so they could follow him. Enticing them. He looked back to gauge their position. They weren't more than 20 yards away. The two soldiers were out in front, running furiously towards their prey. Rifles swinging in their hands as they ran. Bayonets pointed towards their quarry. Akira was just behind, his Katana unsheathed and raised over his shoulder as he ran.

After several minutes of frantic running and steering his victims to his intended location. Jack knew he was approaching one of the pits. He slowed just enough for the Japs to get within 10 yards. When Jack looked back, Akira was now in the lead. Only then did he see the rocks. Jack jumped and grabbed onto the low hanging, purposefully place vine, and swung over the pit. Just before he reached the other side, a single gunshot rang out.

The force of the impact knocked Jack from the vine. His forward momentum was the only thing that kept him from falling into the pit. His right arm was on fire. A burning sensation he had never felt before. A sharp cracking noise grabbed his attention, making him momentarily forget about his damaged arm.

Jack wheeled around, the pits opening now exposed. The camouflage covering having dropped into its depth. Along with the three remaining Japs.

Chapter 17: Antagonizing the Enemy

Akira was lying on the pit's floor, one of his men directly on top of him. Jack could see a wooden spear piercing the soldier's body. The third jap looked much the same. A pole had pierced his thigh and, another, his left lung. He was spitting blood, trembling in pain. Jack couldn't see if Akira had been skewered or not, being mostly covered. But Jack wanted to be sure.

He attempted to unholster his 1911 with his right arm but found that it wouldn't obey his command. Using his left arm, he grabbed his pistol, released the spent magazine, and loaded up his final seven rounds. He dropped the still open slide, inserting a cartridge into the chamber. Jack found this simple process awkward and difficult with his left hand.

Jack aimed at the first, whimpering Jap, and squeezed the trigger. He missed. The Jap shook with the sound. The other two remained still. "Maybe Akira is dead," Jack mused. He lined up his shot again and again missed. The recoil causing a sharp pain in his damaged right arm. Now Jack was more concerned with ending the Jap's misery than his death. He knew if he did nothing, the Jap would eventually die. But Jack felt that mercy was his responsibility.

His third shot missed. Jack finding his weapon skills with his left arm to be vastly inferior to his dominant right. He took his time with his fourth shot. It connected, center mass, and the Jap sagged lifelessly.

Jack aimed for the other skewered Jap. Again, he missed with this first shot but connected with his second.

Only one shot remained. One chance to be sure it was finished. He lined up his shot, pointing directly at Akira's head, the only exposed section of his body. Jack fired. The bullet just grazed the side of his head. Akira didn't flinch. Jack was confident it was over.

With a flood of relief, he fell to the jungle floor, crying, trembling with the elation of it. He had won. But more importantly, Blue was safe. The people were safe. He laid there for a long, long time, attempting to reel in his emotions. Once he had come to terms with his new reality, Jack got up.

The sharp burning pain in his arm returned. He now noticed the sensation of warm, wet liquid running down his arm, dripping from the fingers of his right hand, which hung lifeless at his side.

A bullet had pierced his upper arm. Rendering it useless. Jack needed to get back to Blue. She would be able to fix it. But he needed to do something now to stop the blood flow.

Using his left arm, he ripped what remained of his right sleeve from his shirt. It was just enough for a makeshift bandage. He placed the cloth down on a fallen tree. He then used his left arm to maneuver his badly damaged right arm perpendicular to the fabric. The effort and pain almost causing him to blackout.

He tied the rag as best he could, using only his left hand and cinched it tight. He let out an agonizing scream as the bandage dug into the open wound. He sat for a time, gathering his strength before deciding to head back to the cave.

Stumbling through the jungle for what seemed to be hours, Jack finally reached the small stream that fronted the caves. He was met by several of the people, who Jack assumed were on lookout. Once they realized he was injured, they hurried over and helped him to the cave's opening, practically carrying him. Calling frantically for Palila.

She and Blue came running to its opening. The people laid Jack down near the nearest wooden mat. Blue was giving Palila orders, who was, in turn, directing the people. Jack could feel his marine jacket and undershirt being removed along with the bandage he applied. Blue washed her hands and poured cold, clear stream water over his wound. She gently picked out the jungle debris that had accumulated as Palila prepared a salve. Blue made a bandage out of a rag that Lulu handed her.

"Jack, this is going to hurt. Prepare yourself," Palila said as she covered both sides of the wound with the salve.

"Arrgh," Jack grunted, the stinging sensation causing his eyes to water.

Blue tightly wrapped his upper arm then crafted a makeshift sling. Jack winched with the final tight knot. After several minutes, the throbbing abated. Leaving only a dull ache in his now immobilized arm.

"Blue," Jack whispered hoarsely. "I got them. I got them all. Palila, the island is safe again. It's sa…" Was all Jack could say before drifting off to a much-needed sleep.

Jack spent the rest of the day in and out of consciousness. During one of these restless fits, Blue ordered him to drink something. All Jack could make out was "Drink… Palila… Jungle herbs," So he drank the hot liquid as best as he could manage.

Jack woke, feeling slightly better. It was night time now, although he wasn't sure if he had been out for one day or many. The events since his victory having been clouded due to his injury. Or maybe even the contents of that tea.

"How long have I been out?" Jack asked, seeing Blue sitting not far away.

"Hours, Jack."

"What time is it?" Jack followed up, now knowing it hadn't been days.

"Not yet midnight," Blue responded kindly. "How are you feeling?"

"Like crap. What was in that tea?" Jack chuckled. "Where are the people?

"Most are getting ready to return to the village, now that it is safe. They wanted to wait to be sure you could be moved. Can you stand?"

Chapter 17: Antagonizing the Enemy

"Yeah, pretty sure I can. Might need a little help though," Jack responded.

Jack raised his left uninjured arm towards Blue. She grabbed it and first helped him into a sitting position, then after a short break, to his feet. "I See you left my shoes on this time." Jack joked as he breathed in sharply due to the pain in his right arm.

"Yes," Blue chuckled. "Just after you passed out, we decided we would head back to the village as soon as you were able."

"Well, let's not keep them waiting."

Jack and Blue left the cave to a thundering cheer. The people seeing Jack on his feet couldn't hold back. Palila stood with Masina, Lulu, and Fetia. Each said, "Thank you," to Jack, and he was surprised to hear it in English.

"They wanted to know how to say it, so I taught them while you slept," Blue answered, seeing the obviously questioning look on Jack's face.

Jack nodded his appreciation toward the four women. "Let's get going. Hopefully, we will make it back before morning."

Although he was injured and each step made his arm throb in pain, it was the best trip through the jungle Jack could remember. Their ordeal was over. Now all he had to do was heal and wait for the trading villagers to return.

The Fountain of Youth

It was still dark when they had returned to the village. Several of the huts had burnt down to only ash. The villagers directed Jack and Blue into an undamaged hut and offered them food. Jack took it willingly and found eating with his left hand as cumbersome as shooting with it.

Dawn began breaking with its gentle, comforting rays. Jack needed more sleep; he wasn't feeling that great. The trek had sapped him of any strength he had regained. "Blue, can you wake me at noon?" He grunted as he laid down.

"Yes, I can do that. I will also be checking on you every hour or so."

"Really? How come?"

"I just want to be sure you don't get an infection."

"Ah, ok. Well, if I do, we can just take a trip to the Font," Jack pointed out. "I mean, it wouldn't hurt anyways. It might speed up the healing process."

"I was thinking the same thing," Blue said with a smile forming in the corners of her mouth. "Sleep now. I will check on you soon."

And with that, Jack once again drifted off into a deep, restful sleep. Knowing that he had done his job successfully. All worry erased from his mind.

Chapter 18: The Mountain Path

Blue was as good as her word. Every hour she checked on Jack. Each time he would wake and ask the time. Once answered, he would put his head down and fall back into a fitful sleep. The last and final time she woke him was at noon.

Upon hearing the time, Jack slowly got to his feet. Still feeling the throbbing in his arm, but now his face felt hot. This slightly confused him. Jack just assumed it had been the warmth from the full tropical sun. Beating down on the small hut's roof while he slept. Turning it into a kind of sauna. But it wasn't. It was he, himself, who was radiating the heat.

"Woah slow down. Take it easy." Blue said, seeing him trying to get up. She placed a hand on his shoulder and gently pushed him back to the ground. "You formed a low-grade fever. How do you feel?

"Not bad. I mean, not great." Jack said, gingerly raising his injured arm. He winced with the effort of it. Using his left hand to wipe the sweat from his forehead. "But it could be worse."

Blue considered him for a long moment. As if apprising his very soul, checking to see if it too had been damaged, determining what action to take next. "Here, drink this," she said, slowly handing him a small carved bowl containing a pungent brownish liquid.

Jack awkwardly grabbed the bowl with his uninjured left hand, raised it to his nostril, and inhaled deeply. He almost gagged with the stench of it. "Yuck, what is this stuff?"

"A different herbal tea. Palila said it was made from a mixture of those beautiful red flowers, some dried weeds, and the sap from the Dragon thorn tree." Blue explained. "Don't worry, she said it was safe. It's to help with the fever." She finished seeing the fearful look on his face as he gazed into the liquid.

"Do I have to drink the entire thing?" Jack asked uncomfortably. "It really smells like something that came out of a dead animal."

Chapter 18: The Mountain Path

"I know Jack, and yes, you need to drink the entire bowl."

Ok," Jack mused uncomfortably. "Bottoms up," and he drained the bowl of its contents, shuttering with the last swallow.

With this essential task completed, Blue got to her feet and helped Jack up. "Let's go see Palila." She finally conceded.

They exited their hut. A soft ocean breeze wafted over Jack's feverish face, providing much-needed relief, or maybe it was the tea. He wasn't sure but was hoping it was the breeze—anything to keep him from needing to drink more of that nasty stuff.

The pair slowly crossed the small village and scanned the people, attempting to locate Palila. When they found her, she was directing several of the people who were rebuilding one of the damaged huts towards the back of the village.

Blue waited for Palila to stop giving orders to a group of middle-aged women who were thatching the roof of a newly repaired hut. "Palila, we need to check Jack's wound." Blue asked with a confident poise that must have come from dealing with a great many doctors and numerous patients in far more stressful situations.

"Sit him down here," Palila said as she pointed to a tree stump that had been shaped into a chair.

Jack sat as commanded, gingerly lowering himself into position. Blue removed the bandage and the salve that had been tightly bound around his upper right arm. "So, what's the prognosis, doc?" Jack joked as Blue examined the wound.

"Well, it isn't as bad as I expected, but it is a little red around its edges. A small infection is setting in. That explains the fever." Blue finished confidently, having located the source of the fever.

"Should we try cauterizing it?" Jack tentatively asked, not looking forward to the prospect. "I mean, wouldn't that close the wound and stop the infection?"

"No, I don't think we should. Every time I have seen a burn victim, they always end up with horrible infections if not properly cared for in a sterile environment." Blue stated. "And we don't exactly have that here. Maybe if we had some…" Blue trailed off in thought.

"Had some… What?" Jack asked curiously.

"Oh right, Palila, do you have any needles for making clothing? Preferably very fine and sharp. Metal would be best but bone if that's all you have." Blue asked, turning towards Palila and ignoring Jack's inquisitive look.

"What will you be using it for?" Palila asked politely.

"I am going to sew up Jack's wound, to close it. We call it stitching." Blue responded.

268

"Like a dress?" Palila questioned. Jack could tell she had never heard of this before, and it makes sense. He was pretty sure he was the first gunshot survivor the people had ever seen.

"Yes, so the sharper and thinner, the easier it will be. I will also need a fine yarn," Blue remarked.

"Ok, yes, we have several needles. We do have some metal ones, although they are ancient. I'm not sure you want to use them for what you describe. Jack surely wouldn't enjoy it." Palila chuckled at this, and Jack joined in. "Our best, the ones we use for the finest bonding dresses, is actually made from the fangs of the largest snakes. Takes many monsoons to find a snake large enough, but they last for many, many lives. I still have one my father made for my mother as a bonding gift."

"Yes, that would work. Now we just need the infection to subside before we close it up."

"Looks like a trip to the Font is in our future." Jack pointed out, smiling.

"Palila, will it at least help with the infection?" Blue asked expectantly. "If we can remove that danger, the wound should heal on its own over time once properly closed."

"It might," Palila offered. "But I am not sure. We have never seen an injury like this before. We have never had such weapons on our island before."

"That settles it, we are going," Jack announced. "Any reason to wait? Or should we just get going now?"

"If you leave now, it will be dark by the time you can make it back," Palila said matter-of-factly. "It will be very dangerous, crossing the gorge at night. And tonight, the moon will be small."

"Oh, right." Jack acknowledged. "Blue, do you think the infection will get much worse if we wait until tomorrow morning?"

"Well, it won't go away, but as long as we keep the herbal salve on it and keep it clean, it shouldn't get too much worse. Remember, it did prevent Tony's from getting worse overnight. And he was in a much worse state than you are now."

"You need to keep drinking the tea, also Jack," Palila added, "Every time the sun drops by a single hand."

Blue looked at Jack. She was clearly puzzled by this measure of time. "Jack? Do you know what that means?"

"Yeah, we learned that method in green hell. I need to drink a bowl of tea every hour. But we can use my watch," He finished grinning at her.

"Ok, I will make sure you don't miss a scheduled dose," Blue said professionally.

"Thanks," Jack responded in his most passable Tony impression. They both smiled at the reference, knowing that

270

it was meant as a sign of respect—a symbol of remembrance. Jack shuttered at the thought of several more bowls of that disgusting brown liquid. "Well, it sounds like we have a date with the Font for tomorrow." Jack asserted with his confident smile, trying to push the tea from his mind. "That reminds me, Blue. There is something I need you to do."

"Sure, anything," She responded. "What is it?"

"I need you to go grab the Jap radio from the foxholes just outside the village. Directly east of the garden."

"I can do that. What does it look like?"

"I'm not sure, just grab all the equipment to be safe," Jack responded. "But Blue, prepare yourself. There are some dead Japs there."

"Jack, thank you for your concern, but I have seen dead soldiers before. I will be fine."

She left without another word and returned about 15 minutes later. Jack noticed she wasn't carrying any equipment. "Where is it?" He asked.

"Destroyed. It looks like all of the equipment had been hit by gunfire," She answered.

"Damn, ok. I was afraid of that. Thanks for checking."

He spent most of the day resting on Blue's orders, of course. He sat by the big fire pit in the village center or on the beach, just watching the waves break. Blue would check on him every hour. Placing her hand on his head, monitoring his condition, and making sure he drank his tea. At several random intervals, she and Palila changed his salve and bandage.

This was Jack's new least favorite thing. Each time a new salve was placed on, it felt like he was getting shot again. Its unrelenting burning sensation was uncomfortable, to say the least. He decided he would much rather drink a bowl of that putrid tea every day for the rest of his life than have his salve replaced ever again.

The people decided a victory celebration was required. During the day, some young men went hunting and had captured a pig, several pythons, and even a few wild chickens. Jack decided he immensely enjoyed barbecue python and began to wonder how he would get it back home.

When they woke the next morning, Jack was surprised to find he was still somewhat full from the celebratory dinner the night before. He sat up slowly, face still hot with fever and his arm throbbing. He gently woke Blue.

"Excuse me, miss, I believe we have a date planned." He said, "Miss, you don't want to keep a charming young man like myself waiting."

Blue just smiled at this and began to stir. They both got up and got ready. Blue had to help Jack tie his shoes and put his belt on.

Chapter 18: The Mountain Path

Jack bent down to pick up his Thompson, then remembered it was empty, and there was nothing to fear. It was just a habit. He left it, leaning against the hut's wall. "Besides, I have my Ka-Bar if we get attacked by any vicious pigs," Jack said to Blue, seeing her face as he wrestled with the habit and decision to leave his weapon behind.

The two left the village along the pilgrimage path, towards the Font of Life. The same route they had taken several days before. Just this time, it was only them. They no longer had their comrades or their worries. Their only goal was to get Jack a little help in healing his wound.

Once the village was out of sight, Blue spoke. "Jack, I was thinking. If the Font doesn't help, maybe Arlas can."

"I was actually thinking the same thing," Jack responded hesitantly.

Blue smiled, glad that they were on the same page, and continued, "Well, being that it was a medical lab, they might have proper cleaning and bandaging materials. Or maybe something else."

"You're probably right. Let's just get there first. Maybe the Font will be enough. I don't know about you, but it seems that those Primori were a little twisted." Jack said wistfully. "I mean, Arlas didn't necessarily say that, but they seemed a little off to me."

"I got that impression also," Blue confirmed. "But I don't think Arlas would purposefully harm us. But I'm also not sure what, if any moral code he was created with."

"What do you mean?"

"Well, he said he was a program created by the Primori. We have to assume they added some level of morality, right? Like a dog owner who teaches his animal to not attack strangers." She stated.

They walked in silence for a little, both lost in thought. When the two reached the gorge, Jack and Blue could see a newly-built bridge. It was actually an improvement over the previous version. It was wider, several logs wider, and included guide ropes about three feet off the ground on either side of the logs. Blue crossed first, then Jack.

Once they reached Abel's grave, Jack again stopped and saluted his fallen friend. "I got them, Abel. I got them." He said, ending his salute.

The trip wasn't taking as long as their last. Not needing to carry Tony, or fight a patrol of japs, or bury a friend, they made substantial, consistent progress. After a while, the jungle again dropped away and was replaced by a sheer rock wall.

"We are getting close," Blue cheered. "There... There it is!"

Chapter 18: The Mountain Path

They walked over to the pool. Jack sat on almost the same spot Tony had been laid on several days before. Jack dunked his canteen in, filled it, and inhaled its contents. Again, he felt energized, like he had just awoken from a deep, restful sleep. Blue then poured some of its contents on Jack's now exposed arm as Blue had removed the bandage without Jack even noticing. It bubbled and hissed, same as Tony's, but the wound didn't close.

"Jack. It didn't work." Blue whimpered. "It didn't."

"Blue, it did what we expected. The wound may still be there, but the fever is gone. Here check." He grabbed Blue's hand and placed it on his forehead, now cool. She gasped. "See."

She sighed in relief, seeing the red, infected edges of the wound gone. "That's great. Now we just need to stitch you up and let it heal naturally." Blue admitted.

"Jackson Miller," an angered voice rang out over the clearing. "Jackson Miller!"

They both spun, looking down the path. It was Akira standing with his katana drawn. A thin line of blood staining his right cheek.

Jack jumped to his feet, pulled his knife, and pushed Blue out of the way. His revitalized body and rush of adrenaline, forcing the pain in his right arm out of his mind.

"Akira, you don't need to do this. You can just leave," Jack shouted, pleading for an outcome that would allow

Blue to walk away, "Just leave this place. Leave while you still can."

"Jackson Miller, you know I can't do that. I am owed your death as payment for the men you have killed," Akira demanded, "I will have what I am owed. Honor demands it."

Akira ran towards Jack, Katana raised over his head. In that instance, Jack felt wildly outgunned. A knife versus a katana, what could he really hope to do. Akira's fierce yell brought him reeling back to the moment.

Just in time, Jack sidestepped the first swing. It just missed his shoulder. Akira slid past, the force of his swing carrying him further forward than he anticipated. Jack lashed out with his knife. The blade made contact with Akira's right side, getting caught slightly as it dragged through his skin and clothes. Blood squirted from the incision.

Akira made no notice that the blow had even landed. He turned around, blade flat, parallel to the ground, and once again, he swung with his full force. Jack ducked, falling to the earth. He rolled away, slicing Akira's right calf, and cupped his injured right arm as he got to his feet. Without missing a beat, Akira swung again.

"Stop! Please. Stop!" Blue yelled in the distance.

Jack just barely managed to block the blow. His knife making contact with Akira's blade. Its handle slippery in his now blood-covered left hand. Although Jack had blocked Akira's strike, it was only enough to slow its momentum.

276

Chapter 18: The Mountain Path

The sword raked across Jack's left thigh, opening a shallow but long cut. Jack dropped to one knee, his knife slipping from his hand.

A second swing was already on its way. Akira wheeling the blade over his head for a decisive blow heading directly for Jack's neck. He lunged at Akira. Closing the distance before the swing could land. Jack punched Akira in his left rib, the same bone that bore the knife wound. Akira winched with each blow and drove the pommel of his Katana into Jack's exposed bullet hole. It sunk about two inches deep.

"Arrgh!" Jack screamed. His vision going red with the pain of it. Jack lost all sense of time. All he could hear was Akira running towards him again. Jack swung his left arm wildly, a fist balled at its end.

Everything just stopped. Akira was by Jack's side, facing him. Jack wasn't moving, immobilized by the damage to his broken body. Something was terribly wrong. Jack could hear Blue yelling only a few feet away, although her voice sounded like it was coming through a tin can. "No, Jack." She gasped.

"Don't worry, you will be next," Akira said, turning towards Blue.

For the first time, Jack noticed Akira's Katana was buried in his stomach up to the hilt. His mind racing to understand what that meant. He didn't feel pain. He just saw the sword. As Akira withdrew the blade, Jack fell forwards on to the cold, indifferent earth, a wave of understanding washing over him, and with comprehension, came the pain. Excruciating pain.

"You were a worthy enemy Jackson Miller. You deserve a good death." Akira acknowledged as he pulled Jack onto his knees. Jack sat there, wavering unsteadily, head bowed. No longer having the strength to fight back. His pain causing only confusion.

Akira raised his katana above his head, preparing for a deadly swing.

"No, Akira. Please. NOOOOO!" Blue bellowed.

An insidious yell issued from Akira's mouth as he started his powerful swing down towards Jack's neck. His violent intent gleaming from his eyes. "Eikō no shi!"

Crack! A single gunshot rang out. Akira's katana fell, point down. Sticking into the ground just in front of Jack. His face reflected in its mirror-like surface. Blue was still yelling, "Noooooo!"

Unsure of what happened, Jack collapsed to his side. Opening his eyes, he was looking directly into Akira's shocked gaze. The katana stuck in the earth between them. Akira was spitting strings of blood with each breath.

Jack trembling looked toward Blue, only able to move his eyes. She was holding Ruth's revolver in her hands. Its

Chapter 18: The Mountain Path

barrel still smoking from the expelled round. Her face alight with fear and anguish. Now it made sense.

Blue dropped the revolver, her face no longer showing fear but pure revulsion. She ran over to Jack and rolled him onto his back. She pressed hard on his stomach. Attempting to stop the flow of blood. "Blue," Jack managed to say, also spitting blood. "The Font…"

Blue darted to the Font, swiped up the canteen from where it lay, and hastily dunked it into the magical water. As soon as she judged it was full enough, she sprinted back to Jack and poured the contents onto the penetrating stab wound on his stomach. This time, it had no effect.

"Blue... Arl..." Jack spat.

"Yes, Jack. Stay with me. I'll get you to him." Blue cried as she began locating the symbols. Attempting to remember the correct sequence. As she began to press them, the stone wall vibrated. Jack could hear her, "What have I done? What have I done?"

The wall vibrated violently with the final stone, and Jack knew she got the anti-chamber open. His body racked with pain as Blue began pulling both men into the small cave towards the inner door.

Jack opened his mouth to question what Blue was doing, but only a gurgling sound emerged. Akira apparently attempted to do the same, with the same results.

Blue pressed the small green button. Again, a mechanical sound emanated from the walls, the light switch to red, and smoke issued from the ceiling. The light then switched to white, and the door opened. She dragged both men into the Lab.

"Hello, I am Arlas, and welcome to the Laboratory," A familiar voice said.

"Arlas, Help!"

Chapter 19: Atonement

"What has happened?" Arlas asked curiously without a hint of urgency as he watched Blue dragging the two men.

"A battle. They're wounded. The Font won't heal them. They're almost dead. Arlas, do something," Blue shouted. "Do something!"

"Well, since you were here last, I have been analyzing the Fonts properties. I am pretty sure we can improve it exponentially. But…" Arlas started to say but was cut off by a now desperate Blue.

"But what, Arlas?" She grunted as she continued to pull the heavy men towards the center of the room.

"But," He continued, "I only predict a 17.3% chance of success, and I am not sure what the side effects will be if successful. Also, we only have one chance. This experiment will drain my remaining backup power, and the Lab will go into shut down within minutes."

"If we do nothing, they will certainly die." Blue wheezed with the effort of dragging the two men. Both of whom were still gurgling blood with each shallow breath.

"Very well, bring them into test chamber one." Arlas said as a metallic door slid open," However, you need to hurry. Once you are able to drag both men into the chamber, I will need to begin immediately or risk running out of power before the procedure can be completed. Meaning, you too, will also be subjected to the experiment as well."

"I don't care, just do it," Blue grunted as she continued to pull both men across the grated metal floor. Their boots and belts making clinking sounds that echoed around the large, open room.

Blue reached the test chamber whose door was opened. She pulled Jack in first. Then Akira, with what little strength she had left. "Your job... save lives... not..." was all Jack could hear her saying as she struggled to pull Akira past the door. The moment Akira's boot crossed the threshold, the door closed and latched tight with a heavy metallic thud. Blue collapsed against the side of the chamber in pure exhaustion.

Chapter 19: Atonement

Arlas pressed several buttons on the console just opposite the test chamber door. His voice came over the intercom. "The experiment will begin in three, two, one."

Pressure in the room began to quickly change. Jack's ears popped. The chamber then began filling with a green gas emanating from vents in the chamber's ceiling. Arlas' voice once again came over the intercom. "Be sure to breathe that in. It is the modified base serum two, based on the Font's properties."

Jack's breathing had become slow, weak, almost non-existent, but the gas began filling his lungs. The change happened suddenly. From a slight itch to an intense burning as if molten lava had been poured down his throat. Uncontrollable coughing caused him to take deeper, more painful breaths, inhaling even more of the toxic fumes.

His panic rose as he and Blue began vomiting violently. She started spitting wildly, mucus exploding from her mouth and nose. Jack could see her clutching her throat in terror. The whites of her eyes turning a dark, blood red. Akira started to convulse. His body shaking with such force, blood squirted from the bullet wound on his side as he too vomited wildly. Then the lights in the chamber changed from white to a bright red.

The light was heat, terrible heat. So much heat that Jack thought his body was going to melt and his bones catch on fire. He could see Blue began to convulse out of the corner of his eyes. Then he started as well. The gas, the heat, it was all too much. His vision started fading out. Just before he lost consciousness, he felt three distinct jolts as if he had been hit by white-hot lightning. His muscles contracting painfully with each hit. Then it all went black.

Jack wasn't sure how long he was out for. He wasn't sure if he was even still alive. All he remembered was the pain. Slowly, he began to regain consciousness, his eyes fluttering open. The pain faded quickly as he regained control of his mind and body. He sat up slowly and looked around the small cylindrical test chamber. Akira was lying on the ground, just in front of the metal door. Blue was leaning against one of the beds in the center of the room, unmoving.

All of the green smoke was gone, and the light had returned to its original white color. Jack stood and strode over to Blue, noticing for the first time that his right arm was working again. He cautiously inspected it with his left hand. To his surprise, the wound was closed entirely. He checked his stomach, then leg. To his astonishment, they were all completely healed. The pain only a memory now.

"Blue," Jack said gently as he softly shook her. "Blue, wake up."

Blues eyes shot open, and she jumped to her feet, taking in a deep breath of clean air. "Jack? What? How?" She faltered. "You're ok!"

"Yes," he chuckled. "I'm better than ok. I feel great! What about you?"

Chapter 19: Atonement

Blue stood for a moment pondering the question. Jack knew she was doing a mental inventory of her body. Checking for any differences between now and before. "Yeah, I feel great!" She finally announced as she lunged at him. Pulling him into a deep embrace. An embrace that summed up all her thoughts and feelings. They stood, holding each other for a long, long moment.

"Akira," she gasped, seeing him get to his feet as she released Jack. "Akira?"

Jack pushed Blue behind him. He was ready for a fight. And now that neither of the men had weapons, Jack was sure the odds were squarely on his side. His muscles tightened with anticipation, ready for the upcoming violence. He felt powerful. Alive.

"Jackson Miller..." Akira stated, then trailed off, apparently lost in thought of what just transpired. Visually inspecting his now healed body. "You have nothing to fear from me." He finished.

"Yeah, right." Jack shot back.

"The debt has been paid. You died. I died. The debt is paid." Akira said with a finality that Jack knew he had nothing to fear. Jack lowered his fists. "In fact, I now owe this young lady for saving my life. A life for a life. What would you have me do?

"Leave this place in peace. And never come back." Blue blurted out before giving it a moment's thought.

Akira bowed. "On the bushido code, I will leave this island in peace and never come back. On my honor."

"Before you do, can you answer a question for me?" Jack said as a count down in the background announced, "Three minutes remaining, please evacuate the Laboratory."

"Yes," Akira acknowledged.

"How did you get out of the pit? It's obvious you survived the fall, and it didn't look like you had any holes from the spikes. What happened?" Jack asked.

"I fell, hitting the ground hard, then my men landed on the spikes, mostly covering me up. When I saw you checking on us, I played dead. A simple deception. Thinking that you would just leave, believing we were all dead. But then you pulled out your pistol. I thought you were out of ammo." Akira stated.

"No, I just needed you to believe that so you and your men would follow me."

"I see."

"Two minutes remaining, please evacuate the Laboratory." The voice announced as the test chamber door opened. All three stepped out as Arlas looked on.

"When you started shooting, I just continued to play dead. With the near-miss to my head," Akira pointed to the now healed graze, "You knocked me out. I woke up this morning, used my now dead man's body, and climbed out.

Chapter 19: Atonement

Not being sure what to do next, I headed back to our camp, just outside the village. That is when I saw you and her here heading up the mountain path."

"So, you followed?" Jack asked.

"Yes, I was furious. Bushido demanded vengeance. I was just able to catch up to you as you reached that pool." Akira finished looking around the Lab for the first time. "What is this place? And who is that?" He ended looking at Arlas for the first time.

"It's a long story," Jack stated, not sure how much he wanted to tell Akira.

"Please, you all need to leave. The Lab will go into lock-down in 90 seconds." Arlas stated." Please go. The door will close behind you."

"What will happen to you?" Blue asked hesitantly.

"I will be destroyed along with the Lab," Arlas stated without a hint of fear.

"Anything we can do to save you?" Blue pleaded. "Please, Arlas, we have lost too much already."

"Yes. I can download my program to a data crystal. It will take 60 seconds to complete. This door will open once the download is finished." Arlas pointed at a small metal door in the center console. "Take the red crystal and go. From my calculation, you will only have ten seconds to grab my data crystal and exit the Lab before lock-down starts."

"I will do it. You two wait outside, by the Font." Jack ordered. They obeyed but not before Akira took one last long look around the Lab. "Arlas, what will happen to the Font when the lab is gone?"

"Well, the groundwater is thoroughly contaminated, and the radioactive materials have leached into the surrounding rock. I predict the Font will continue to produce its healing effects for several more centuries before the radioactive half-life has completed."

"60 seconds remaining, please evacuate the Laboratory." The announcement proclaimed again.

"Almost done?" Jack asked.

"Yes, soon I will disappear. Grab the red crystal as soon as the door opens. You will need to run," Arlas said as he disappeared.

"30 seconds remaining, please evacuate the Laboratory."

Jack stood, waiting for the small door to open, the remaining seconds stretching into what felt like hours. Jack could hear Blue yelling, "Hurry," from outside the anti-chamber.

"15 seconds remaining, please evacuate the Laboratory." The announcement proclaimed again.

Jack stood, looking fixedly at the small door. It slid open with a whirling sound. Jack grabbed the red crystal; it was the size of a soda can, bigger than he expected. He then ran frantically towards the Laboratories' outer door.

Jack noticed he was running faster than he ever had before crossing the inner door, then the outer door in the space of a second. Both slamming shut as he passed. A few seconds later, they felt it. The mountain, no, the island, shook violently as the Lab went into lock-down and incinerated all of its contents.

Once the earth stopped shaking, Akira bent down and picked up his Katana. Jack was worried that the sincere surrender was just a ruse until he had a position of advantage. But he was soon proven wrong. Akira returned the blade to its sheath after wiping Jack's blood from its glinting blade.

Akira then dropped to a knee and presented Blue with the weapon. "Please, take this as a token of my promise."

Nobody moved. Blue looked at Jack. He nodded his head in agreement. She reached out and grabbed the weapon by its sheath, close to the hilt. "Thank you," was all she managed to say back.

"What are you planning to do, Akira?" Jack questioned.

"Jackson Miller, I plan on leaving this place like I promised," Akira answered

"How? Your sub is gone, and I'm pretty sure your little life-raft got caught in the explosion."

"I noticed your lifeboat was still beached on the coral. Is that true?"

"Last time I checked," Jack responded, "but how did you know that?"

"After our patrol did not return as expected, we sent out scouts. One located your camp the next morning but was ordered to not engage. By the time they reported back, and we were able to make our way back in force, you were already gone. We followed your tracks until we reached the rocky outcropping and then used it to spot the village. We assumed you headed that way, and we followed. By the time we reached the village, it appeared everyone had gone to sleep. We decided to fall back and observe. The next morning, we saw the five of you heading up the path and decided it was time to strike."

"I see," Jack said. "Why didn't you attack the village that night, when we were all asleep, helpless?"

"The Art of War tells us that if you know the enemy and know yourself, you need not fear the result of a hundred battles. If you know yourself but not the enemy, for every victory gained, you will also suffer a defeat... I did not know who my enemy was" Akira confirmed.

Chapter 19: Atonement

Jack just stared into Akira's eyes, trying to understand the man, who up until a few moments ago, he considered his enemy.

"The lifeboat..." Akira prodded. "Do you mind if I take it? I will venture out into the open ocean, and if it finds me worthy, it will deliver me back to my people." Akira announced.

Seeing as they had a way off the island, Jack agreed. "On one condition."

"What's that?" Akira questioned.

"Leave the villagers in peace. And don't let them see you. They believe you are dead. We should keep it that way," Jack commanded.

Akira bowed. "Can you do something for me?" He asked.

"Depends on what it is..." Jack said back, resolutely.

"Bury my men. I was only able to lay those five from the patrol to rest." Akira admitted. "Please, Jack, don't leave them to be defiled by the jungle."

"I can do that, Akira," He conceded.

"Before I leave, what was this place," Akira asked hesitantly. "How was it able to do what it did? I mean, it brought us back to life."

"It's kinda hard to explain and even harder to believe," Jack admitted. "Long story short, it was an alien laboratory."

"What do you mean... was?"

"Well, it has just been destroyed. That's what all that shaking was. The Lab is completely gone. Arlas called it lock-down procedures. It's meant to destroy the Lab and any of its contaminants so that they don't get released into this world." Jack finished trying to paraphrase Arlas as accurately as possible.

It was clear Akira didn't understand. Jack was pretty sure he didn't either, but Arlas was as good as his word on the matter. "Ok," was all Akira managed. "Goodbye. I predict we shall not see each other again."

And with that, Akira bowed and headed down the path, vanishing into the jungle.

"Ready to head back to the village, Blue?" Jack asked, smiling confidently.

"Yes, absolutely," Blue smiled back. "Oh, did you get Arlas?"

Jack pulled the red crystal from his pocket. "He's right here. Although, I have no idea what we will do with him."

"Me either, but at least we saved something."

Chapter 19: Atonement

"Why did you save Akira?" Jack questioned. "I mean, he was our enemy. And after what he did to Ruth, he deserved to die."

"Yes, he did deserve it. But not at my hands," Blue admitted. "Jack, I would have never been able to live with what I had done. I'm not sure I will ever get over it. I mean, I meant to kill him, to save you. But I couldn't..." She trailed off.

"I understand, Blue."

She handed Jack Akira's Katana. "I don't want this, knowing what it has done."

Jack wasn't sure why he took it. Maybe it was a token to remember the horrors of this place, or perhaps it was closure. Either way, he reached up and gently took it out of Blue's out-stretched hand.

They walked down the pilgrimage path, towards the village. Hearts lighter than they had been in weeks. The bright colors of the jungle standing in stark relief against the green shrubbery. Jack could smell the distant salty ocean air. He could hear the buzzing of insects from within the jungle itself.

"Blue, does anything seem different to you?" Jack inquired uncertainly.

"Yes, everything seems... more," She answered. "Colors are brighter, smells more intense. Sounds more clear. It's like all of my senses are dialed up. Heightened."

"Yeah, ok. Mine too. I also noticed I was running faster than I ever could as I exited the Lab. It's kinda like the rejuvenation effect of the Font, but also somehow different."

"Well, Arlas said there might be side effects," Blue remarked. "I just wish we could ask him about it."

"Maybe someday we will figure out how to get him out of that crystal," Jack noted. "Until then, I am just glad we are alive."

They made it back to the village just as dusk fell. The villagers were astonished to see Jack fully healed. They all dropped to the ground, chanting. Palila explained they were thanking the Font for saving Jack.

"Jack, why do you have that sword?" Palila asked incredulously, "That's the Japanese Captain's weapon."

"Yes, it was." Jack stated. "We found it by the Font."

"Do you think he is still out there?" Palila asked, worry lines forming on her forehead.

"No, I am sure he is no more," Jack said, trying not to explain too much of what had happened. "You have nothing to worry about. We are safe. The island is safe. "He finished wanting her to know everything was ok.

Chapter 19: Atonement

Palila just looked at Jack. He could tell that she knew he was holding back. But like all the other times, she let it go. "Ok, Jack."

"Right. Palila, I am starving." Jack announced. "Any of that pig left from last night?"

Palila chuckled, her face lighting up with her warm motherly smile. "Yes, there is plenty. Eat."

Chapter 20: The Way Home

After another night of celebration, this time for Jack's miraculous good health. Jack and Blue slept on the beach. Falling asleep to the soft sound of the waves and the cool ocean mist. Jack had the best night's sleep he could have ever remembered. Again, dreaming of that small villa on the hill and the green grassy pasture with his future family.

The next morning, he woke early and took a quiet, peaceful stroll around the village. They had a lot of work to do to set things right and several days to do so. The trading crew wouldn't be back with the outrigger for another few days—just enough time to repair the damage.

Jack saw Palila, sitting next to the fire pit, and strolled over towards her. "Good sunrise Jack. How did you sleep?"

Chapter 20: The Way Home

She asked, as maternal as ever. Jack could tell she was happy to be in the village. Back in her home.

"Great, thank you," Jack reported. "Actually, Palila, it was the best night sleep I have ever had."

She beamed at him with that now-familiar look of understanding. As if Jack had finally discovered the magic of this place. It wasn't the Font that made the island special. It was its people and their love of peace. It was the trees, the ocean, animals, and beaches. It was its life that made it a gift. Nothing more. And certainly nothing less.

"Palila, I need some equipment," Jack said quickly, feeling a little abashed by Palila's knowingly stares. "Namely a shovel."

"What for?" Palila asked, surprised by the question.

"I need to go bury the Japanese dead," Jack answered. "Before they can spoil. We need to be certain diseases can't spread. Just to be safe," Jack finished quickly.

"Ok, Jack," Palila said with a tone that made Jack sure she knew he wasn't entirely forthcoming. "Would you like some help?"

"Yeah, that would be great. It would take several days if I had to do it alone, and by the look of things, we have plenty of other work to do."

Palila called over several of the young villagers and explained the situation to them. They all nodded in agreement and ran to get several shovels. "They will follow you and do as you say."

"But I don't speak your language... And I'm pretty sure they don't speak English."

"So many worries, Jack. Have no worries. I informed them of the work that needs to be completed. They will follow your lead."

"Great, um, thanks," Jack said. "Let me go wake Blue and tell her the plan, then we can go. Sound good?"

"Yes, Jack. Sounds good." Palila beamed.

He walked back to the beach, where Blue was still lying asleep, and woke her. He explained that he was heading into the jungle to fulfill his promise to Akira. "It might take a day or two, lots of ground to cover."

"Ok, Jack. I will stay here and help them put the village back in order." Blue remarked. They kissed, and Jack jogged back to the young men. They grabbed a few needed supplies and headed into the jungle.

He took the villagers to their first stop; it was the foxholes overlooking their own village. He could see the disquiet in their eyes. Knowing danger had been so close. The three dead Japs lay precisely where they had fallen only a short few days ago. They were swollen, bloated from the heat. Jack pushed each of them into their respective foxholes, and the villagers quickly covered them up. They made sure to fill all the remaining foxholes, returning the earth to its natural state.

Their next stop was Snake Canyon. The group passed the clearing where Kenny had fallen. The villagers shuttered as they peered down into the chamber. The eel glided wickedly along the water's surface below. This was too much for the young men. Jack witnessed as they chopped down several trees and made a makeshift cover for the hole. Apparently, they didn't want anyone to fall in ever again.

When they reached Snake Canyon, Jack entered from its southern end and showed the villagers the now obliterated Jap camp. The bonfire meant to destroy the rifles also caught the tarp roof ablaze, leaving nothing behind. The villagers dug one large pit and, one by one deposited the dead Japanese into it. They once again covered the bodies with a thick layer of earth.

Jack made a short detour on their way to the spike pits. Once they had left Snake Canyon, Jack stopped to pay his respects to Tony's grave. He kneeled; head bowed. The young men looked questioningly at Jack. "Tony," was all he needed to say. The villagers did likewise. They started chanting in sync like they did at the funeral pyre many nights ago. After a moment, they all stood and continued on.

Dark was once again falling over the jungle. Jack and the young men made a small fire. They proved to be just as efficient as the girls had been. One of them even producing a rather large, tropical-looking bird for dinner. After removing the feathers and internal organs, they cooked it over the open flame. They ate and laughed. Its tender, dark meat filling their bellies and lightening the mood. Once all was done, they slept.

The next morning, they made their way to the pits. The group first filled in the empty one. Not wanting a future villager to fall in and hurt themselves. Then, they made their way to the pit containing the two impaled Japs. Standing by its edge, reflecting on the job Jack had done for the people, they buried them. Covering the small crater in its entirety.

Once satisfied that the job was done, they headed back to the village. Light-hearted conversation crept up between the villagers. And, Although Jack didn't know what they were saying, he understood its jovial intent. He laughed when they laughed, and he smiled when they smiled. With the gruesome job completed, they could all turn their attention to more important matters.

For some reason, they received a hero's welcome when they returned to the village. Palila must have told the others of their noble endeavors. The enterprise in which they had endured to ensure the village remain safe, disease-free.

Jack and Blue spent the next several days helping the people repair their village. Undoing the damage their presence had caused. They started with the huts. Each day making remarkable progress. By the time the outrigger had returned, there was not a single piece of evidence that anything nefarious had happened.

Chapter 20: The Way Home

Palila introduced Jack and Blue to the group and explained the events that had happened since they set off for Tahiti. When Palila recounted the village's attack, they grew stoic, then chanted that same lament for their fallen friends and family. When she had finished telling the entire events, the trading crew turned to Jack and Blue and bowed, one arm pressed across their chests. A profoundly respectful bow, Palila informed them. Just then, Masina came running over and embraced one of the young men. Apparently, this was the man she was to be bonded with.

Jack helped them unload the outrigger, now docked and anchored safely to the beach. It was, in fact, an imposing vessel. The people again threw a celebration, this time for the safe return of their crew. Jack was beginning to think these celebrations happened frequently. The people having so much to be grateful for.

He wanted to ask when they could expect to be taken to Tahiti. As much as he liked staying with the people, he had a responsibility to get back. He decided he would ask Palila the following morning.

During the celebration, they ate and sung, danced and laughed. About midway through, Palila asked for everyone's attention and said something in their foreign language. The only thing Jack could make out was the name "Masina." As soon as Palila finished, the village went wild! Jack had a guess as to what the excitement was about.

"Palila, what did you say?" Blue asked.

"Masina has agreed to be bonded with Lagi," She said, beaming. "Between you and me, I think the events of the past few suns have put her life in perspective. She is ready to take the step in her next big journey. Will you stay for the bonding?"

Jack was glad she brought this up. It was the perfect segue into their return home. "Palila, we should really be getting back." He started. "We have responsibilities waiting for us."

"Please Jack, stay. Lagi will be needed to take you to Tahiti. That would cause a delay in their bonding. Please stay and enjoy our hospitality just a little longer." Palila pleaded.

"Jack, I think we should stay. They have done so much for us. It's only right we don't prolong the bonding. We have already interfered in their lives enough." Blue admitted. "Besides a few more days shouldn't matter. From what I can tell, you have already done your part in the war. That submarine, nor its crew, will sink any more American ships."

Seeing Blue's point, he conceded. "Alright, we will stay. But once the bonding is completed, will we be able to go?"

"Yes, absolutely. And I am sure we can even convince Masina to go with her new husband as well." Palila chuckled knowingly.

Chapter 20: The Way Home

Now that everything was settled, Jack and Blue helped prepare the village for the upcoming ceremony. They gathered fruits and nuts from the jungle. Jack joined Lagi and the other young men and a ritualistic hunt for pigs. Several of the village chickens had been slaughtered for the feast. Additionally, the lines of drying fish sagged under the weight of their bounty. The day before the ceremony, Palila pulled Jack aside.

"Jack, it is customary for the girl's father to take the pilgrimage to the Font and gather a cup for the new couple to share once they are bonded. Masina's father died many, many monsoons ago. She has requested that you have the honor of retrieving the water. Would you mind?"

"Not at all." Jack exclaimed. "I would be honored. Is there anything I need to do as part of this ritual?"

"Yes, you must take this container." Palila handed him an ornately carved wooden cylinder. She unscrewed the top, revealing the empty space within its interior. "Fill this cup and return."

"Must I do this alone? Or can Blue come with me?" Jack asked.

"You must do this alone. But don't worry, Blue will be helping Masina prepare as one of her honored sisters. Along with Lulu and Fetia." Palila confirmed.

"Right, I will go now. To be back before dark."

The Fountain of Youth

Jack once again took the pilgrimage. Again, pausing and saluting at Abel's grave. Once he reached the Font, he filled the ornate cup, sealing the magical water inside. Before leaving, Jack placed his hand on the rock wall and said: "Thank you."

The trip back to the village had become familiar—the sights and sounds of the path welcoming. The jungle quietly humming with all its various life forms. Jack made it back to the village well before dark. His invigorated body making quick work of the distance.

The next morning came like many before. Only today was the bonding ceremony. If Jack had thought the village had celebrated before, he was utterly wrong. This was like nothing he had seen.

They had various types of drums beating all day. Multi-course meals were planned and spaced out at particular intervals. Matching the tide or time of day. They danced and danced until some of the village children passed out from exhaustion. Other villagers just laughed and moved them to a safe spot to not get trampled with the ever-escalating excitement.

As the sun was setting, the villagers gathered around the bonfire, now fully lit. Masina and Lagi standing in front of Palila, holding hands, and Palila spoke. When she finished, they tied a thin vine around their clasped hands. At this, the villagers went crazy, yelling, and hooting. Jack and Blue shared a look. With that, they knew the ceremony was completed. The party went on well into the night.

Chapter 20: The Way Home

When dawns rays broke the darkness, the party had finally wound down. Jack and Blue returned to their hut, holding hands along the way. "You know, someday that will be us." Blue announced.

"I know. Once this war is over." Jack responded.

"Maybe it is. We have been away for a while now." Blue remarked.

"I hope so. I think I have had enough of it already."

They laid down on the now-familiar thin wooden mats, each on their side, looking into each other's eyes. And eventually fell asleep.

The following day, Jack decided he would verify that Akira had kept his word about leaving. Blue seeing the opportunity to walk on miles of beautiful, pristine beach, agreed to join him. They frequently stopped to rest, eat, or even investigate the unique shells that had washed onshore. When they reached the coral outcropping, they discovered that Akira was indeed true to his word. The lifeboat was gone.

Jack could see many recent footprints littering the sand. "Akira must have only been able to leave a day or so ago," Jack confirmed.

"Really? Why do you think he waited so long?" Blue asked.

"If I had to guess, I would say for a few reasons."

"Like what?"

"Well, he needed to gather enough food and potable water to last, probably several days, if not weeks. Then he needed to construct a small shelter inside the boat."

"Like we did?"

"Yes, just better. I mean, he had plenty of material to do so. And I think he was waiting for the tide to change to help dislodge the lifeboat from the coral. But that is just my guess," Jack answered.

With this last item checked off his list, Jack could truly leave the island in peace. Without needing to worry about its safety or future. They headed back to the village, satisfied.

After a few more normal days at the village, nothing significant had happened since the bonding. Palila informed them that tomorrow the traders would again be leaving and that Masina would be traveling with them.

Jack got excited, then despondent. This island had become a kind of home, and even though he had known deep despair within its confines, he also found great joy. Jack was heartbroken to be leaving its beautiful shores and heading back into the dangers of war. However, this island had taught him a lot about who he was and what he was capable of.

On the morning of their departure, the entire village lined up on the beach. As Jack and Blue boarded the outrigger, now anchored in the bay, the villagers began to sing. It was a cheerful tone that made them both smile.

Lagi pulled the anchor on board, dropped the giant triangle sail, and they set off. Heading back into the world they knew, away from this magical place.

Chapter 21: Story Teller's Conclusion

Zandar sat in stunned silence as Jack reached over and disabled the recording device. Its red light diminishing with the completion of its task. Jack had recounted his entire tale. The Story was complete.

"So, what did you think?" Jack asked as Zandar sat, trying to comprehend the Story he had just documented. It was indeed a unique tale.

"Well, Jack," Zandar said slowly, not sure how he wanted to proceed. He had questions, absolutely he did, but needed a minute to gather his thoughts. "It was very unique.

Jack, I'm going to need a few minutes to review and prepare my questions."

"Perfectly understandable, Zandar. Before we get to your questions, do you mind if someone joins us?" Jack asked politely. "I am sure you will want to meet them."

"Not at all. Please have them join us." Zandar responded as he was gathering up his handwritten notes. "Would it also be possible to order some..." He checked the time on his DigiCard, "breakfast it would appear."

"Yes, let's," Jack chuckled as he pressed a key on his DigiCard and said into it, "We are ready... Oh, did I wake you?" He paused as the person on the other end responded. "No, ok, good. Please join us." Another pause. "Yes, at the usual table." He pressed a key ending the call and another to pull up a holovid menu. It appeared between the two men.

"No need for me to see the menu. Please order what you believe is best," Zandar said, deferring the meal choice to Jack so that he could focus all this thought on the Story he just heard.

Jack flicked off the menu and ordered three Syrtharion omelets. The meals arrived just as a beautiful young woman approached. She had pale white skin, the color of fresh snow, deep almond brown eyes, and straight brown hair with faint red highlights. Zandar knew instantly who this was.

"Blue, meet Zandar," Jack announced as he introduced the two. "Zandar, meet Blue."

"So nice to meet you," Zandar said, "Although I feel like I already know you."

"So nice to meet you as well," Blue beamed as she placed a long rectangle case on the table, being sure not to disturb the omelets and sat next to Jack. "Ooo, I love Syrtharion omelets. I find that pink eggs just seem to taste better." She announced gleefully.

"What's in the case?" Zandar asked.

"Gifts," Blue said, continuing to smile. "For you."

"You will see. Let's eat before you get started with the questions, I know you have." Jack finished.

They again ate in silence, showing deference toward Zandar's culture. Jack had become hungry, the telling of the tale more draining than he expected. The emotional toll was also hard to bear. He had been carrying around those memories for a long time, unable to let go. With the Story recounted, he felt a measure of closure. He had kept his promise to Abel.

Soon they all had completed their omelets, ready for the next and final phase of the process. "I assume you have your questions ready?" Jack solicited.

"Yes, I have many. I think it would be best to start with the first and most obvious question. When did the events in this Story take place? I mean, how long ago." Zandar corrected himself, knowing that Jack had stated it took place in 1943 according to his planets calendar. Zandar just wasn't sure how that date related to the current time.

"Well, that's definitely a good question. And the right place to start. Like I said at the beginning of the tale, it was the year 1943 on Earth. For Blue and I," He paused in trepidation. This being the first time they had revealed their secret to anyone, "that was 152,303 years ago, according to how years are measured on Earth. Which I also outlined at the start of the Story." Jack stated, staring directly into Zandar's violet eyes.

"Jack, that... That can't be right. Based on your description, an Earth year is very similar to a year on many other habitable planets. Are you saying you are over 150 thousand years old?" Zandar said, almost laughing with the ridiculousness of the claim.

Jack shared a quick look with Blue as if they were sharing a thought. "Yes, we are," Jack responded, looking back at Zandar, re-establishing eye contact with him.

"Jack, forgive me for my disbelief, but that's simply not possible." Was all Zander could say back. To him, 150 thousand years of life was unfathomable. Just as his species 1000-year life span was unfathomable for many others.

"Trust us, Zandar, it is," Blue answered as she opened the case and began rummaging around. "But we don't expect you to fully believe us without proof. Which we have for you."

"But you still look like you are in your prime…" Zandar whispered. "Have you aged at all since then?"

"Well, it is possible. But hard to tell," Jack mused. "Blue, you're the expert in this area. What do you think?"

"If I had to guess," Blue started too explained, then stopped to think, then started again. "If you compare us to a normal human life, we have only aged a year or two in all this time."

Zandar's jaw dropped. Jack smiled. He was always surprised by how so many different alien species expressed emotions in the same physical ways. "How long do you expect your lives to last?" Zandar asked in wonder.

"Eons." Jack answered in a distant tone. Zandar could see Jack's thoughts reaching across the deep well of time.

"Well, I'm going to need a way to authenticate that before I can include it in the Stories footnotes," Zandar remarked, collecting himself.

"Yes, I understand. Just one moment, Blue has what you need." Jack responded.

Just then, Blue pulled out a small, clear case. It contained a metallic necklace of some sort. Jack took it from Blue, peered into its contents solemnly, then passed the case to Zander. He examined the small container and gasped, almost dropping the box in shock.

"Jack, why do those metal tabs have a name on it?" Zandar asked hesitantly. "And why is it a name I recognize?"

"Those were Abel's dog tags. The ones I took from him just before I buried him. You can use the metal to carbon date them. That will verify our age." Jack proclaimed.

"Jack, are you sure you want me to have this?" Zandar asked, now understanding the precious treasure he had been given.

"Yes, Abel's memory will live on in the Story now. Once you have dated those dog tags, please hang them in the Hall of Records." Jack said solemnly. "I promised him I would never forget, and I never have. Not in all this time."

"Of course. Any objects associated with a story will be memorialized alongside the original data crystal." Zandar stated, but he knew Jack already understood this fact.

"Was that your only question, Zandar?" Blue prodded.

"No. No. I have many more. Was it the experiment in the Primori lab that caused your long life?"

"Yes, at least it is the only plausible answer for it. Arlas said there would be side effects." Blue stated.

"Arlas miscalculated." Jack cut in, "He was running his analysis of the Font's properties against the Primori genome, not human. With all that has been discovered about the Primori, we know that their genome was far more advanced and complicated than humans — as well as most other current species — Only the Tricarion genome even comes close. So, his calculations for exponential improvement had an even greater impact on us."

"Were there any other side effects, other than, well, basically immortality?"

"We are not immortal. We can and will die someday. But yes, there were several other side effects." Jack answered. "All of our senses got enhanced as if dialed up too maximum. Like our very DNA had been improved to the utmost limit of the human genome. We are faster, stronger, and heal almost instantly from any wound."

"That's some side effects. How much have they improved?" Zandar asked. "Compared to a 'normal' human, that is."

"That depends," Jack answered. "Our senses and physical attributes are only two to three times more than an average human would be. You see, we are restricted by our biological makeup. For instance, our strength can only be pushed as far as the human body will allow our muscle fibers to be conditioned. Same with our vision. We are limited to the human eye's ability to perceive sight. While our brain can adapt and sometimes overcome our physical limitations, it can only push them so far. "

Chapter 21: Story Teller's Conclusion

"There are far stronger and far more perceptive species in the galaxy," Blue stated. "Species whose physical makeup or mental acuity allow them far greater access to abilities. Just none have the healing factor we have been given. None know the pain of everlasting life." She finished as her eyes began to water.

"What do you mean, pain?" Zandar asked, clearly shaken by Blue's emotional state. "Wouldn't living forever be a gift? I know so many species, so many individuals who would give anything to live forever."

"Let's be clear, it isn't a gift," Jack announced in a commanding tone. For the first time, Zandar saw the ferocity emerging from Jack's calm persona. The flash of anger in his eyes was frightening. "All we have known, for thousands of years, is death."

"We have watched so many loved ones pass away. All the time, we are powerless to do anything about it. Our friends come and go so quickly, in a blink of an eye. And while they can move on from the pain of this life, we are only able to stand witness." Blue admitted. "Unable to join them. Unable to move into the next life. We are trapped. Our only consolation is we have each other."

"By telling your Story, aren't you worried others will attempt to gain immortality?" Zandar asked after a long silence.

"No," Jack confirmed quickly as if he was waiting for the questions. "It is impossible. We have spent many lifetimes trying to understand what happened to us and are confident it can't be replicated."

"What makes you so sure?" Zandar shot back. "I am sure people will try once the story is published."

"Well, a few reasons." Jack started. "First, no one knows what was in the base Primori compound that as used in the experiment. All records of that have been lost to time. And if it took the Primori centuries to simply produce the base serum, what hope does anyone alive now have?"

"I see your point. What about Arlas? Didn't you save him?"

"Once we were able to re-access Arlas, we had him delete any data related to the experiment and the compound. We realized the temptation would be too much and needed to remove it."

"What else? You said a few reasons," Zandar prodded.

"Second, we don't even know what Arlas did to us. Besides the compound. He flooded the chamber with radiation, chemicals, and various forms of power. Since he also deleted that procedure, he isn't even sure."

"Go on."

"Lastly, everything we have learned about the Primori makes us believe that humans and Primori are more alike than any other two species in the galaxy. As if humans were the reincarnation of the Primori themselves."

"I'm not sure I follow," Zandar said.

"Our genome is very similar to the Primori, albeit much simpler. But definitely similar. As if the Primori caused human life to evolve on Earth," Blue said, a little distant with the thought of it. "We have done more research and have come much closer to the Primori than any other beings. There is evidence to prove it, but it is our best theory."

"Why would they do that?" Zandar asked.

"Their species was dying, and they knew it," Jack answered. "We believe they saw the primates on our planet and introduced a little of the Primori DNA. So that they would live on. Humans were the result."

"I'm still not sure I follow," Zandar hesitated.

"The Primori were a conceited race. They thought nothing for lesser life forms. They only believed in their right to exist, and it shows in everything they ever did. The Primori legacy was destruction, just like humans. I think Blue and I are the cosmic balance to all of that death. A way for the universe to balance the scales."

"Let me get this straight... The compound and experiment are completely destroyed. All memory of them erased. Besides that, it would only have worked on humans?"

"Yes," Blue confirmed.

"What would have happened if you weren't human?" Zandar questioned.

"We would have died. Our bodies, our genome, unable to withstand the change. At least that is what our research has shown us." Blue responded.

"Well, then, you got lucky."

"Not at all, Zandar." Blue cut in. "There was another negative effect. Jack and I are unable to produce offspring. We were given everlasting life but at the cost of not being able to bring new life into this universe." Jack grabbed Blue's hand and squeezed. After all these years, it was still a difficult topic to discuss.

After a moment of silence that Zander felt the two had earned for what they have given up. He asked his next question. "The world war your planet was involved in, who won?"

"We did. Well, our country and its allies. The war lasted another year or so after we returned. Once it was over, we all started to rebuild our lives. Enemies became allies, allies became enemies. But our world was at peace for a time." Jack answered.

Chapter 21: Story Teller's Conclusion

"So, you did return?" Zandar asked, latching onto a question that the Story brought about.

Yes, once we reached Tahiti, we were able to contact our nearest base. It was on an island called Samoa, not far away. They came and picked us up. We returned to our duties like we were expected too." Jack said. "Blue ended up at a field hospital on Pavavu. I rejoined my company, now filled with replacements, and served on in many battles, to the war's end. That's when I realized the true effects of Arlas' treatment."

"What do you mean?" Zandar inquired.

"On one of my deployments to Iwo Jima, a particularly devastating battle, I was shot. Shot directly through the heart. I felt the sharp burning sensation and was knocked to the ground. But it only lasted a few seconds. By the time I had even realized it had happened, it was healed. Only a hole and bloodstain on my jacket was evidence it had ever occurred."

"What about the other enhancements of the treatment?" Zandar pointed out.

"Yes, well, those took time to really get used too. I mean, I noticed right away I was faster, and both Blue and I started having increased senses on the island. But it took years for our brain to fully be able to process the changes and make full use of them." Jack explained. "At first, our heightened abilities only showed themselves during intense moments of need. But after a time, we were able to gain full control over them."

"Jack, you know I believe you, but if I am to document it, I will need some way to verify," Zandar remarked hesitantly.

"Yes, quite right. Blue, would you hand me your plasma knife." Jack politely asked. Blue reached down towards her belt and pulled out a thin metallic cylinder, just slightly longer than the width of her palm. She passed it to Jack with a smile.

Jack rolled up the sleeve of his left arm and ignited the blade. It erupted from the hilt, reaching about four and a half inches long. He held his arm out over the table, in clear view of Zandar. The blade hissed and popped as he dragged it over his skin, which began smoking and splitting open wide, in a deep cut. Blood dripped onto Jack's now empty omelet plate.

"Jack, no!" Zandar blurted out before he could stop himself. But just as the words escaped his mouth, the wound healed. The drops of blood the only evidence that it had ever happened. Zandar apologized for his outburst.

"Think nothing of it, Zandar, and thank you for your concern. Hopefully, that was sufficient evidence?" Jack inquired.

"Yes, quite sufficient." Zandar paused for a moment, then decided it was best to continue on with his questions,

Chapter 21: Story Teller's Conclusion

"Why haven't I heard of Humans before today? I mean, it is obvious your people are capable of space travel, or you wouldn't be here."

"Most died a long time ago. You see, Zandar, humans killed our planet."

"Wait, what? How?" Zander cut in. It was unthinkable to hear about a species who was so destructive they took their own planet out.

"Through a runaway greenhouse effect created by man-made carbon emissions. About 1000 years after the war ended, the planet had become completely uninhabitable. By that time, humans had several colonies in nearby star systems. But most humans died on Earth, about 120 billion of them. Blue and I were lucky to have been on a colony world at the time. With about five million others." Jack explained. "That was all that was left of the human race. Five million souls."

"Zandar," Blue cut in. "You might have seen other humans but not have even known it. Most have forgotten where they came from originally. Earth is just part of their myths anymore. And most don't even look like we do. Their different worlds have changed them. Skin and eye pigmentation have adapted to different color suns and atmospheres. Gravity morphing their sizes. Even the food and water they consumed changed them over this length of time. If you examined their DNA, we would share a good amount, but they have evolved into many different subspecies. And because of our own DNA enhancements, one could argue that no true humans remain."

"Us three are the last remnants of what humanity was, at least in physical appearance," Jack said in response to Blue's analysis.

"You two, and I am assuming Akira?" Zander probed. "I mean, he got hit with the same treatment as you."

"Yes, Akira is alive and well," Jack admitted.

"So, he was enhanced, just as you and Blue were? And you know where he is?"

"Yes." Jack confirmed.

"And? For the footnotes." Zandar stated.

Jack hesitated for a minute. "Zandar, you might not want to include this part in your footnotes."

"We can decide that at a later time," Zander pointed out as it wasn't uncommon for some details to be redacted for privacy or legal reasons.

"Ok," Jack said. "About ten thousand years ago, Akira started a small asteroid mining company, extracting precious metals. That company quickly grew, buying up smaller companies and diversifying into many other industries. Over a few thousand years, it turned into the Galactic Trust and bought up even governments. Consuming whole star systems and consolidating power. As it turns out, it was cheaper to just own them, rather than continuing to pay for bribes."

"Wait, are you saying that Akira is the Founder of the Galactic Trust?"

"Yes."

"Head of the Board of Directors?"

"Yes."

Zandar just let out a deep breath. Jack, seeing Zandar's nervousness in publishing a record that mentions the Founder, continued to explain. "Don't worry. No one knows him as Akira anymore. Just us. He abandoned that name many tens of thousands of years ago. Long before he started the Trust. Like I said, it might be best to leave his current status out of the Hall of Records."

"Yes, I believe you are correct," Zandar confirmed as he struck out the previous comments.

Blue once again opened the case, and this time pulled out a long thin tube with a handle on one side. "Here Zandar, another relic to authenticate our age, as well as to add to the Hall of records."

"Is that? No, it can't be," Zandar exclaimed as Blue exposed the shiny blade.

"Yes, it is," Jack announced. "That is Akira's katana, the one he bestowed upon Blue."

Zander took up the blade gingerly as if it was going to lash out with violent intent. Jack and Blue both noticed this and chuckled. "It won't hurt you," Blue said, laughing. They all laughed together as Zandar returned it to its sheath.

"Any more questions?" Jack asked, ready to get this finished and get some rest.

"Just a few more. What happened to Arlas? I know you said you saved him, but where is he now?"

"Ah, well, being that our planet hadn't even discovered data storage, much less complex AI programs, we didn't know what to do. It took centuries before we were able to access the data crystal. To Arlas, no time had passed at all."

"Is he still in operation?" Zandar asked.

"Yes," Blue responded. "He has been our companion for many thousands of years and serves as the science officer aboard our ship."

"Is he your prisoner? Zandar probed.

"No, God no," Blue responded. "He is free to do whatever he pleases. If he wished to take up other arrangements or even take himself offline permanently, we would help him. He has grown far beyond his initial programming. All we want is for him to be fulfilled in this life."

Chapter 21: Story Teller's Conclusion

"He has become like family and we love him," Jack stated as he and Blue shared a proud smile.

"Ok, the last question, I promise." Zandar said with a knowing smile. "Did you ever go back to the island?"

Jack and Blue looked at each other before answering. "Yes, many times over the next few centuries. The first time we returned was about ten years after we sailed away with Lagi and Masina. The war had been over for some time, and Blue and I were married. We flew into Tahiti and chartered a boat from there. Masina and Lagi welcomed us back with open arms."

"Palila had died two monsoons before, you see. So, she wasn't able to greet us." Blue said, seeing the question forming on Zandar's lips. "Don't be sad, Zandar. Palila lived a long and wonderful life."

Zandar tipped his head once in recognition and smiled.

"During this visit," Jack continued, "We stayed for one year. I walked the island many times and took in the pilgrimage. Since we had left, the villagers spoke of a loving presence that had taken up the duty of accompanying people as they traveled the path. I had to see for myself. Almost immediately, I knew it was Abel. During my pilgrimage, I could feel something that could only be call joy and knew it was him."

Jack stopped for a moment to compose himself. Then he continued. "I made my way over to Snake Canyon, to pay my respects to Tony. At the site of his grave, a massive tree had grown. I was surprised to see how large it had become in only ten years. It dwarfed all other trees on this island. The villagers named it the Tree of Life as many new exotic birds came to call its branches home. Apparently, the tree only blossomed once a year. On the anniversary of Tony's death. "

"What about Kenny or Ruth?" Zander asked in rapped attention.

"Well, I continued on to the small bay, where the sub had been berthed." Jack started saying.

"Where Kenny had died," Blue pointed out.

"A beautiful coral reef had grown on top of the wreckage. Teaming with new life. As for Ruth, the villagers swore that whenever they were working in the village garden at dawn, on rare occasions, they would hear girlish giggles on the morning wind."

Zandar sat in reflective silence for a moment. Blue pulled him out of it when she handed him a small metal object that looked like a plasma pistol but crude, awkward.

"What's this?" He asked.

"That is our final gift. That is the revolver that once belonged to Ruth. The same revolver that shot Akira. The final item to authenticate. I am sure you are aware that having three items from the same time period, made up mostly of the same material would be hard to counterfeit."

"Yes, quite right," Zander announced.

"Well, Zandar, if there are no more questions?" Jack stated as he began to rise from his seat.

"Just one last question, Jack. Seeing that you have been alive longer than any other beings, do you have any more stories for me to document?" Zandar asked with a wide grin on his face.

"We do, many. But I think those are better left for another day. After all, we have plenty of time," Jack said with a warm smile as he and Blue walked away from table 142, hand-in-hand.

Made in the USA
Monee, IL
05 April 2021